A History of
What Comes Next

A History of What Comes Next

Take Them to the Stars
Book 1

SYLVAIN NEUVEL

MICHAEL JOSEPH

MICHAEL JOSEPH

UK | USA | Canada | Ireland | Australia
India | New Zealand | South Africa

Michael Joseph is part of the Penguin Random House group of companies
whose addresses can be found at global.penguinrandomhouse.com

First published in the United States of America by Tom Doherty Associates 2021
First published in Great Britain by Michael Joseph 2021
001

Copyright © Sylvain Neuvel, 2021

The moral right of the author has been asserted

This is a work of fiction. All of the characters, organizations,
and events portrayed in this novel are either products of
the author's imagination or are used fictitiously

Printed and bound in Great Britain by Clays Ltd, Elcograf S.p.A.

The authorized representative in the EEA is Penguin Random House Ireland,
Morrison Chambers, 32 Nassau Street, Dublin D02 YH68

A CIP catalogue record for this book is available from the British Library

HARDBACK ISBN: 978–0–241–44512–9
TRADE PAPERBACK ISBN: 978–0–241–44513–6

www.greenpenguin.co.uk

MIX
Paper from
responsible sources
FSC® C018179

Penguin Random House is committed to a
sustainable future for our business, our readers
and our planet. This book is made from Forest
Stewardship Council® certified paper.

Please note that all chapter titles are song titles from the years in which this book takes place. You can listen to each song as you read or enjoy the playlist on its own. You'll find the playlist on Apple Music (under "Shared Playlists") by searching for "take them to the stars," or you can re-create it yourself using the song list at the end of this book. It has also been added to Spotify, but its playlist search function isn't as comprehensive. Heading to tinyurl.com/neuvell will get you to the right place.

All civilizations become either spacefaring or extinct.

—CARL SAGAN

INTRODUCTION

We were the Ninety-Eight.

Ahmet found my diary while going through my luggage. It was my fault; I never should have let him come. He said he had questions he needed answered. I could see in his eyes that he had read things he should not have read.

We were Armenian traders in Berlin. Germany has spent decades waging Kulturkampf against the Catholic church. Jews, well . . . There's never been a good time to be Jewish in Germany. In all fairness, 1910 seemed like a bad time to be anything, but we had to be something. Orthodox Christians from a place few had ever heard of was the safest box we could fit ourselves in.

Mother was wise in choosing Berlin. The cultural scene was unlike anything we'd ever seen, and there wasn't a place on Earth with a larger appetite for science. Berlin was hungry for it all. It was the most modern city in the world. It even had a subway, which served us well since Mother didn't drive. She thought owning a car would make us stand out. We were coffee merchants, which seemed a bit cliché, but people find comfort in the familiar. We owned a small shop in Kreuzberg and the three-story building that housed it. We lived upstairs from the store and Mother set up our laboratory in the third-floor apartment that we pretended to rent.

Ahmet was a scholar from the Ottoman Empire. We met at the shop. I was thirty years old, but Ahmet did not mind my age.

He did not mind my daughter Sara. She was almost five when we moved to Berlin. He did not mind that I had a passion for science. He did not mind that I spent my free time in a secret room full of strange contraptions, and he never asked about our past after I told him not to. I did not mind Ahmet. We were married within a year.

Ahmet treated us well. He was a kind and honorable man, kind being the operative word. There were lots of honorable men in those days. When Franz Ferdinand was assassinated by Serbian nationalists, honorable men in Austria declared war on Serbia. Honorable men in Russia did what honorable men do: they honored their treaty with Serbia. The honorable thing to do for Germany was to stand with Austria. France sided with Russia, because it, too, had honor. Seventeen million lives later, the war was over, everyone's honor intact.

Mother died during the war. She hanged herself after breakfast on a crisp April morning in 1915. She thought it was our time, my daughter and me. There can never be three for too long.

Mother had performed her duty well, as her mother did before her. She and I were the Ninety-Seven. My daughter and I were now the Ninety-Eight. I had learned all that I was to learn and I had set a path for myself as instructed. I was as certain of what was expected of me as I was of the sun coming up every day. That certainty would not last. While removing Mother's personal items from the laboratory, I stumbled upon a box of papers I had never seen. In it were handwritten notes and a dozen scientific papers from the previous century. There was a brilliant paper from 1824 by French mathematician Joseph Fourier in which he calculated the temperature of an Earth without an atmosphere, another by John Tyndall, an Irish physicist, about the effect of certain gases on infrared radiation. The one that caught my attention was from an electrochemist, of all people, a man by the name of Svante Arrhenius. In 1896, he had presented at the Stockholm Physical Society a paper titled "On the Influence of Carbonic Acid in the Air upon the Temperature of the Ground." In it, he performed calculations on the effect of increased or decreased CO_2 concentrations on the temperature of Earth. I was not so much interested in the paper itself as I was in the countless scribbles my mother had added, no doubt over years, judging by the different inks she used.

Mother had spent most of her life working in physics. Her passion was electromagnetic waves, but like all of us she also spent a fair amount of time dabbing in anything from astrophysics to propulsion and flight dynamics. One year before I was born—I suspect the moment she decided it was time to bear a child—Mother had copied all her notes on EM waves and sent them to a promising student at the University of Berlin. From then on, she would sporadically perform new experiments but spent a good portion of her time collecting and analyzing air samples. She had regular correspondence with professors at various universities doing the same at her request, and carefully logged thirty years of data from across Europe inside notebooks. Mother was a brilliant physicist. This was tedious, unrewarding work at best. Why would she waste her time caring about the weather?

I found the answer in her diary. Mother was worried we would run out of time. If carbon dioxide levels kept rising, plant life, and soon all life on this world, would eventually come to an end. She wanted to know how fast it was happening and whether or not we could do anything about it. If Earth was doomed, her life, and that of the ninety-seven that came before her, had been a colossal waste of time. She had read our journals, felt the pain and sacrifice of each of her ancestors. She had watched her mother die. Was all of it for nothing? Every cell in her body was aching for an answer. She needed to know if our lives meant anything.

Answering that question also became my life's work. I make it sound like it was a calling. It was not, at least not at first. The war had infused my mother with a deep sense of urgency. I was still a child when it ended, and what suffering I remembered served as a reminder to enjoy every moment. For me, our lives were about the journey, not the destination. I took up Mother's research as a pastime. I spent most of my days teaching Sara everything I knew, a task that proved much more challenging than what I had imagined. This was my way to escape, like scrapbooking or playing biritch. Perhaps more than anything, it was something I could share with Ahmet. I will never know if it was the work he enjoyed or my opening up to him—I like to think it was both—but he poured himself into it. He was with me the whole time. He helped collect samples. He even traveled to France to get a better spectrophotometer. For nearly twenty years, he was a competent assistant, a constant supporter, a faithful husband. He was also a great father to my daughter.

On the eighteenth day of July 1925, Hitler published the first volume of *Mein Kampf*, and Sara gave birth to our granddaughter. We named her Mi'a, the Arabic word for one hundred. When the New York stock market crashed in 1929, we knew it was time to go. Hitler's popularity was on the rise, and the United States would undoubtedly pull back all the loans it had made this country after the war. Hell was coming to Germany.

We had to leave earlier than expected. Mi'a was only seven at the time. In hindsight, it was a blessing. Hindenburg won the election in April of that year but it wouldn't last. Hitler would soon take power. We left in September. 1932 was the year of everything.

Amelia Earhart completed her solo flight across the Atlantic. We were ecstatic. It was one of many things that inched us closer to our goal that year, but mostly we were indulging in a bit of vicarious living. None of us had ever been on a plane.

Across the Atlantic, Karl Jansky detected radio waves coming from space. To Sara and me, it was as if we'd found a window to a whole new place. We could see more of what was out there, expand our knowledge of the universe. We spent entire evenings speculating about what we could find. What would the death of a star sound like if we could hear those frequencies? What kind of radio signal would a whole civilization be putting out? We designed radio telescopes in our minds and imagined giant dishes aimed at the sky, searching for life.

What else? They discovered the neutron, finally. I'll admit, it was somewhat less exciting than watching a woman fly across Earth or eavesdropping on aliens. It was a whole lot less exciting for my granddaughter. Mi'a only talked about crossing the ocean. Nonetheless, particle physics was a lot easier with all the particles. I was happy.

We'll never know if we played a part in any of these things. Perhaps some of our research from the past . . . It did not matter. We had an ocean to cross. We boarded the SS *Milwaukee* of the Hamburg-Amerika Linie on September 18, didn't tell a soul. The trip to New York would take eleven days.

On the third day, Ahmet found my diary. He was seasick and going through my luggage, looking for medicine. It was all my fault; I should never have let him come. I could see in his eyes that he had read things he should not have read. I could see he would not let it go. I could see the entire chessboard, and every move led to the same outcome. Checkmate. Panic is knowing there is a way out but not knowing what it is. Calm is the absolute certainty there is not. I smiled. I told him: "We are the Kibsu." I pulled a pen out of his shirt pocket, put it in his nostril, and drove it into his skull with my palm. I do not think he suffered. I waited until nightfall and I gave his body to the sea.

I won't tell Sara. Some things are better left unsaid. I left the passports I had made in Berlin on the bed. When we dock at Ellis Island, Sara and Mi'a Balian will be no more. Sarah and Mia

Freed will take their first steps into the world. I wish I could see it, that New World, but my time has come and gone. We are the Ninety-Nine now. There can never be three for too long.

A bag of silverware tied around the ankle should be good enough. I think I will wear the blue dress . . . Ahmet will like that. It was always his favorite.

ACT I

1

Sentimental Journey

1945

What's a little girl like you doing so close to the front lines? That's what he said, in German, of course. It's a very good question, though "little girl" is a bit of a stretch. I'm nineteen years old, not five. We *did* always look younger than our age. Anyway, I think a better question is why I walked up to the SS instead of sneaking in. It seemed like a good idea not five minutes ago. Relax, Mia. This is going to work.

Needless to say, I didn't want to come. It's 1945 and it's fucking World War II. Pardon the language. I've been hanging out with American GIs for a month. Still, I was seven years old when I left Germany. I never dreamed I'd see it again. I don't remember much, but I thought . . . I *hoped* being here would feel—I don't know—special. Childhood memories, familiar smells, anything.

They flew me into France with US soldiers from the XXI Corps. A bunch of rude loudmouths, swearing and spitting everywhere. I liked them the minute I saw them. They snuck me into Germany through an unmanned gap in the Siegfried Line. I walked a dozen miles through farmland before I found a German farmer willing to drive me to the nearest town deserving of a train station. From there I spent—I don't know exactly—what felt like a decade on a near-empty train making my way northeast.

I slept through Bremen and Hamburg. The Allies pummeled Hamburg to dust. I didn't want to see it. Not the crumbled buildings, not the shattered lives. Certainly not the dead. I've seen the war in black-and-white. Fifty thousand civilians burned alive is not something I need in living color. I stayed awake for barley. And beets. Beets and barley and the endless sound of train tracks. Clickety-clack. Clickety-clack.

I watched people come in and out. Little vignettes of human resilience. Children in soldier's uniforms hovering between tears and laughter. Haggard nurses leaving one hell for another. A man and his boy fleeing the night raids. Like most, they don't speak, except for the occasional "Put your head down, son" when gray-green greatcoats and jackboots plod the aisle. Ordinary people in extraordinary times. We all stare at the yellow fields, pretending none of this is real. Clickety-clack. Clickety-clack.

We crossed a small bridge near Rostock. There was a body floating in the river below. A woman. She was drifting face-down, her red polka-dot dress bulging with air. She could have been anyone. Sixteen or sixty. All I know is she was dead and no one seemed to notice her but me. I kept waiting for someone to see her. They didn't. I stared for as long as I could. I twisted my neck backwards, hugging the window until she vanished behind us. I had to see her. I don't know why. I couldn't let her . . . not matter like that.

The man and his boy got off at the last station. An hour later I was here, Peenemünde Army Research Center, where Wernher von Braun is building the V-2 rocket. It's a city, *was* a city. Airport, power plant, miles and miles of train tracks. Twelve thousand people lived here, I think, before the Brits bombed the shit out of it. The factories are gone now; so are the slave workers. All that's left are the scientists. A few thousand brains in a town too big for them.

This place gave up a long time ago. The main building sits alone, as if they forgot to build the world around it. It's ugly, functional, as nondescript as it gets. The walls don't bother to hide their scars anymore. Burnt bricks. Boarded windows. Empty streets and run-down structures. Whoever kept things up around here is either dead or gone. Even the grass knows it lost the war. Everything smells . . . I don't know what it smells like. Musty. Sad, mostly. I shouldn't be here. I miss my home, my bed. I miss . . . I miss Mother.

She said I had to come. "It has to be done, Mia." I understand. It was her work that enabled them all, including Wernher von Braun, the man I'm here for. A hundred lifetimes had led us to Berlin. Our work, our legacy was here, spread around in the minds of thousands. Willingly or not, they were all working for the devil now, using the knowledge we gave them. Soon, Germany would lose and all that knowledge could be gone. We can't have that. Preserve the knowledge. That's the rule. Mother said that's all she cares about, but I know she can't stand Hitler using us that way. I just wish she'd come herself.

Hitler should have had von Braun executed six months ago. They've already lost. They just don't know it yet. Everyone else is playing another game, fighting for the spoils. To the victors, they say. Well, the victors will pillage this country. They'll pick it clean like vultures. The only question now is who gets the meatier parts. The Americans really want von Braun, but the one thing they want even more is to make sure no one else gets him. That's why they sent me. I'm nineteen and I'm supposed to shoot a German rocket scientist if they can't get their hands on him before the Russians do. I say shoot. I'm sure they'd be fine with strangle, drown, tickle to death, but men sent me, so I know they had a gun in mind. These are the same folks who think a woman's place is in the kitchen. Either there, or in a German compound. Go figure.

Mother set it all up. She works as a mathematician for the OSS. The Office of Strategic Services. There's nothing particularly strategic about them. Mother had the right résumé, she made sure of that, but these people will recruit just about anyone. They hired a player from the Red Sox—the Boston fucking Red Sox—to pose as a Swiss physics student and—I love this part—kill Germany's top nuclear scientist if it looked like they were close to building an atomic weapon. They hired Julia Child. The chef! They'll also send someone's daughter behind enemy lines without thinking twice, apparently. They call it Operation Paperclip. I don't know why they call it that. I didn't ask. Mother said I had to come, so I did.

Here I am, five months later, making puppy eyes at the SS. That's, literally, what the OSS asked me to do. They used *those* words. Look pretty and make puppy eyes if you get in trouble.

I think I am. I messed up. I told them I was Wernher von Braun's niece, Lili. That's what I said. I said niece. I was supposed to say cousin, but I'm so scared I should be glad I managed to say anything. Niece is bad, though. A cousin is vague enough. Everyone has cousins they've never met. Niece . . . He'll say: "What niece? I don't have a niece named Lili." Even if he's curious enough to play along, the SS will know something's up just by the look on his face. Stop thinking, Mia. What's done is done. Puppy eyes.

It almost sounded easy the way Mother put it. "Von Braun will understand. He's a smart man, and he's a scientist. He only cares about the work, Mia, not who he does it for." I hope so. Our plan, the one where I come out of this alive, sort of hinges on that man's survival instinct. I just wish . . .

I know why I came, I can see it from here. The steel tower. The high-sloped sand wall. That's Test Stand VII. Von Braun's V-2 launched from there and became the first man-made object to make it to space. Right over there, October 3, 1942. I am standing here, legs shaking, in the cradle of spaceflight. This is a place of science, home to one of mankind's greatest achievements. Wernher von Braun perfected that rocket on the top floor of the building behind me. *That's* what Mother wants me to see. She wants me to see the top floor, not the empty concentration camp in the basement.

There's a concrete footway going from this building to the next. Whoever designed it made it turn at a right angle. Aesthetics, I guess. People, of course, took the direct route. The dirt path they made is three feet wide, and a good eight inches deep. It would take . . . megatons of cumulated pressure to do that. Droves of starved people in striped uniforms walking to a slow death over and over again. This whole town was built by slave workers; so were the rockets. This is a place of science, and a place of oppression, and a place of suffering.

Countless died—That's not true. I'm sure the Germans counted them. They all died and not a single person here ever did anything to stop it. Not the young SS staring at me in his one-size-too-big uniform. Not the engineers, not the accountants. Certainly not Wernher von Braun. His rockets rained on London by the thousands—death falling from the heavens—but they killed more people making that weapon than they did using it. I doubt he could have stopped any of it, but we'll never know because he didn't try. His commitment never wavered, even after the Gestapo arrested him for treason. Von Braun is a man of science. He's also an SS officer. How many good men own an SS uniform?

I suppose it doesn't really matter. The US would want him if he hunted kittens for sport, and I won't come out of here alive without his help. If von Braun is a true believer, he'll turn me in to the SS. If he's a bad actor, he'll turn me in to the SS. If he wants to surrender to the Soviets, he'll turn me in to the SS. All he has to do is stay here if that's what he wants. Russian troops are less than a hundred miles away.

I've been waiting for a good thirty minutes now. Something's wrong, I know it. I'm not sure I can make it out if things go south. Maybe. Grab the kid's rifle with my right hand, raise it under his chin. Force his trigger finger with my left. I can take him, but there's lots of open space once I get out of here. I need to be rea—Oh shit, that's him. That's von Braun.

Dear God. The groomed hair, the tan. He looks more like a Hollywood actor than a physicist. Mother might be right. I see vanity here, not conviction. This is a man who does research in a fancy suit. He doesn't have to be a good man. He just has to be smart enough to realize the Germans have lost. Selfishness will do just fine. I just hope his ego wants to hear what I have to say. He's coming this way. Be ready.

—Lili!

A smile. I'll be damned. This might just work.

2

The Honeydripper

—Sit down, Lili. I'll be back in a minute.

He doesn't speak a lick of English, but all I hear is Cary Grant. He's all smiles and graces. I don't think he ever turns the charm off. This is a man who likes to be liked. I wouldn't be surprised if he slept with half the secretarial staff here. His office is meant to impress. Mahogany desk, fancy carpet, wall-to-wall bookshelves. The room belongs at Oxford, not in a concrete building littered with metal scraps. I suppose most of this would feel normal if it weren't for the war outside, but right now it reeks of denial. This is wall-to-wall pretend, like a movie set. He's made himself the star of his little world. All I need now is to convince him I deserve a role in it. Only I don't know how. I sure don't feel like Katharine Hepburn.

I feel like a child. I certainly look like one. I cut my hair. I don't know why I did it. I was leaving for Germany the next day. There were a million things to do but I went out and got my hair cut. There is this fancy salon not far from our house. I walk by it almost every day. I see rich people coming out of there and they look so . . . happy, confident. I wanted that. I never wanted it before but I did then. Going on a secret mission for the government. It was scary, but exciting. I wanted to feel . . . special. Ha!

Shoulder length, and bangs. As soon as I looked in the mirror, I knew I'd been lying to myself all along. It was stupid, really. I told myself I wanted to feel special, but I wanted to feel different. It's the first time I've done anything by myself. Me. Just me. I didn't want to look like my mother. Now I look like my mother when she was a teenager. I'm sure I inspire about as much confidence as I have in myself. I don't think I'd follow me if I were in von Braun's fancy shoes.

Not like my mother . . . Funny. Who else is there? I don't even know who I am without her. I don't know why I can force a door open without breaking a sweat, why I find people more cryptic than differential equations. Mother is the only person I relate to. I am *exactly* like her. I look like her, think like her. There is nothing *but* my mother. I spend my life following the rules she taught me, pursuing the one goal she told me to pursue.

Take them to the stars, before Evil comes and kills them all. My mother's words. *Her* mother's words, and her mother's, and her mother's. Our lives boil down to a single sentence, a handful of symbols on an ancient piece of jewelry. I thought it was a gift when Mother said I could wear it. Now that necklace hangs heavy like a manacle.

The world is doomed, and we must get people off of it. That's what's important. Not this war, not the first one or the next one. Not the woman in the river. Our fight is against gravity, and von Braun can help us win it. Mother said all that, of course. She's the one who believes. I only know we're the same, so I follow. Maybe that's how it's supposed to work.

3

Begin the Beguine

—Do you know who I am? Look around you. I created all this. I made the V-2! If the Americans were serious about this, they would not have sent a little girl.

He's smiling. What a creep! Yes, mister. You're a big wheel. We're all impressed. The good news is he didn't make a pass at me. That and they all agreed they should surrender to the US three weeks ago. The bad news is he won't listen to anything I say. I don't know if it's my gender, my skin, or the fact that I look like a fourteen-year-old nerd. Probably all three, not that it makes a difference. What does he think? That I *want* to be here? I want to go home and drink a milkshake, listen to Big Boy Crudup while a B-17 carpet-bombs this place. But I can't. I have to be here, with him. Him and a townful of Nazis. Time for some Olympic-level pride-swallowing.

—I'm nineteen, sir. And I understand. I do. You're a very important man, and a brilliant one. I know that, and the United States knows that. They will stop at nothing to make sure you get out safe. You see, they didn't send a little girl. They sent Patton's Third Army. All of it. I'm only here to make sure you're still alive when they reach us.

—Flattery will get you nowhere, young lady. . . . How long until they get here?

He knows I'm fawning over him, but he can't help himself. Now for the hard part.

—Soon, sir. Soon. Unfortunately, not before Soviet troops reach Peenemünde.

— . . .

—What I mean is we can't stay here, sir. If we stay, you'll be dead in a week. Either dead or learning Russian. I need you to come with me.

—Come with you where?

That is a very good question. One that the OSS answered only with "away from the Soviets and towards US troops." It kind of made sense when they showed me on the map with their small toys. They like pushing toy figures on maps, with a stick. It's a small map, they could reach with their hands, but they think the stick makes it look serious somehow. Red Soviet figures, blue American figures. Get away from the red toys and head towards the blue toys. Simple enough. What was missing on their little map was about a million little German figures filling all the space in between. One step at a time, I guess. We need to get away from tiny red people.

—Anywhere but here, sir, and preferably without being fired at. The Germans must know they'll lose Peenemünde. Do you have orders to go anywhere?

—I do indeed.

. . . Really? That's it? Maybe it's a European thing. A friend of Mother's went to Paris before the war. She said she asked a lady if there was a post office nearby and the lady answered: "Yes."

—Where, sir? Where did they ask you to go?

—How do you Americans put it? Oh yes. *Take your pick.*

Wow. I knew German command was a mess, but this . . . Right there on his desk, ten, maybe a dozen written orders, all from different people. Here's an army chief who wants him to pick up arms and join the fight on the eastern front. I don't think we'll follow that one. Another one asking him to stay put. The wording on these is fascinating. Failure to comply. Blah blah blah. Summarily executed. Blah blah blah. Firing squad. Here it is again. Orders to stay, orders to go. This one is from Kammler himself.

Technically, Kammler is von Braun's boss. Official title: Beauftragter zur besonderen Verwendung Heer, Army Commissioner for Special Tasks, something like that. *Less* technically, Kammler is about as close as you can get to the devil himself. Before dealing in advanced weaponry, Hans Kammler was chief of Office C, the same Office C that built all the concentration camps. Now this asshole is ordering von Braun and his men to Bleicherode in central Germany, near the Mittelwerk weapons factory where they build the V-2.

—I think Kammler is our best bet, sir. We should head southwest to Bleicherode.

—No! You said we had to wait for the Americans. Now you want to take us away from them.

It does sound counterintuitive. We'd like to get out of Germany, not deeper into it. But we'll never get near the border without getting caught. What I told him was kind of true. The Americans really have no plan to get us out other than to plow their way through the German army until they reach us. The best we can do for now is to bide our time.

—I know, sir. But we can't stay here, that means going somewhere else. We also need to stay alive. We're going to need help doing that, and since we're in Germany, I think the Germans are in a better position to help us than anyone else. You can't hide from your own army for weeks, sir. Follow orders, any orders. All we need is time.

Silence. I think he knows I'm right. Either he doesn't like what that means for him, or he really doesn't want to listen to me.

—Then tell me, Lili—is that even your real name?—I'm the chief scientist in the V-2 program. I have nearly five thousand men under my command. Why would I listen to *you*?

—Mr. von Braun, I—

—You can go back to where you came from, Lili. I will handle this myself.

I should tell him I have orders to kill him if he doesn't play along. Maybe I should just kill him and get it over with.

—Forgive me, sir, but I don't think you have much of a choice.

—Who the hell do you think you are?

I have absolutely no idea, so let's not go there. I get it, though. Creep or not, he doesn't know me from Adam. I might not listen to me either, but we're running out of time.

—I don't mean any disrespect, sir. I only mean that your options are very limited at the moment. Unless you want to put your fate in the hands of a Russian general, you have to leave. You can run, but you and I both know it won't work. You need to understand, you . . .

—What? What do I need to understand?

Here it comes. Kid gloves, Mia. Kid gloves.

— . . . You're a brilliant man, sir. I said that already. The work you've done here is impressive, very impressive. But you're not . . . irreplaceable.

—I built the V-2!

Good Lord! I almost feel bad for what I'm about to do to him, but someone has to shrink him down to size. I need to speak a language he understands.

—You did. And it's great, but it's not perfect. I think a lot of it isn't your fault. Working conditions haven't been ideal, but that engine . . . I suspect you just couldn't build one that size that fast, without it going BOOM, so you tied together eighteen smaller ones, fed their exhaust into one large mixing chamber, and hoped for the best.

—How dare you? What do you know about building rockets?

—Enough to know there are limits to what the Americans will do for two hundred and three seconds of specific impulse. . . . I don't mean this as an insult, sir. I understand. You scaled up your design and the rocket started shaking like a leaf.

28

—Nonsense! Are you saying the Americans will kill me?

I need to make him trust me. Me, not the plan. He has to see me as an ally, a kindred spirit or something. I need . . .

—I'm saying . . . I'm saying you couldn't find the right geometry to get rid of those transverse gas vibrations. I'm saying maybe you should try adding baffles around the injector face.

— . . .

He's still smiling, smug as a cat, but I think he understands.

—And we should follow Kammler's orders and head southwest.

— . . . Baffles, you say? Anything else?

—No, sir, just the orders.

Progress. Not much, but progress. At least he's willing to hear what I have to say.

—It will not work. There will be checkpoints along the way. There will be checkpoints everywhere. The SS will stop us.

—We have Kammler's orders.

—We have many orders, from people just as important as Kammler. Someone will find out we disobeyed theirs.

—Who?

—It does not matter. Any of them. The SS will call the wrong person, and they will arrest us, or they will round us up and shoot us all. We will *never* make it all the way to Bleicherode with these orders.

I'm tempted to disagree on principle, but the man does have a point. He also works for the SS. He *might* know a bit more about them than I do. Problem is I don't have another plan, so I sort of need this one to work. How do we make sure the SS will let us through? We have good orders, ones we want to follow. We just need to make sure *these* orders supersede every other set of orders on that table. Problem solved. . . . I have absolutely no idea how we're supposed to do that. . . . Maybe *he* does.

—Sir? Is there anyone the SS wouldn't stop, anything they wouldn't check on?

— . . . It would have to be something above their clearance, some top-secret project they are not allowed to know about.

So what we need is some sort of *school note*, from Hitler. Sure. Why not?

—Could we . . . forge some documents?

Von Braun is *soooo* not going to like this.

—There *is* the letterhead . . .

What letterhead? Oh, I forgot about their weird manners. I'm probably supposed to ask.

—What letterhead?

—We received these from the printer last month. I was about to destroy them.

He's fetching a cardboard box from behind his desk. Looks like . . . paper. One big pile of Nazi paper, eagle, swastika, and all, and the initials "VzBV" across the top. I don't know what it means. BzBV, with a B, is the department Kammler runs, what von Braun actually works for. This . . . I've never heard of it.

—What's VzBV?

—It's nothing. It's a typo.

—It doesn't exist?

—No. Just a misprint.

Let me get this straight. We need to forge some documents from a secret project and he just *happens* to have a boxful of letterhead from a place that's not real, in his office, right now. This all seems a little too convenient, but I'll take it.

—Well . . . There's your project. VzBV.

—What does it stand for?

—I don't know. It's your project.

—Vorhaben zur besonderen Verwendung?

Project for Special Disposition. I like it.

—I think it's perfect. It sounds important but it's vague enough it could mean anything. How long do you need to get your people ready?

—A few days.

30

Days! How long does it take to throw some clothes into a bag?

—That seems like a long time, sir. The Russians will be here in a few days.

—All my research. The Americans will want it.

—I understand, sir. You have some boxes to pack. That should take a few hours, not a few days.

—There are nearly five thousand of us. It will take time.

I don't know what he's talking about. We can't *all* leave. There are—He just said it. There are nearly five thousand of them!

—What? No, sir. I'm supposed to get *you* out, you and your top scientists. You are . . . how can I put this? . . . (Off your rocker. Nutty as a fruitcake. Cuckoo bananas.) . . . underestimating the risks involved. Those fake papers might be enough for them to let a car through, not a town. A few people, sir. That's the mission.

—Then you need to rethink the mission, Lili. The Russians will exterminate anyone we leave behind if the German army does not do it for them. There are families here. We have to take them with us. Those that want to come, at least. I will not leave without them.

He *is* insane. Even if half of his staff stays behind, there's no way we can move thousands of people without being stopped everywhere. He also sounded genuinely sincere right then. He even dropped the radio-host voice for it. I realize I have no idea who that man is. Thousands of people died here building his rockets, and he let it happen. Mother says he only cares about science. I thought that made him a coward, but he'll apparently risk his life in the thick of war to save the people he works with.

What *does* that make him? Did he believe them when they told him who was human and who wasn't? Or did he just . . . wish all the horrors away, pretend they didn't exist? Did he sleep through the rubble and watch yellow fields through the window? Like most things, it's probably more complicated than this or that. I wanted to save a good man, or kill an evil one. Von

Braun might be neither. The world is flooding with egotistical men concerned only with their needs and wants. Another place and time, he might just be . . . unremarkable in his own self-serving way. Von Braun is no hero, that's a fact, but this is the first remotely selfless thing to come out of his mouth. If I'm going to do this, I need to believe there is something inside that man worth saving, something other than knowledge.

I must be as crazy as he is. We'll need boxes, lots of boxes. We can't fit all these people in cars or trucks. We'll have to put them on trains. This won't be subtle. We're moving a town. I'll start making stencils while they pack. I want those four letters painted bright on everything. Red and white, something you can't miss. I want the boxes painted. I want jackets painted, armbands. I want the toilet paper to say VzBV. I want them to see it, everywhere. That department didn't exist yesterday. By tomorrow, it will have trains and a few thousand employees. This can work, right?

What the hell am I thinking? We have *zero* chance. We're all going to die and we're going to do it the stupid way.

4

I Wonder

I sent my daughter to Germany. I wish I knew what kind of mother that makes me.

It all began about six months ago. German major general Walter Dornberger contacted someone at the General Electric Company through their embassy in Portugal. The note was short. "I wish to come to some arrangement," German for "I know we are losing the war and I am willing to help you if you can guarantee my safety." The US government liked Dornberger because of his rank and what he might know about Hitler's strategy. I liked him because he built rockets. He recruited Wernher von Braun in 1932—the two of them went to school together— before he was given military command of Peenemünde. When the V-2 first launched successfully, Dornberger said: "This is the first of a new era in transportation, that of space travel." I wanted him. After the assassination attempt on Hitler, the SS were put in charge of everything. Kammler took over Peenemünde and Dornberger was pushed aside, sent away to command training batteries. The OSS arranged for him to meet the Ninth Army in the north.

Dornberger can help us reach the stars, but he cannot do it alone. Wernher von Braun is the brains behind the V-2. Unfortunately for him, and me, von Braun does not have the rank to escape on his own. I convinced the OSS they had to send someone. It took some effort. Those men did not have the required intellect. They did not realize it was the Soviets they were racing against, not the Germans, that the prize was more than a piece of land in Europe. A friend at Caltech had performed an analysis of German rocket capabilities for the army, but they missed the point in its entirety. I showed them what could have been, had the Germans been given enough time. Bombs dropping from space with absolute precision. Wars waged halfway across the globe without ever leaving home. Acquiring the V-2 became a top priority, but they wanted the hardware, not the brains that created it. They would improve upon it themselves. Only they could not, and they would waste a decade figuring that out. The Germans were better at this. We had made them that way, Mother and I. I did not dare attack their unshakable belief in American exceptionalism, but I hinted at what Russia could do if they captured Germany's best and brightest. I did it over dimly lit dinners, so men could claim the idea for themselves the next day. It worked with painful predictability. They can live with failure, so long as no one else succeeds. Operation Paperclip was born within days.

Part of me wanted to go. I wanted to see Germany again, but we are more fearless when we are Mia's age. We also see the moment, the uniqueness in people. We can find value in *one* life. As we grow older, we realize the scale of it all, and the insignificance of everything and everyone. I would kill von Braun and those around him at the first sign of trouble. I would not hesitate. We gave them the knowledge, we can give it again. We are the Ninety-Nine but we will be the One Hundred, and the Hundred and One. Mia . . . Mia will not spend her life retracing my footsteps if she can make her own. She is at that age when we see ourselves as special, unique. She still believes she is not us and she will not give that up easily. She will take risks. She will be scared, but our instincts will take over. I hope.

Preserve the knowledge. That is why I sent Mia. I followed one rule, only to break another: survive at all costs. I risked everything, all that we have worked and died for. I put us in harm's way. Was it wrong of me? Perhaps the question is meaningless. If there is such a thing as right and wrong, I doubt it was meant for us. We are the Kibsu. We are the path.

I cannot tell if these are rational thoughts, or the weakness of a mother fearing for her child. I question everything, every choice. I question the life I have made for ourselves, moving to Washington to join the OSS. Every time we step into the light, we make it easier for the Tracker to find us. Don't draw attention to yourself. Another rule I broke or bent. I told myself it was worth the risk, that we were saving lives. I hope it does not mean the end of ours.

Part of me wishes I were there with Mia. Part of me wishes I *were* Mia. We arrived in America the same year *Buck Rogers* hit the airwaves. For years, those fifteen minutes I spent with my ear glued to the radio were the highlight of my day. I did not want to be the Kibsu. I certainly did not want to be my mother. I wanted to be Buck Rogers and go on a myriad of adventures.

I met my next hero when I joined the OSS. The Gestapo called Virginia Hall the most dangerous of Allied spies. I called her . . . I called her Virginia, but I . . . I envied her. I wanted to *be* her. She was in Paris when the war started. She joined the ambulance service there before France fell and ended up in Nazi-controlled territory. She got out, went to London, and volunteered to work for the British SOE. She went back to Vichy and, for over a year, helped coordinate the French underground while posing as a reporter.

When the Nazis seized all of France, Virginia escaped to Spain, by herself, over the Pyrenees mountains. She did that on foot, singular. Virginia was missing a leg. She used a prosthetic she nicknamed Cuthbert. If I ever remarry, I shall name my husband Cuthbert.

In hindsight, I did not particularly *like* Virginia, not as a person.

We trained together only briefly. She was not very close to me, or anyone else for that matter. I liked . . . the *idea* of her.

Now my daughter is on a secret mission in Germany. As much as I fear for our safety, part of me is glad we are on this adventure. We are Buck Rogers now. We are Virginia Hall.

5

Crawlin' King Snake

We saw the river first. A refreshing punctuation after five hours of spruce trees. It's been one of those soupy days where the rain refuses to rain and everything is its own shade of gray. We were still on the bridge when their silhouettes appeared through the mist. I see them clearly now. All of them.

—*Zeig mir deine Papiere.*

Skull and bones on the hat. Four pips on the collar. He took his raincoat off before coming over to make sure we noticed. This one is a *Sturmbannführer*, a major, maybe. Someone important for about two hundred feet, like the store manager at the local Woolworth's. Blotchy eyes and a day-old beard. They must have painted the night in the village across. That's where the trains will meet up with us. If we make it. These guys are Waffen-SS, and they are all over us.

—*ZEIG MIR DEINE PAPIERE!*

Von Braun is out there handing him our orders. I just realized these two hold the same rank. Easy to forget I'm bowling along with a ranking SS officer. Von Braun asked for the major's name but I couldn't hear over the dog's barks. It sounded like *Asshat*. Whatever his name is, he's not too impressed with our letterhead. Everyone is louder now. Asshat wants to confirm our orders. You can't, Asshat. We're the VzBV! That's more or less what's coming out of von Braun's mouth.

I'll roll down the window. It's getting hot in here. The dog is barking up a storm, tugging at his leash and—oh shit!—Asshat's pistol is out of its holster. It's pointing at the ground but the two behind him just pulled the bolts on their submachine guns. They're not scared, they're itching for it. It's not about rules or orders. This is all territory, pissing on lampposts. VzBV may be above Asshat's head, but if you reduce the world to a small enough size, this road or this bridge, Asshat is king. He won't bow to anyone, least of all Wernher von Braun in his fancy suit. Why is it so hot in this car?

I shouldn't be here. I don't have the moxie for this. There's no way out if this escalates. I'm stuck in the car on the passenger side. I don't have a gun because I'm Lili the fucking *niece*.

SOMEONE SHUT THIS STUPID DOG UP!

I'm burning hot. It's not the car, it's me. I must be coming down with something. Everything feels . . . slower. Crisper. I can see . . .

I can see everything. Thirty, forty men in front. Three are messing with von Braun. The rest are sitting by the road, making crude jokes and rolling cigarettes. They'll shoot us all if it gets to that, but for now we barely register. Fucking with people is what these guys do. This is their normal. The light truck to my right is empty, but the one Asshat came in on has a Flak 38 on top. One man at the wheel, one in the back, smoking. Elevated position. That's where I need to go.

What on earth is happening to me? I can see it go down. Clear as day. Everyone dead in thirty seconds flat.

I get out of the car. The SS holding the dog leash turns and yells at me: "Get back in the car." I smile and keep walking. Five seconds. I lean inside the truck window and snap the driver's neck while he checks the inside of my blouse. I reach down and take his sidearm. Ten seconds. Now I'm a girl with a weapon.

I saunter to the back of the truck. The man up there smiles. I wink. He throws his cigarette on the ground before stepping down. It's still burning when I raise the gun to his chin. Bam. Fifteen.

This fever. I must be losing my mind. I can't end a platoon of Waffen-SS on my own.

But I can. The gunshot gets everyone's attention. A handful of SS start aiming everywhere. Most just lie on the ground when they hear gunfire. I climb up the back of the truck—twenty seconds—and mow through the crowd with the Flak 38. No one shoots back through the pandemonium. I can't hear them if they do. The only sound is the roar of the gun. I throb and pulsate two hundred times a minute while two-centimeter projectiles dig into the ground, halving people along the way. The world turns red when the incendiary heads ignite. The heat wave hits me like a brick and I let go of the gun. I cover my seared skin with my hands while pentaerythritol tetranitrate consumes what's left of everyone.

Thirty seconds.

. . .

Breathe.

. . .

Breathe. None of it is real.

. . .

It soon will be. Asshat poked von Braun in the chest with his pistol. The men around him are raising their weapons. That's it. I can't save von Braun anymore but I can save myself.

I'm getting out of the car.

—*Fräulein, geh* zurück *ins Auto!*

"Miss, get back in the car." Right on cue. Focus, Mia. Breathe. Just smile your way to the truck.

. . .

Holy cow! Von Braun grabbed Asshat's gun and pressed the barrel against his own head. He's screaming now.

—Call Himmler! Call Himmler or shoot me in the head, and *then* call Himmler. Either way, you'll be facing a firing squad by morning. . . .

Asshat hasn't pulled the trigger yet.

All right. I'll give you three seconds, then I'm doing this my way.

One . . .

—*Geh zurück ins Auto!*

Two . . .

Pistol down. He's holstering it.

Everyone's heartbeat is slowing down. I feel a cool breeze coming in.

I guess calling the head of the SS wasn't on Asshat's to-do list for the day. It's a good thing he didn't. Von Braun spent two weeks in a Gestapo cell because of Himmler. I don't think there's a lot of love between those two. Von Braun is back inside the car. Somehow he seems in his element in all this. Fake smiles to everyone. I feel a Heil Hitler coming. Here it is.

The SS are leaving, just like that. Moving on to God knows where to mess with someone else. I don't think Asshat liked having to back down. I pity whoever crosses their path next.

I was going to blow them all to smithereens. If it weren't for von Braun . . . I would have killed them all. I knew how. This was a close call, but the Waffen-SS aren't the ones I'm scared of right now.

I need to go home, but a drink will have to do. We'll spend the night in the next village. The trains will be there in the morning.

6

Lili Marlene

This place is loud. Must be the only bar here. Sticky floors. It stinks of old beer and . . . I can't quite put my finger on it. Something. The girl at the bar is younger than I am. Sixteen. Seventeen. I should relate but I can't read her at all. She's phlegmatic, neither happy nor sad, isolated from the world by a ten-foot oak slab.

—*Einen halben Liter Weißbier, bitte.*

I can still hear my heartbeat. Thump thump. Thump thump. We got lucky, but it was a mistake to send me. I'm going to get us all killed. Me and von Braun deserve whatever we get, but there are three thousand people I've never met on those trains. Three thousand flavors of guilt and innocence. Janitors, secretaries. Wives and children. I shouldn't be the one to—

—Sara Balian?

Silence. My heart stopped. I'm trying to swallow the beer in my mouth as if nothing happened, as if I didn't hear anything. But I did hear. That's my mother's name, *was* my mother's name before we moved out of Germany.

—*Sara Balian, du bist es!*

Keep calm. Just ignore him. What are the odds he'll just go away? Nil, he just tapped me on the shoulder.

—Sara!

I need to get rid of him while there's no one else within earshot.

—I'm sorry, sir, I don't know who that is.

—Sara! You're Sara. How—

He's probably fifty, scruffy beard. The eyes. He's drunk as a skunk. He seems . . . broken, but I can tell he was a good-looking man before all this. This is someone who was happy once.

—My name is Lili, sir. You have me confused with someone else. I don't know anyone named . . .

—Sara.

—Like I said. I don't know who that is.

—You haven't changed one bit. Not one bit. How is that possible? It's me, Sara! Dieter!

He knew my mother when she was my age. He remembers her that way. I knew her, too, or course. But I remember her through the eyes of a kid. To him it must look like I traveled through time.

—I just told you. My name's Lili. I've never seen you before in my life, sir. I've never been here before.

—No. I know who you are. Your clothes . . . they're different. Your hair. But you're still the same. How can you be the same?

I'm not the same. I'm not my mother.

—I think you need to go, sir. Now.

—I have to tell Bernhard. He'll be so happy to see you. BERNHARD! Over here!

That name. I don't think I've ever met a Dieter, but Bernhard, I know. He came to our house many times when I was young. I see him now, a couple of tables back . . . in a fucking SS uniform. Dang! He's older, but that's him. That's the man I knew. Now he's just another soldier. I keep forgetting they're people, but this is Nazi Germany. The Nazis are your neighbors, your parents, your childhood friends. Five more gray-green shirts around him. Beer spilling everywhere. They're just as drunk as Dieter; that should give me a few seconds. I need to leave before Bernhard sees me.

—I have to go. Goodbye, sir. I hope you find that friend of yours.

—Don't go, Sara! You have to see Bernh— Wait! Wait!

Don't follow me. Please don't follow me out.

Ding. The door hits the bell as it closes behind me. . . .

Ding. It rings again.

—SARA!

Don't draw attention to yourself. I'm sure Dieter means well, but he's going to get me killed.

— . . .

—SARA!

—SHHHHHHHH!

I can't let him do this. I don't look German. One of them says "Gypsy" and they'll tear me to pieces. All I have are fake papers. Lili papers. I'm not having a sit-down with the SS trying to explain why I'm not who Dieter and Bernhard say I am. There. There's an alley behind the flower shop.

—Over here, Dieter. Come with me.

—Oh, Sara. I never thought I'd see you again. I didn't think you'd come back, not after what happened in Bad Saarow.

Bad Saarow. Why does that ring a bell?

—I'm not Sara. I keep telling you.

—Don't do that. Don't lie to me. I was there when it happened, Sara. I—

—Sara's my mother.

—Mi'a?

He knows me. I thought . . . I was hoping this was all a mistake.

—Mi'a . . . I can't believe it's you. You look so much like her, it's . . . You don't remember me, do you? Dieter? Uncle Dieter?

That voice. I sort of remember now. He . . . He played with me. NNNEEAOOWWW! I was in his arms. I was an airplane. He carried me around while I pretended to fly. It's more a feeling than a memory, but I think I liked him. Dieter . . . Didi? I remember Didi. Mother trusted him, she . . . She left me alone with him. Mother never left me alone with anyone.

—Are you Didi?

—Yes! It's me, Didi! You were this high the last time I saw you. I knew you when you were a baby, Mi'a. I held you in my arms for . . . You peed on me!

Mother and he were close, but she never talks about him. It seems like they were on good terms, but he said . . . He said he never thought she'd come back, not after . . .

—What did you mean, about my mother? Why would she not come back here?

— . . . I meant it's been a long time. I thought, after so many years, you know.

That's not what he said.

—You said you were there, Dieter. There for what?

—Is your mother here? Is she . . .

He doesn't want to lie to me. Why?

—What happened, Dieter?

—Nothing. I—

—What happened in Bad Saarow?

We had to leave Germany because the Tracker was getting too close. That's what Mother always said.

—You should ask your mo—

—My mother's dead.

Why did I lie?

—I'm sorry. She was . . . She was special.

What does he mean, special? Special to him? Special how? It doesn't make a difference now that he knows who I am. This is a nightmare. I shouldn't have come. I shouldn't be here.

—Are you okay, Mi'a? Is anything wrong? I'll go get Bern-hard. Just stay here, I'll be right back with Bernhard. He's an important man now. In this town, he—

—Don't. Not now.

—What's the matter, Mi'a? You remember Bernhard, don't you?

That face, the way he smiles without smiling. I see . . . pain, sorrow. Did my mother do that to him? Did she break his heart in Bad Saarow? There's still kindness in his eyes, though. Like that's the one thing life couldn't take from him. He cares about people, despite everything. He still cares, about my mother, about me. I don't think I can do this.

—Why are you crying, Mi'a?

—I'm fine.

I'm not fine. Whom could he tell? He doesn't know anyone . . . I wish that were true. He knows Bernhard. He knows the fucking SS. I can't explain any of this. Our house burned down thirteen years ago and we haven't been seen since. Don't leave a trace. I learned that rule while I was here. I learned it while Didi and I were flying across the house. I . . . Please stop looking at me that way. I'm not even sure who he's looking at. Me or my mother? What do his eyes say? Are those the eyes of a friend? A lover? . . . A father? Don't think, Mia. Just get closer.

—I'm here, Mi'a. I'm here.

He's hugging me. He must be twice my size. I feel . . . safe wrapped inside his arms. He has strong hands. He's a worker now, not a thinker. This is a good man. It's men like him we're supposed to save. Only, not him. Not *this* man. This one's guilty of knowing me, knowing *us*. Mother tried to prepare me for this. Here, let me hold your face, Didi. Let me be my mother for a minute. See her one last time. Feel her fingers running through your beard. Let her hold your head with both hands.

You won't feel a thing, Didi. I promise.

7

God Bless the Child

I have been combing through intercepts of German radio traffic. There is no mention of von Braun, or my daughter. I did, however, stumble upon disturbing news from Berlin. There was an *incident* in Kreuzberg—war is a seedbed for euphemisms—at the tavern across from the house I grew up in. Nine people were killed, mutilated. Jews, or Roma, I assumed; German jingoism rearing its head with wonted cruelty. This was different. Half the victims were Brownshirts. One girl belonged to the SS-Helferinnen. Nine model Aryan citizens slaughtered. This was not the work of the SS *or* the Gestapo. The police have no suspect, but I do, and it makes my blood run cold.

For three thousand years, the Tracker has hunted us. Like us, he is one and many. Like us, he has survived the passage of time. Our ancestors called him the Rādi Kibsi. My mother called him Spürhund. Whatever his name, these murders could very well mean he is getting close. Thirteen years behind us is a heartbeat away.

It seems unlikely. We did not leave a trace. But we did not leave a trace in India, Morocco, or the Philippines. We followed the rules for three thousand years, yet the Ninety-Two lost her mother. We followed the rules, and the Tracker might be in Berlin at this very moment, just as Mia travels through Germany. I have never been one to believe in coincidences. I need to bring my daughter back. We need to disappear.

I have no way to contact Mia. She and von Braun are heading

to Bleicherode and I cannot send a telegram to a German rocket factory. I did the one thing I could, played the last card left for me to play. It will cost me my job, but our time here is ending anyway. I only hope it works.

All I can do now is wait. That is something I am usually good at. Progress is inconspicuous, the world often perceptually still. Ours is a slow march towards something we will not see for ourselves. We plant the seeds; our daughters reap the fruit. Thus is the life of the Kibsu. My mother told me so many times, but now Mia is missing and every minute of every day feels like watching a pot that refuses to boil.

I thought I could keep my mind occupied with my mother's research. I have been collecting samples, logging data from a dozen locations. It is tedious enough not to require my undivided attention—that is something I cannot give at the moment. The data we collected shows a rise in carbon dioxide, but I have no way to know if this is an exceptional phenomenon, nor can I isolate man's contribution to this increase from that of the planet's natural mechanisms. I find myself at an impasse in all matters.

I am restless. Mia has gone astray and there is no one to turn to. Without her, I am completely alone. I realize how deft I have become at avoiding relationships. The only one I keep is with a man I have met only once. I know our correspondence is not paramount to him—though he still makes it a point to write every month—but Hsue-Shen Tsien is the only person I would label as friend.

He came from China in 1935 on a Boxer Indemnity Scholarship. We met at MIT during a lecture on fluid dynamics. He was a brilliant student, but struggled mightily adapting to his new culture. Both of us stood out like sore thumbs. It was only fitting that we would share a table for lunch. I introduced myself as Sarah Moussa from Cairo. It is somewhat ironic that my truest connection began with a lie.

Through time, and a fair amount of serendipity, we ended

up sharing a lot more than lunch. After his master's, he moved to California to study with Theodore von Kármán. It was there that he struck up a friendship with a handful of bright budding rocket scientists. Von Kármán and this tight-knit group of students founded what they call the Jet Propulsion Laboratory. They attach rockets to planes to accelerate their takeoff.

After graduating, Hsue-Shen Tsien chose to stay. He found himself directing research on a small ballistic missile for the army. His rockets are light-years behind von Braun's, but few people understand mathematics the way Hsue-Shen does. We have been bouncing ideas off each other for almost a decade, and I just wrote to him about my CO_2 conundrum. I told myself he could shed new light on the problem, but what I really need is someone to share with, someone intelligent enough to comprehend. There are so many things I cannot tell him, but I can at least be candid about the science.

As for the rest, I confide to him in half-truths, overtones. "My dear Hsue-Shen, Please forgive my belated reply. My daughter is traveling abroad and the void she left behind gets louder every day." Hsue-Shen is just as fluent in the unsaid. In the end I think he and I understand each other perfectly.

8

Hot Time in the Town of Berlin

—Eyes on the road!

Whoa. Maybe I shouldn't be driving. I haven't slept in two days. I can't. We're traveling at night now, trying to cover as much ground as we can while it's dark. We've had some close calls. Allied planes are bombing everything that resembles the German army. Our VzBV convoy sure looks the part; we've gone out of our way to make it look important. I'm driving in the dark with the lights off. Von Braun and I are alone in the truck, and I'm helping him with his homework. The idiots at German command want to ramp up production of the V-2 rockets by September. The war will be over long before that, but they want the V-2 to be more accurate, and to stop blowing up in midair. Those aren't entirely unreasonable demands, if we weren't relocating a whole town while doing it.

—I'm sorry. You know, sir, I was thinking . . .

—About something other than the road, obviously.

—I . . . Yes. I know a good quarter of your V-2s blow up at launch, or you just throw them out because they're unusable.

He won't like that. He'll say it's not his fault.

—It's not my fault if—

—No, I know. I know. But I was thinking, and . . . Why not build them in sections?

—Here we go again. And tell me, Lili, why would I do that?

—Well, you could assemble them at the last minute on the launch site. Transport would be a lot easier, for one thing, and

49

that way you'd throw away one-third of a missile instead of the whole thing if it doesn't pass QA.

—Someday, Lili, you and I will need to have a serious talk about who you are and what you do.

—I'm sorry, I just . . . You could also make the warhead detachable while you're at it. You need that big rocket to go up, you don't need it going down. There's no point in keeping it along for the ride.

—Just watch the road, will you?

I will, I am. But helping him keeps my mind busy. Not busy enough, though. I keep thinking of Didi. The look on his face, his brown eyes disappearing into squints when he smiled. I now have this crystal-clear image of him in my mind. He's holding me in midair. One hand on my chest, one on my back. I'm laughing, screaming, flying to the sound of lip trills. I can't be more than two or three years old, so I know these memories aren't real. But I see it. And I ask myself who that man was. Mother and I rarely talk about Berlin. If ever one of us brings up the past, the other reminds her of the rules. Don't leave a trace. The Ninety-Eight is dead. We say it often and we believe it, even, but that doesn't make it true. I knew that man. Mother knew him for over a decade. Who was he to her, to me, before I put him in a dumpster?

I've never met my father. . . .

Mother always said she didn't want a man around. She told me my father was a sailor, that he'd done his part and went on with his life. I never questioned that. Men aren't exactly our strong suit. What if she lied to protect me? What if he was there all along? A friend. There were many of those. Dieter, Bernhard. Maybe one of them was a really good friend, a special friend. Just one time, and we'll never talk about it again. Maybe she lied to *him* and he didn't know. Maybe . . . Maybe my father was a sailor, had done his part and went on with his life. I suppose I'll never know what happened in Bad Saarow. I do know I shouldn't be here. I shouldn't have come.

There's this dream I keep having. I'm wearing a pink dress, and a boy is picking me up for prom. My father walks me to the door. The boy looks nice in his tuxedo. He pins a corsage to my dress and we walk away, my arm under his. We walk into the dance and all my friends smile at me because he's so handsome. We dance, and my heart jumps when he kisses me on the lips. It's a fantasy. Prom was two years ago and I went alone. I don't have any real friends, and all the boys I've met wouldn't be content with a kiss on the lips. I'm nineteen years old and I dream of being seventeen. I would trade places with a child right now if it meant I could be normal. I can't be with anyone. I can't get close. I'm alone.

Maybe I could live in that fantasy. Forget the rules, forget everything. I didn't choose this life. Someone chose it for me, even if that someone was me. . . . Maybe I'm losing my mind.

I think I was twelve when Mother and I had the talk for the first time: "When the time comes, Mia, you'll know what to do. We cannot let a single life get in the way." I didn't want it to be true. I still don't. All I want is to close my eyes and wake up in my bed, eat some eggs and tell Mother about the crazy dream I just had. I want to close my eyes so bad, but I'm afraid of the things I see. A woman in a red dress, floating into forgottenness. A man I knew facedown in the garbage.

I felt my muscles tense, first in my hands, then my forearms. I heard his collarbone snap. His head became heavier and heavier, until I let his face slip through my hands and watched his limp body collapse on itself as if someone had cut the strings off him. I could see it happening, and I try to convince myself I thought it through, but I didn't. It was all instinct. I didn't think. I just . . . happened.

Mother said I would understand when I grew older. I don't want to. I don't want to be like her. I do what she tells me to do. It usually means learning new things, and I'm happy to do it. This. I don't have what it takes for this. We're supposed to protect people.

Dieter wanted to help. "Why are you crying, Mi'a?" I could have told him the truth, that I'm—

—LILI, WATCH OUT!

—OH SHIT!

I've lost control. We're gonna crash.

—AAAAAAAHHHHHHHH!

. . .

I can't . . . feel my . . .

ENTR'ACTE

Rule #4: Don't Draw Attention to Yourself

AD 1608

The front axle on their carriage broke as they hit a hole. The rain and hail had left the road to Amsterdam in the worst shape they had seen it. There would be no one to fix it in the nearby villages, and as much as Sura dreaded the long walk home, she hoped it would help her shake the feeling of disappointment.

The sawmill they had just seen was a remarkable feat of engineering. Powered by the wind, it was the first of its kind, and she knew others like it would soon fill the landscape. It was fast enough to make the men toiling in sawpits look like they were standing still. It would allow the Dutch to build ships faster and cheaper than anyone else, to control shipping routes and claim more colonies. Sura knew this was more than a piece of technology: that machine would change the map of the world.

And yet, she felt let down by the experience. Perhaps it was because she had spent too much time building it up in her head. The ride there was long and uneventful, and her daughter Ariani slept for most of it. Sura let her imagination run wild. Magnificent castles stretching their long arms into the sky to catch the breath of the gods. Timber conveyed from the hills by endless loops of moving link chain.

What she saw was clunky and noisy, completely devoid of aesthetic consideration. The sails, she thought, were poorly angled and the cap couldn't be turned in to the wind like that of the tower mills she had seen in England. She tried to find awe in seeing the contraption move on its own, powered by an invisible force. For a moment she considered building one herself. She quickly gave up on the idea but left open the possibility of an afternoon spent putting what she imagined to paper.

—Mother, look! A traveling show!

Street artists were a staple of Amsterdam life, especially in the fall. Surrounded by a perimeter canal, the city couldn't grow with the population. It was bursting at the seams with factory workers, traders, and migrants arriving every day from the four corners of the world. What Amsterdam lacked in space, it more than made up for in entertainment. Despite her mother's warnings, Ariani, who was now a very precocious ten, often ran outside to chase the sound of crowds gathering for jugglers or fire breathers.

There were, indeed, people up ahead—thirty or forty, probably the entire village. All were facing the river, arms raised, cheering and screaming. As they drew closer, Sura made out the words. The hair on her arms stood on end and she squeezed her daughter's hand harder and harder as her heartbeat quickened. This, alas, was no traveling show.

—Ariani, put your hood up and don't say a word.

Sura took off her necklace and hid it inside her boot. She had seen mobs like this one before. She had seen women hanged or burned alive. No one knew why, but the temperature had cooled in recent years. Weather patterns were chaotic, thunderstorms appearing out of nowhere and laying waste to fields and farmland. Entire crops were lost. People were hungry, angry. Unable to explain the phenomenon with the knowledge at hand, they found their answers in superstition.

—Mother! There's someone in the water.

—Ariani! Not a word. Keep your head down.

In the river, a young woman was screaming for help, struggling to keep her head above water. Her hands and feet were bound together, and a rope was tied around her waist so she could be brought to shore.

—She needs help, Mother!

Ariani had a good heart, always had. In the city, she fed birds and dogs and starving men, brought soup and blankets to the homeless. Her mother disapproved—the streets were not safe for a child her age—but she could not bring herself to forbid it. This was different.

—There is nothing we can do for her, Ariani. Remember the rules. Do not draw attention to yourself.

Ariani was not a rebellious child—far from it—but it was difficult for someone so young to weigh something concrete, like the screams of a young woman drowning, against something as abstract as a rule. She let go of her mother's hand.

—Ariani!

The child ran through the crowd, to the bald man holding the end of the rope.

—Bring her back, mister! She's drowning!

—We'll bring her back if she sinks, but she won't. She's a witch! Have you ever seen a witch, little girl?

This was a "swimming." If the accused was innocent, she would sink and hopefully be brought back before dying. A devil worshiper, on the other hand, would float. Having renounced her baptism, she would be rejected by water.

—She doesn't float because she's a witch, mister. She floats because she has little muscle and she's a little fat. Fat has a lower density than water.

—Density?

—Yes, mister. Density is how much matter is in an object divided by how much space it occupies.

Ariani said it with a smile. She had repeated that formula many times but had never found a practical use for it until now.

—That is utter nonsense!

—No, it is not. *You* would most certainly float if they threw you in, mister.

The man did not take kindly to the accusation, but Ariani

ignored the screaming and cursing. She was still proud of her scientific explanation. She had turned vague knowledge into something tangible. She remembered that air is also not as dense and turned to the woman in the river.

—Exhale, madam! Exhale! Get the air out of your lungs and you will sink!

The woman did as instructed and, as Ariani predicted, her body disappeared underwater.

—The heiden speaks the devil's tongue. She spoke of density and put a spell on the witch!

Heidens, often called Egyptians by the locals, were societal pariahs throughout Europe. The skin tone of the Eighty-Seven was a common enough sight in Amsterdam, but there were few immigrants in rural areas and heidens were persecuted for their mere presence. Fearing for her child, Sura did what she could to defuse the situation.

—We are not heidens. We are traders from Amsterdam. We work with the VOC.

It was true. Upon her arrival in Amsterdam, the Eighty-Seven had purchased a fair number of shares in the Dutch East India Company and were selling goods from the colonies to the wealthy. True or not, it did not matter to the villagers, who were now screaming for more blood.

—Hang the witch!

Sura heard the words and kneeled without thinking. Visions of the past rushed into her mind. The wind blowing louder than her cries, driving sand in her eyes. Her small arms wrestling those of a man, trying to rip the next stone from his hand. Her mother's lifeless face warped and distorted like wax on a burning stove.

Sura pleaded for her daughter, she begged as she had done for her mother. She knew full well the villagers wouldn't listen. She had seen what fear could do to people. A woman grabbed Ariani by the arm. Two men ran to her aid and tied the screaming child's hands behind her back. A rope went up and around a high branch. The two men pulled, and pulled, until Sura's daughter was hanging in midair. Her small body twisted like a worm while the bald man stood in front of her watching.

Run, save her child, or kill them all. Sura did the math before her fever got too strong. The weight of the child would spread evenly through the surface of the rope around her neck. The thicker the rope, the smaller the pressure. Seventy-eight pounds of child spread over twelve square inches of rope meant that either the rope was too thick, or the child was too light. Either way, Ariani did not need saving, and Sura was done running.

She picked up two broken branches and hid them in her palms. With an uneven end, a hundred pounds of force should suffice to break skin. Sura let the fever take over.

She walked behind the man nearest her, stabbed him three times through the kidneys. Quick blows, arms close to the body. The man groaned and felt his back with his hand. His wife got stabbed in the carotid artery. She didn't scream. Everyone kept staring at Ariani. Sura's steps were brisk, her blows precise and controlled. One. Two. Three. The wooden sticks went in and out of bodies faster than anyone could see. Four, five, six. Most just stood in shock, unsure of what had happened. They were all dead, they just didn't know. Nine were hit before the first one fell to the ground. Five more before someone pointed at Sura. Eighteen were done for before anyone did anything about it.

The first to come at Sura was a skinny man in a green suit holding a pitchfork. Sura grabbed a teenage boy paralyzed with fear and impaled him on the incoming tines. The man in the suit tried to hold on and fell forward. Sura ignored him and removed the weapon from the boy. She threw it at a woman who was running away. If everyone had run, the woman might have been safe, but they didn't. She fell face-first into the mud, a long wooden handle sticking out of her neck.

The bald man was still staring at Ariani when the child swung forward and grabbed his head between her legs. She pushed herself up to relieve the pressure around her neck.

At the front of the remaining crowd, a man stood still holding an ax. Sura walked up to him at a steady pace, tore the ax from his hands, and split his head in half in one swoop. She let her anger loose. The twenty people left standing thought they could find safety in numbers and huddled together. The Eighty-Seven cut through them like a ship through fog. None of them were whole after thirty seconds, their parts mixed together like a jigsaw puzzle someone had dropped on the floor.

It would take another hour for the first eighteen to bleed out and stop moaning, but Sura didn't hear them anymore. She took a knife off one of the dead and cut her daughter's hands free. Ariani passed the noose over her head, her legs still wrapped around the bald man's head. She took the knife her mother handed her and cut the man's throat from shoulder to shoulder. She jumped off him and pushed him in the river.

—You see, mister? I told you you would float!

Without a word, Sura examined her daughter from head to toe. She turned her around to make sure there were no wounds.

—Mother, look! She's alive! The lady's alive!

They pulled the young woman out of the water. Ariani rolled her on her side to set her hands and legs free, but her mother stopped her.

—What, Mother? Why?

Sura did not speak. She did not need to. Ariani looked around and she knew. Remember the rules. The Eighty-Seven had just slaughtered a village. What were the odds this young lady could keep that a secret?

Ariani's eyes filled with tears but she stopped herself from crying. She handed her mother the knife and gently stroked the woman's hair. What seemed so abstract an hour ago was now painfully concrete. Do not draw attention to yourself.

ACT II

9

Death Valley Blues

I can't get the smell out of my nose. Outside, the war smells like piss and wet cement, but in here it reeks of burned flesh and pus. Human beings broken down into their ingredients. A million odors competing with one another. The putrid smell of rotting meat. The sweetness of caramelized fat. Charred leather, singed hair, and the metallic smell of blood. The worst part is these people are still alive. This; this is what Dante wrote about. The stench is so thick I can taste it. I can feel it crawling all over my skin.

I woke up in a hospital near Berlin. One of the Peenemünde engineers found us on the side of the road. Pure luck. We could have died alone in a ditch. Von Braun's left shoulder is wrecked. His arm is fractured in two places. He'll live, no thanks to me. I'm okay, except for a nasty cut above the eye.

There was an air raid not far from here. Allied forces dropped incendiaries by the thousand near a tire factory. The firestorm spread ten blocks in every direction. Thousands died in the inferno. The ones in here only wish they did. Most are civilians, some military. We can't tell which is which because their clothes fused with their skin when the air around them reached four thousand degrees.

They wanted to keep von Braun for surgery, but we can't wait. There are three thousand people making their way to Bleicherode, and von Braun is the man in charge. He knows it. He insisted they set his arm in a cast and let us leave. He is loyal to his people, maybe even a little brave. It bothers me, somehow. The world is easier to grasp in black-and-white. This war . . . it's nothing but gray.

The other person in my room is a ten-year-old girl. I know that only because I heard the doctor say it. She has no skin left, none. She's just a dark red shape, scabs in the form of a human being. I can't bear to look at her, but she has to, because her fucking eye-lids are gone. I wish her a quick death. Her, and the people who dropped those bombs on her, and the Nazis, and the German police. Maybe the whole world should burn. We don't deserve to live if we're capable of this.

I want to go home, but for now I'll have to be content with leaving this hospital. We'd better do it soon. A nurse came in five minutes ago to draw my blood. Mother said they can't look at our blood. No one can. I told her to stop. I did. I told her twice, then I snapped her wrist in half.

10

This Land Is Your Land

Dear Sarah,

I can only imagine your disquietude for I do not have children of my own, but I know all too well the iciness of an empty house. May your daughter return to you safely and expeditiously.

Thank you for inquiring about my situation. I am still teaching at Caltech but my research for the American government now takes up the bulk of my time. Sentiment towards the Chinese being what it is, my continued involvement in this project never ceases to surprise me. Nevertheless, this morning I received news that our program had been fully funded. I must admit to some trepidation but I am also filled with excitement. There is a small celebration scheduled for tonight and I promised to attend. As you know, social events are not my forte but I have been told these things only come with practice. We shall see. It is a momentous event for our group and despite my intermittent misgivings, I feel mostly at home in the company of these men.

Outside our lab, I remain very much a stranger. My colleagues are encouraging me to seek citizenship now that the Chinese Exclusion Act has been repealed. I am touched by their support, but a piece of paper will not put a stop to the stares and whispers. Citizen or not, they will not let me own a business, or marry whom I please. Perhaps it is simply our nature to mistrust what we do not know. Please forgive my grousing. I know you have endured your own share of prejudice.

I find your research on carbon dioxide both fascinating and daunting. I am baffled by the amount of measurements you have managed to collect in so little time. I have given your theory some thought and it shames me to say I do not have a proper answer. I would tell you that this is not my area of expertise, but it seems like a poor excuse knowing it is not yours either. You truly are a Renaissance woman.

Your data unambiguously suggests CO_2 concentrations are on the rise, but a correlate in global temperature seems much more difficult to establish over a short period. As for mankind's contribution to the phenomenon, it is worth considering the possibility that CO_2 concentration has always been on the rise since our planet developed an atmosphere. From my limited perspective, the only way to properly answer these questions would be to extend your study over millennia instead of decades. I know how impractical that may seem since you do not have CO_2 measurements from a thousand years ago. I also realize air from another era might prove difficult to obtain. With that said, I am fully confident in your ability to resolve the issue.

With your permission, I would like to share some data of my own. I am wrestling with the limits of fin stabilization and I would welcome your perspective on the matter if you are so inclined.

Yours faithfully,
Hsue-Shen Tsien

11

Y'a Pas de Printemps

All three thousand of us arrived in Bleicherode. We didn't leave anyone behind. No one died. We kept families together and we made it. The Russians took Peenemünde. We just found out. The Americans, well, they're so close, we can hear artillery fire from here. They'll take Mittelwerk soon. Too bad we won't be around when they do.

Kammler found out we followed his orders. I'm sure he was ecstatic. But with Germany losing ground, he has "concerns" about von Braun being captured by the Americans. No kidding. Now we're surrounded by soldiers all day. There's a whole lot of them, too. Major General Walter Robert Dornberger arrived this morning to meet us. He and von Braun hugged like long-lost brothers. Clearly these two like each other. Dornberger did pretty much the same thing we did and moved *his* men here to get away from the Allies. He's in charge now. We're not a group of scientists anymore. We're the German army.

At first, I didn't understand why Kammler wanted to keep us here. I thought he was just being stubborn. Give up, already! You've lost the war! I'm such an idiot. He knows he's lost. I'm sure he's known for a while now. He's not thinking of Germany, or Hitler, or anything else. He's doing all this for himself, holding the scientists hostage as a bargaining chip. I should have known. These people are evil and if there's one thing the devil is good at, it's saving its own skin. He'll have to move us soon, but his first order of business is to increase von Braun's value.

Kammler ordered all the classified documents we were carrying destroyed. Boom. All the science, all the research, the notes, the microfilms, he wants it all burned. Von Braun will be worth a whole lot more if everything exists only in his head.

Von Braun had his own men load everything into trucks. He's maniacally methodical. I'm sure he'd insist on loading it all up himself if his arm weren't in a cast. There must be thirty tons of documents in these trucks. Decades of passion and dedication, all sorted inside neatly labeled boxes. It must be strange, watching your whole life being hauled away to the incinerator. The last box is being loaded now.

This will set us back . . . years, maybe decades. Years of watching hundreds of the most brilliant minds wasting their time doing things they've already done. The knowledge in these boxes is what I came for, why I'm risking my life and the lives of everyone else. I killed someone for it. Now it will burn and there's nothing I can do to stop it. I only get to watch.

Time to go. The SS are getting into their cars. General Dornberger will escort the cargo himself. I'm in one of the trucks, with an engineer from Peenemünde and our SS driver. The uniform makes me sick to my stomach, but I'm glad I'm not behind the wheel. Off we go. It's out of my hands, now. I can't hijack a convoy by myself.

This is a nightmare—a gorgeous, heartbreaking nightmare. This whole place would be like a postcard without the barbed wire and the five thousand soldiers. We're in the Harz mountains and spring is in full swing. Melting snow is making its way down, painting the rock face with miniature waterfalls. I see flocks of black storks returning home from their African winter. Everything is coming alive after a long, cold death. I can hear it, smell it. I feel . . . light, in the most horrible way. All the weight on my shoulders, all the pressure, gone. I'm like a twig in a river, just floating along and taking in the view. In some ways, it reminds me of home. Not the mountains, but the inevitability of it all.

That's what being around Mother feels like. That's why I follow her. If she sets her mind to something, just strap yourself in and enjoy the ride. Mother *always* has a plan. She's the river. I just go with the flow. Only she's not here right now and this river leads to a deadly fall. I've failed. I did it all for nothing.

You have to admire Kammler in some ways. He's a rare breed. No honor, no love for his country. He doesn't care for a moment about his place in history, how the world will remember him. He just wants to save his own neck and he'll kill everyone in Germany in the process if he has to. A perfect little machine built for one purpose only: survival. He's a rat. I almost envy him. I don't mean the evilness, just the simplicity of it. Never having to consider anything but yourself. It must be very . . .

I suppose we all have something we care about more than anything else, that one thing we'd kill for, die for. I know I do, but watching von Braun pack up his notes, I realized how much it all meant to him. I'm not comparing him to Kammler, but it was obvious that science is higher up on his list of things that matter than, say, people. I shouldn't be surprised. Mother said so before I left. He only cares about the work, not who he does it for.

I miss her. I miss small things about her. Breakfast. Mother makes the best eggs. I miss my room, my clothes. I miss music. Our trucks don't have a radio. I wish I could play my own records. Someone should invent that, a portable record player. Hamburgers. Forget breakfast, I wish for a hamburger. A real hamburger, not a stupid Hamburg steak. I want a bun, and fries, and a milkshake.

Our driver is smiling. He looks genuinely happy. I wonder what he's thinking. He's probably just enjoying the ride. I see the uniform and I forget these people are even human. Most of them would probably be decent people under normal circumstances. Not great people, not particularly brave, or nice, or smart. Just . . . okay. Like an extra on a movie set. I can tell this one doesn't care what we're hauling, or that he's been asked to burn more knowledge than he can fathom. He wouldn't understand if I explained it to him. He's been on the wrong side of a war for too long, following orders that make no sense to him most of the time. Today, his orders are to drive a truck on a beautiful road in the Harz mountains. He doesn't have to walk in the rain or lie facedown in the mud. He doesn't have to kill anyone. I'd be smiling, too.

We're slowing down. This must be the last village before our destination. The SS car has stopped and we're pulling over beside them. Our driver is straightening his collar. It seems Major General Dornberger wants to talk to us.

—*Du solltest alleine gehen. Eine SS-Eskorte würde auffallen.*

You should go alone. An SS escort will attract attention. I wish I could say it the way he does. He has a great voice. It's not particularly deep, not very loud either. But there's something . . . leathery about it. Soothing and commanding at the same time. It makes you feel like everything will be fine if you do what he says.

Our driver is getting out. I don't understand. Dornberger just dismissed our entire escort. Are they going to kill us? All the SS are getting into Dornberger's fancy black car. But not him. He's walking towards us. Towards me it would seem. There was a pen in between the seats a minute ago. There it is. I'll hide it up my sleeve.

There's a piece of paper in Dornberger's hand. I think he wants to give it to me but he wants to say something first. He wants me to bring my head closer. I let the pen slide into my palm.

—Your mother sends her best. She wants to know where you are.

Mother. I should have known. It makes sense. Dornberger is an engineer. This whole project was his before Kammler kicked him out. The V-2's his baby as much as it is von Braun's. He wouldn't want our cargo to burn any more than I do.

That's it. He's gone now. There's no one watching us anymore.

It's just me, and the two engineers von Braun trusts the most. Let's see what's on that piece of paper.

There's a map with some coordinates. We're not driving to the incinerator. We're heading to an abandoned mine about three miles from here. I think I know what the plan is. We'll hide the documents inside the mine, seal it closed with dynamite if we can. When this is all over, the Americans can dig it out and von Braun will get all of his precious research back, all sorted and in neatly labeled boxes.

I guess I haven't failed yet. I can get von Braun out of Germany. I needed help and Mother sent me a major general in the German army, all wrapped up in a neat little bow. Mother always has a plan. She—Wait. The map is pretty clear, but these coordinates makes no sense. 21–3–15 26–5–19 23–3–10. They aren't coordinates at all. This is a message from Mother.

Letters to numbers, I suppose, but she'd have used a cipher. For a short message like this, she'd probably go with a one-time pad no one can break. Now I just need the pad. There's no point in trying to guess, so I must already have it. Mother would have given it to me. Think, Mia. Think.

"Your mother sends her best. She wants to know where you are." Mother knows exactly where I am, or she couldn't have sent Dornberger to meet us. Bleicherode. That must be it. Bleicherode is the pad. I need a pen.

Twenty-one. That's a "t" . . . Three . . . Fifteen . . .
. . .

Let's see what we got.

                    Trkrclslv

Does that mean anything? Tracker . . . close. Tracker close. Leave.

Fuck me.

12

Stormy Weather

I have not heard from Mia since she arrived in Bleicherode, and there are few intelligence reports coming out of the area.

I know General Dornberger rendezvoused with them as I asked. I know he delivered my message. I did not want to risk burning him, but I had no choice. I told Dornberger his escape route in the north was compromised, that he had to join von Braun and head south. He could not do it on his own without arousing suspicion, so he took all of his troops with him. He will help as much as he can. He is an intelligent man, enough to know he is more valuable with von Braun than on his own. Dornberger could betray us. He offered to help only to save himself, and there is no reason to believe his priorities will change if the Germans find out. There is also no point in thinking about it. He is on our side for now, and there is very little I can do if he chooses to not uphold his end of the bargain. In fact, there is very little I can do, *period*.

I am out of focus, distracted by the smallest thing. I am grateful to Hsue-Shen for his insight but muddled by his suggestion. I cannot go back in time, nor can I walk to the general store and order air by its vintage year. Perhaps some form of container, sealed shut and conserved for centuries . . . I am nowhere near a solution, and my train of thought keeps veering in a more existential direction.

I became interested in climate change because my mother did. She became involved for the same reason. My grandmother is the one who started it all, but why? Why would she choose to go down that path? I realize how important the outcome is for the future, ours and everyone else's, but we are the Kibsu. Our path is to the stars. More puzzling is the fact that my mother stumbled upon her mother's notes by accident. My grandmother abandoned her life's work to pursue this inquiry, and she did not tell a soul. Take them to the stars. That is what we do. Preserve the knowledge. That is how we do it. Why did my grandmother break the rules? And if it was that important to her, why did she not want her daughter to know about it?

More questions and not a single answer. Mia is missing. The Tracker might be closing in on us.

I will pour myself a bath and read from the *Enūma Anu Enlil*. That should calm me down. I do not know why I like reading from it; it is nothing but the ramblings of ancient Akkadian fortune-tellers. Perhaps it reminds me of who I am. No one knows how we came to lose the knowledge that was once ours, but we did. At some point, one of us had to start from scratch, learn everything from nothing. I cannot imagine what it must have felt like for the Eleven, knowing there was so much beyond the sky but having no way to see it. Dreaming of civilizations a galaxy away, machines that can cross the heavens in an instant, yet stuck in the middle of the Iron Age. We were living in huts. Science was the domain of soothsayers. Somehow, we got our hands on these. The *Enūma Anu Enlil* was a series of tablets containing omens, some type of briefings for the king, warning him of things to come. Most of it is utter nonsense, but many of these omens were based on celestial phenomena: the way the moon behaves, the position of the sun, some stars and planets.

The tablet I am reading from is particularly grim. Whoever wrote it was not in a good place.

"If on the first day of Nisannu the sunrise is sprinkled with blood: grain will vanish in the country, there will be hardship and human flesh will be eaten."

Human flesh will be eaten. It would take a severe drought, or perhaps a long siege, to reach that level of desperation. Even then, I doubt cannibalism as a means of sustenance was really a thing. What is more interesting is the idea that a red sky in the morning is a bad omen. There is some truth to it. In high-pressure areas where good weather is found, there is more dirt and dust in the lowest layers of the sky. That dust scatters colors with a shorter wavelength and lets the red shine through. Where most people live, the weather moves from west to east, and if we see the sun rise through good weather that has already passed, that good weather likely made way for some bad. "Red sky at night, sailor's delight. Red sky in the morning, sailor's warning."

In these tablets, the red sky brings with it much more than bad weather. "If on the first day of Nisannu the sunrise looks sprinkled with blood and the light is cool: the king will die and there will be mourning in the country. If it becomes visible on the second day and the light is cool: the king's high official will die and mourning will not stop in the country."

Those first two days of the month of Nisannu must have been quite stressful. For the king, obviously, but also for the scholar who wrote it. If the sunrise did look bloody and no one died, there would be some explaining to do. Things get better for everyone on the third day.

"If the sunrise is sprinkled with blood on the third day: an eclipse will take place."

It goes on and on. Some parts are more interesting than others. One of the tablets is a crude mathematical scheme to predict what the moon will look like on a given day. It all seems childish now, but this was information worthy of a king back then. For us, it was a place to start.

To reach for the stars must have seemed an unsurmountable task, like finding air from a thousand years ago, but here we are, closer than ever. We are the Kibsu. We will prevail.

13

Trouble So Hard

Tick.

Tock.

Tick.

Tock.

It won't be long now.

Tick.

Tock.

They should have let me leave.

"I just want to go for a walk," I said.

"No, ma'am. We have orders to keep you safe."

Orders to keep me safe. What he meant is I'm a prisoner. We all are. Thousands of German engineers, wives, children, and nieces held prisoner by the Germans. The Third Reich is falling apart, and the Nazis are scrambling to keep it together any way they can. That includes holding their own people captive. Trust has never been one of Hitler's strong suits. It won't last, the Allies are nearby. It's just a question of time before they get to Bleicherode. I suppose that's good news, though the SS have orders to shoot us all when that happens. Sore losers. They'll do it, I'm sure. The real prize isn't here anymore.

Kammler sent them farther south, to Oberammergau, a small internment camp in the Bavarian Alps. Them. He sent *them* there. Von Braun and five hundred of his top people. No workers, no wives. No nieces. He had General Dornberger make the list. I guess he still doesn't trust von Braun. I find the irony slightly amusing, but it doesn't make up for the mess they've left behind. All those families we worked so hard to keep together, they broke them apart faster than they could say goodbye. I don't know if I was more heartbroken by the crying children or pissed we did all of that for nothing. The SS shoved everyone of value into trucks and they drove away. Dornberger went with them. It's so absurd, I don't know why I'm doing this anymore.

Guarding your own people isn't that hard. There are only a handful of soldiers left here to keep us company, and shoot us all if the Americans get too close. The rest of Dornberger's men are busy dying in the mud somewhere. I've been lying in my bunk for . . . almost three hours now. I don't know where everyone is. I have the whole room for myself. The light in here is something else. I opened all the windows to let the cool breeze in. The wind is picking up now. I can hear it whistle along the window frames. Inside there's paper flying everywhere, posters flapping on the concrete walls. I don't care. I'm burning hot.

Bombs are dropping all over Europe. Thirty, forty, fifty million dead—*million*—and I'm here trying to save a handful, or one. I've already killed someone doing it. All so I can hand them over to the Americans for them to make even bigger bombs. The craziest part is the Germans are doing the same thing. Kammler is trying to save the *exact same people*! And he's doing it so he can hand them over to the Americans as well! You think this would be easy, right? Hell, they could make a deal with Kammler right now and be done with it. Maybe they will. I hope they don't. I really do. I want to see that evil prick burn. I want to light the match myself.

Maybe it's the absurdity of it all. Maybe it's the notion that the Tracker could show up any minute. Maybe I'm still shaken by what happened with Dieter, or that nurse, but I can't stop thinking about the people here. Ordinary people, expendable people. There are kids *everywhere*. There's a boy, maybe seven years old. His name is Frank. He traveled with his parents from Peenemünde. Days cooped up inside a shitty transport truck on a bumpy road

74

with a bunch of people in brown suits. He didn't say a word, never complained. He played with a toy motorcycle—probably the one personal item his parents let him take along—a piece of twine, and some paper clips I stole from von Braun's office. Now he's here. He's found a couple of kids close to his age. They play marbles all day in the yard. His parents weren't on Dornberger's list. They aren't on anyone's list. Dad is an accountant. I'm not sure about Mom. They don't matter, to anyone. Kammler will have them rounded up and shot if the Allies make it all the way here. God forbid the enemy get their hands on another accountant. It might not happen. The SS might take to their heels when they see the Americans. These people aren't worth dying for. Not Frank, anyway. Not his parents. Kammler wants them killed anyway. He has no idea who these people are, but there are too many folks here to sort through. Mom and Dad just aren't important enough to justify the effort, and no one gives a shit about Frank.

I'm not supposed to care either. I'm supposed to find a quiet way out of here and head home. Dornberger will take it from here. I know that's what Mother wants. She wants me to escape and leave all those families here to be killed when the good guys get too close. Fear the Tracker. Always run, never fight. Mother made me repeat the rules every day as a child. She still does sometimes. I'll admit, that one always struck a chord. Eight-year-old me dreamed of giant monsters, fire-spitting dragons burning down cities. Mother said the Tracker was just a man, but it didn't matter. How can the devil just be a man? I know better now, but thinking about him still makes me nervous. Run from the Tracker. Always run.

I've never seen him, of course. Mother's never seen him. We haven't met the Tracker in . . . seven generations. Not since the Ninety-Two found her mother's bones boiled clean in a wooden box. He had left a note: "I'll see you soon." I wonder if that's true. I know the Ninety-Two was as real as I am—I've read her journals—and I have no reason to doubt her mother was killed by an evil man. But I wonder if the stories we're told weren't embellished, even a little, for our benefit. A bit of flair for dramatic effect. For all I know the Tracker is just a name we give evil when it crosses our path. Something for naughty children to fear. Our boogeyman.

Fear the Tracker. I suppose I do. I *should* run. That's what they expect of me, von Braun, the OSS, my mother.

Well, fuck von Braun and fuck the OSS. It's been three hours, that should be enough. I bought rat poison when we left Peenemünde. It was just a precaution, a way to kill myself, or von Braun if things went south. I made my way into the kitchen this morning and poured all of it in the stew. Not ours, the good stuff they serve the SS. The meat they have isn't that fresh. They put enough vinegar and spices in there to mask the stench, and the taste of the strychnine. Mother said they still use it as medicine in some places. Put enough of it inside someone and it will do a number on their central nervous system. The muscle spasms should have started before they got to dessert. Thirty minutes later they would have been on the ground, convulsing. They probably broke some bones, bit their tongues off or split their heads open. If they were lucky, their lungs seized and they died gasping for air. If they weren't, well, it took a bit longer. However long it takes to exhaust yourself to death jackknifing on the concrete floor. I don't care either way. It's over by now. I'll stop by the officers' mess on my way out and take care of those who weren't hungry.

These people are safe now, as safe as anyone can be. They can go wherever they please. I can go and finish what I started. This is *my* mission. I killed a man to get this far. I'll be damned if I give up now because of some mythic creature I've never seen. I'm scared, yes, but I'm not leaving Germany without von Braun. Kammler did me a favor. Five hundred men is a lot easier to move than three thousand. There's a train leaving in an hour. I can make it. I'll be in Oberammergau by morning.

14

Dream

There's no one on this train; it's quiet. I should be asleep by now, it's . . . shit, 3:00 A.M. I'm exhausted but my mind won't rest.

Twenty-seven. Twenty-seven men lying dead on the ground. I did that. I did it to save thousands, but if I'm honest I didn't care. I was angry. I didn't feel remorse when I saw them lying there. I didn't feel anything. They were Nazis. They were going to kill everyone and I killed them first.

Dieter. That little girl without skin. The SS I killed, the ones I thought about killing on that bridge. They're all blurring into one another, slowly fading in the background. It's all part of the scenery. A woman in a red dress floating in the river.

I'm good at this, somehow. I don't want to be. "We kill to survive, like every other living thing." That's what Mother said. I didn't believe it. Not me.

. . .

I didn't want to be like them. I *never* wanted to be like them.

Look at me now. I'd never hurt anyone before. I've been here a few weeks and I've killed twice already. It's getting easier. Dieter was hard. I couldn't care less about the SS lying on the kitchen floor.

I'm not like that. It's this war, this place. The Nazis keep redefining insanity. They've turned their country into a satanic ritual.

It's in the air we breathe, the water we drink. I'm swimming in it and it's changing me. I'm losing my fucking mind, one chunk at a time. I need to get away from the war before there's nothing left of me to find.

15

L'Âme au Diable

I almost missed them. By the time I got to the Oberammergau camp where von Braun and his men had been moved, General Dornberger had already convinced the superior officer there that it was a bad idea to have all of Germany's top scientists in one place. One lucky bomb and boom. No more scientists, and a firing squad for the man in charge. The officer agreed to let everyone stay in the villages around the camp, even gave them some civilian clothes so they could blend in. Dornberger delivered in spades. Everyone is free, more or less.

I found von Braun and Dornberger in this café an hour ago. They've arranged for some vehicles from Bleicherode to come get us, but they apparently don't have enough gas to take us anywhere. I don't know who they talked to in Bleicherode, or if they found out about the guards. They didn't mention it if they did. I don't think either of them would care.

This is crazy. I thought I'd have to break them out of an internment camp. I imagined a firefight, bombs going off, blood everywhere. Instead I find two dandies drinking espresso in an upscale café. Their idea of "roughing it." You can't get coffee anywhere nowadays, no sugar, no tea. The owner of this place must have friends in high places. Von Braun saw me when I came in. He nodded at me, got me a chair, and went on with his conversation as if nothing happened. I had to interrupt for them to fill me in. In a nutshell, we need to find gas and enough food for five hundred people while we wait for the Americans. I don't know how long that will be. Still, this all seems petty compared to what I had in mind. It could be as easy as—

—Forgive me for interrupting again, gentlemen, but do we have any VzBV letterhead left?

They're smiling. I guess they hadn't thought of that. Dornberger doesn't seem all that convinced, but von Braun is getting up. Oh, they're both leaving now. Thank you for ignoring me. You're welcome! All they need is a typewriter and the project-for-whatever-we-said-it-was will requisition all the fuel and supplies we need. The only thing left to do now is to wait for the Americans to come to us and drink some coffee. I need one. I haven't slept a wink.

This café is like Neverland. Outside it smells of death and dampness. In here it's fresh coffee and chocolate pastries. Where on earth did they get chocolate? It's like the war never made it past the front door. White china, white linen, white chairs. Come in! The world's gone to hell, but we've got Franzbrötchen!

Here comes the *Kellnerin*.

—*Einen Kaffee, bitte.*

I— Shit.

The war's back. Waffen-SS just walked in. Wow, there must be a dozen of them. I can see their reflection in the window. They're moving on either side of the door. One of them is just behind me, I can hear him breathe. They must be making way for someone. I wonder—Here he is. Oh, great! Two oak leaves on his collar patch. He's an *Oberführer*. That's a . . . I don't know what that is, an über-colonel or something. A very important asshole. You can tell how full of themselves they are by how slow they walk. This one is sloooooow. I hope he wants his coffee to go. I also wish he'd come in five minutes ago, when I had a major general sitting beside me.

Happy thoughts. A week from now, I could be back in Washington eating pancakes. Oh, here's my coffee.

—*Danke.*

Über-colonel is staring at me. It's making me nervous. I'm

sure he knows. Could *he* be . . . ? Nah. I'm being paranoid. Then again, if the devil is walking the earth, I can see him wearing this uniform. There's enough evil to pass around in these parts.

—I'm sorry. Do you mind?

Shit. He's talking to me. My blood pressure shot through the roof. He didn't wait for me to answer. He just sat down across from me. Now I'm *really* being paranoid.

—I—no. Please.

—*Kellnerin!* Coffee!

No knives on the table. I can't run. I'll have to go through a dozen men if he decides to stop me, and I won't kill them all with a spoon.

How would I know if he's the Tracker? Our ancestors described them as ghostly and ashen. That's what Mother said. I'm not entirely sure what that means. We lived in Asia back then, so my bet is they'd never seen a white guy before. There weren't that many around those parts a thousand years ago. This man—I don't know. He's not the whitest fellow I've seen. He won't win Aryan of the Year but he could use some time in the sun. I'm freaking out now. He might be—Really? He's staring down my shirt.

—Sir?

—What a beautiful necklace.

My necklace. My heart's throbbing. That medallion is the one thing that survived us all, the only tangible proof of who we are, short of looking in a mirror. That necklace belonged to the One. I didn't even want to touch it when Mother gave it to me. We've held on to that thing for three thousand years. I didn't want to be the idiot who drops it in a lake.

—Thank you, sir. It's a family heirloom.

—That stone. Is it a sapphire? I've never seen one this orange.

—It's just a garnet, I'm afraid.

—May I?

He wants to touch it. I don't think he means to harm me. In fact, he's not paying attention to me at all.

—Here. Let me take if off.

He's holding it to the outside light. That stone is so close to his eye now . . . What is he—

—You're right. Not a sapphire.

—How can you tell?

—Believe it or not I was a jeweler before all this. Seems like a million years ago. The refraction's not right for a sapphire.

—I told you it—

—It's not a garnet either.

—Then what is it?

—I don't know. . . . It seems I'm a little rusty. Here, you can have it back. Thank you for the company.

He's leaving. He's no Tracker, that's for sure. This isn't the depraved rabid animal Mother described. I look at this man and I see . . . dispassion, indifference. That wasn't wrath or furious anger sitting in front of me. That was apathy.

What would the Tracker have done? Slash my throat right here at the table? We left this country because of him. Mother said he, they, were getting close.

How did she know? How does she know now?

I suppose it's as good an excuse as any if you have to convince a child to leave everything behind. Then again, maybe she did know. A stranger asking too many questions. Old friends turning up dead. We've never met any of them, but we have hundreds of people working for us. Maybe they knew. It's kind of funny when I think about it. I'm a carbon copy of my mother, but there's still so much I don't know about her. What would she have done in my place? Would she have killed Dieter? Would she be angry that I did?

I'd still look exactly like Mother no matter who she slept with, but maybe *I'm* what he was there for. Maybe they *fucked* in Bad Saarow. "I didn't think you'd come back, not after what happened." Maybe she broke up with him there. Maybe . . . Maybe I need to get some sleep.

16

Down, Down, Down

Hitler is dead. We heard it on the radio.

Berlin has fallen, Hitler is dead, and we're still here. We've "set up camp" in a small town near the Austrian border. That's what they said, Dornberger and von Braun. "We'll set up camp here." There's no camp. We're in a resort hotel, for crying out loud. Haus Ingeburg, that's what it's called. There's an indoor pool with a view of the Alps. There's a sauna. Von Braun is in the fucking sauna.

We wait. We wait and listen to the radio. The Americans can't be more than a couple of miles away, but so are the Germans, and no one wants to risk getting caught. Not when we're so close. Wait. Wait. Wait.

Mother must be going mad. I know I am. I haven't slept in three days. I need Mother. I need to ask—I don't even know what I want to ask. Dieter, the Tracker, Bad Saarow. I have a thousand questions stampeding in my head. I can't formulate a single one. It doesn't matter. She'll make sense of all this. I just need to get home.

I cut myself. I didn't even notice. I was playing with a switchblade I stole—confiscated—from a kid in Bleicherode, scratching my name on a wooden table. It's a nice table. I don't know why I was doing it. Von Braun walked by. He looked at me and screamed my name. I thought he was angry about the table, or looking at my leg jumping like a jackhammer, but he grabbed my arm, hard. I . . . I cut myself. Long cuts—not too deep but deep enough—across my forearm. Lots of them. Maybe a dozen. I must have been at it for a while. I was as shocked as he was when I saw the blood. I didn't know what to say. There was nothing *to* say. No matter how convoluted a story I could come up with, there was no way to sell this as anything but what it was. I tried, though. I really tried.

Von Braun didn't say anything. He didn't scold me. He let me pretend. I thought that was nice of him. I suppose normal isn't what it once was. That or he didn't care. Here he is now. Oh, no. That's Magnus, the *other* von Braun. He's younger than his brother. An engineer. Everyone likes Magnus. I do, too. I suppose it doesn't hurt that he speaks English.

—Hi Lili! What are you doing?

—Just reading a book. You?

That's not true. I haven't opened it.

—Getting some fresh air.

He's smiling. Magnus is always happy. Always. I don't know how he does it. Then again, I don't know how he builds rockets for Nazis.

—Why did you do it, Magnus?

—Oh, that was easy. We despised the French, we were mortally afraid of the Soviets, we didn't believe the British could afford us, that left the Americans.

—I didn't mean that. I meant . . . Never mind.

I shouldn't have asked. I want them to be good people. I want all of this to be worth something, the dead, all that we did. If that's not true, if they're like Himmler . . .

—What?

—Building weapons, working for Hitler. Why did you do it?

—Says the girl who wants us to do the same thing for the United States.

I *am* a hypocrite.

—You're right. I don't want to know.

—They didn't leave us much choice.

He feels the need to justify himself. That's not the way to go. Getting up every morning is a choice. Not putting a P38 to your temple and blowing your brains out is a choice.

—You didn't have to do it. You certainly didn't have to be good at it.

—Do you know why Himmler had my brother arrested?

—What?

—You heard me. A year ago, why did they have him arrested?

—They said it was on suspicion of treason.

I just heard myself saying it, and I realized it doesn't make any sense. You don't suspect someone of treason then have him lead your biggest weapons project three months later, no matter how indispensable he may be. Von Braun wouldn't be alive if they thought he could betray them. They trusted him.

—That's funny. Suspicion of treason. Have you met Helmut Gröttrup?

—He was at Peenemünde, wasn't he?

—He was a manager, yes. Smart man. He and my brother didn't always see eye-to-eye, but they respected each other. Anyway, Helmut, Wernher, and—who else was there? Oh yes—Klaus Riedel, another scientist. It doesn't matter. They were all having dinner one night. A casual event, friends, engineers from the research center. They were all having drinks. Gröttrup, at some point, said he'd heard the war wasn't going well for the Germans, to which my brother replied that they should all be building spaceships anyway, not missiles. Rockets want to go up, he said, not down. It was innocent enough. But there was a young woman at dinner, a dentist, who turned out to be spying for the SS. Just Germany being Germany. She reported all of them to Kammler, who told Himmler. You know the rest.

—Spaceships?

—He meant it, you know. That's all he can think about. He wants to go to space himself. Only no one wants to fund that, so he does the next best thing. He builds rockets, the biggest ones he can.

—And you?

—Oh, I'm not as smart as he is. It doesn't really matter what I believe. I just like working with my brother.

I didn't know von Braun wanted the same thing we do. Listening to Magnus talk about his brother, there's something profoundly endearing about family. Unconditional love. That's worth saving. That's worth dying for.

—Is he still mad at me?

I snapped at von Braun this morning. No reason, just me being . . . The way he broke the shell on his boiled egg, the way he held his spoon. There was a spit bubble on the corner of his mouth. I . . . It was like time slowed down, almost to a halt. Everything was loud, screechy. I could hear my heartbeat, his chewing. Constant. Chewing . . .

—Oh, I'd be surprised if he rememb—Lili! what are you doing!

I have no idea. All I know is I'll lose my mind if I stay here another second. I need to do something. I can't drive to the border, there'll be checkpoints, soldiers. I'll take that bicycle and cut through the woods. With any luck, it'll be Americans at the bottom of the hill.

—I'm getting us out of here!

That is one ugly bicycle. It's heavy as hell with those milk churns in the back. Perfect for going downhill, and it's all downhill. I know I'm being stupid. We could wait it out. All we have to do is wait, but I can't sit still anymore. Even if I get caught, I did my job. They'll make it if I don't.

—Stop! Wait for me!

Magnus is following me. Now *he's* being stupid. There's no point in the both of us getting caught. Whatever. His call, not mine. Damn, this hill is steep. I hope I don't break my neck. I hope *Magnus* doesn't break his neck. I don't think von Braun will like me very much if I get his brother killed.

We're going too fast! We're like two rockets speeding through space. Except gravity is working for us, not against us. More weight, more speed. It's the milk churns. If I get rid of them, it'll slow me down. Ditch some weight . . .

I'm getting tunnel vision. The trees are flying by faster than my eyes can focus. We'll never be able to stop. If there's anything blocking that path, we'll drive right into it, or into a tree. It doesn't matter what it is. If it's solid, we're doomed. What happens when an unstoppable force meets an immovable object? You split your skull open, that's what happens.

I need both hands on the handlebar to keep the bicycle straight. This. Is. Not. Goooood.

I see someone down there. Forget the someone. I see a ditch. There's a fucking ditch!

—MAGNUS! WATCH OUT!

This is gonna hurt. OOOOOOOHHH NOOOOOOOO!

That pop. I dislocated my shoulder. Damn it hur—

—ON YOUR KNEES! NOW!

—No! Don't shoot! PLEASE DON'T SHOOT!

I can't tell if it's a German muzzle I feel on my neck or an American one. I'm sure the bullets feel the same. I can't feel it anymore. Whoever it is, he's coming around.

—Do you speak English, miss?

—I . . . Yes, I do. What's your name?

—PFC Frederick Schneikert. I need to see your hands, miss. Raise your hands.

Schneikert? But he speaks English. This is confusing.

—Who are you with, PFC Schneikert?

—324th Infantry Regiment, 44th Infantry Division.

Americans. We made it.

17

Going Home

My daughter has returned to me. She led von Braun and the best of his people into the hands of the Americans. She accomplished her mission, but all that matters to me is that she is safe and sound. I can tell it was not easy for her. She has been distant ever since she came home.

—Say what's on your mind, Mia.

If there is one thing we do not do well, it is hide things from one another. She saw things, or did things, that she was not prepared for.

—It's okay, Mother. I don't want to talk about it.

Of course she does. She does not know how.

—What happened in Germany, Mia? Did anyone hurt you?

—No, Mother. No one hurt me. I'm fine.

—Obviously, you are not. Why did you not come back when I asked you to? I know you received my message.

—I couldn't.

—What do you mean you cou—

—Mother, stop! Have you . . .

—Yes?

—Have you ever done bad things because you thought you had to?

She's killed.

—What did you do, Mia? You can tell me.

— . . .

I did not want to talk about it either. I was thirteen. The war had not ended yet. A German police officer stopped me on the street and asked for my papers; I did not have them. He said . . . He said it was people like me that ruined his country. He said he thought about "my kind" every time he had to eat turnip. The Jews, the immigrants were eating what little food there was, taking it away from the "real Germans." He was going to take me in, said I would go back to where I came from. He offered to give me a chance, one chance because he was a *nice guy*. That chance meant I had to go with him behind the post office. I did. I was scared beyond words. I thought he would send me away and I would never see my mother again. I grabbed a steel bar from a pile of rubble while he undid his belt. I remember being surprised at how hard it was to break through skin with a blunt object. He was strong, and struggling for his life. I gave up trying to impale him after a few tries. I shoved the iron bar inside his mouth and pushed through his palate. I was still shaking when I got home. I could not tell my mother. I was afraid we would have to move again because of me. Mother knew right away. She came into my room, stroked my hair, and asked: "Was he a bad man?" I nodded. She said: "Survive at all costs, Sara. You're alive. That means you did good."

—Mia?

—What can you tell me about my father?

—Where is this coming from?

—Do you remember a man by the name of Dieter?

I do. I was still a teenager when I met Didi. He studied music history. He could talk about opera until morning if you let him.

—You saw him?

—He thought I was you.

I was about Mia's age the last time we saw each other. The re-semblance would have been confusing. He would ask questions, too many questions.

—Mia. Dieter was not your father. Even if he were, it does not matter.

—It matters to me.

—It matters to you that you have a father. It does not matter who it is. You would be the very same person no matter who it was.

—No, Mother. Call me crazy but it kind of matters to me whether I killed my dad or not.

—You did not kill your father. You did what you had to do, Mia. I would have done the same thing. We kill to survive, like every other living thing.

—What happened in Bad Saarow?

—What?

—You heard me, Mother.

I did, but I was not ready for it.

—What did Dieter tell you?

—Nothing. He said I should ask you, so I'm asking you.

—There is nothing to tell, Mia. What happened in Bad Saarow is between me and him. It does not concern you.

She knows I am lying but it does not matter. She does not need to remember. Not now.

—Why did we leave Germany?

—I told you, Mia. The Tracker was closing in on us, as he is now.

More lies. I have started something and I cannot stop it.

—How do you know?

Doubt is hard to get rid of once it sets its roots. Dieter planted the seed and I am feeding it with lies. Ragweed.

—Because my mother said so. . . . I know you are upset, Mia. You have every right to be. I wish there were something I could say to make you feel better but there is not. All I can tell you is that you did the right thing. It will take time, but you will learn to make peace with what you did.

— . . .

—You will, Mia. I promise you.

—It's not so much what I did that bothers me. That's not true, it's eating me alive, but what bothers me most is that I knew how, Mother. I didn't hesitate. Fuck, I—

—Watch your tongue, Mia.

—I'm sorry, but I did. I stood in front of a whole platoon and I knew exactly how I could kill them all. What's wrong with me?

—Nothing, Mia. We are . . . percipient. We have always been. You knew what to do for the same reason you can do physics in your sleep.

—What does that make me?

—I'm not sure what you mean.

—What *are* we, Mother?

—We are the Kibsu.

—Don't do that. We're not the same thing as everyone else, are we?

—Our blood is somewhat different when you look at it under a microscope, but it *is* blood. Beyond that, you know as much as I do. We lost the knowledge a *long time* ago.

—When?

—What does it matter, Mia? Around twenty-eight hundred years ago. The Eleven is the first of us we have any knowledge of. Her mother died before she could tell her everything.

—So you don't know why I'm like you? Why I can tell exactly what my daughter will look like?

—You are upset.

—I'm not upset!

—Fine. And no, Mia. I do not. Do you think I would keep it from you if I did? We do not know why *any* children are the way they are. Most of what we know comes from work on pea plants almost a century ago.

—I'm sorry, pea plants?

—Pea plants. A monk named Mendel—he was a botanist— bred lots of pea plants and looked at different traits, like the pod shape or color, the height of the plant. He found that traits do not mix, that one always wins out over the other.

—What does that mean?

—It means tall plants and short plants do not make medium plants, only tall plants. Mendel described the ways in which pea plants inherit these "traits"—he called them factors—from their parents. He published his findings in 1866. No one cared at the time but most of what we know is straight out of Mendel's work. People talk about genes now but we have no idea what they are. Some researchers think they are proteins. There was a paper last year that showed a nucleic acid was involved in how bacteria inherit certain traits. We simply do not know.

—What does that have to do with us?

—Everything. Whatever these genes are, *our* children seem to inherit all of them from us, and none from their father.

—We could find out. We could help with the research.

—No, Mia. We will not waste time indulging personal curiosity. That is not our path.

— . . .

—Tell me what the path is.

—Mother!

—I mean it.

—Take them to the stars, before Evil comes and kills them all. That is the path.

—You should find comfort in that. Most people do not have a clear purpose.

—But what if . . . Never mind.

—Mia . . .

—What if we're wrong? We've lost the knowledge. You said yourself we don't know why we do what we do. Why do we keep doing it? Take them to the stars. It's just words on a necklace, Mother. Why do we follow them like scripture?

—Because they are *your* words. You see the person who wrote them every time you look in the mirror. You see her sitting across from you now. I do not know why we set ourselves that task but we did. We made a choice and you would make it again if it were yours to make.

—I don't—

—You *do* know. I've seen you tear through our journals as if you'd read them before. The events are unfamiliar, but the choices feel obvious. You know what these women will do before you read it, and you know why they did it even if it is not on the page. You convince yourself otherwise because you crave what everyone else has, but you know who you are. Deep down, you have always known. It scares you, the same way it scared all of us, until . . .

—Until what?

—Until you see your own daughter and realize she is you. Then you will know. You will know you are me, and my mother, and the Eighty-Seven, and the Ten. And you will know that those words are real.

—All right, that's enough. I'll be okay, Mother. I'm okay. Let's talk about something else.

—We do not need to talk about anything. You have some personal items to pack.

—Do we really need to move *now*?

—Tomorrow. He is too close for us to stay.

—How do you know?

—I told you. There was a murder across the street from—

—People get murdered every day, Mother. It doesn't mean it's the Tracker.

—It was not a murder. It was a bloodbath.

—There are deranged people ev—

—It happened across from our *house*! I will not take that chance, Mia. Tomorrow we move to Moscow. Pack what you can. We will burn the house in the morning.

—I just . . .

—You just what, Mia?

—I just don't think he's real.

—Then let us make certain we never have to find out.

ENTR'ACTE

Rule #5: Don't Leave a Trace

AD 1945

The war was coming to an end when the Tracker made it to Berlin. As always, the brothers were late—thirteen years behind the traitors. The store the women ran had burned down. Friends had moved away or had died in the trenches. For George, the eldest, this was the end, a final attempt at capturing the traitors before retiring to have children. His brothers would continue without him until his boys were old enough to hunt on their own.

Years of failure had taken their toll on George. He would honor his father's wishes and spawn a new generation, but he had long stopped believing in their cause. All he had hoped for was to kill his prey and put an end to this pointless chase. Now, staring at the ashes of an old spice shop, he had to come to terms with the idea of watching small versions of himself grow up to live the life he had so resented. That, he decided, would be better achieved with large amounts of whiskey. He sat at the bar in the tavern across the street and asked for the bottle. The barkeep obliged, turned to wash some dirty glasses, and started talking to the wall.

—Shame what happened to Ahmet's place.

George grimaced as he downed a full glass. The barkeep kept talking.

—Rough day?

George's throat was still burning. He looked at the patron next to him, facedown on the bar, slowly adding width to a small puddle of drool. He took a deep breath, let the smell of stale beer and cheap cigars fill his lungs, before he acknowledged the barkeep looking at him in the bar mirror.

—Are you talking to me?

—Yeah! I said you look like you're having a rough day.

—What were you saying *before* that?

—I saw you looking at the rubble. It's a shame what happened to Ahmet's shop.

Two words: Ahmet's shop. George's breathing got shallow. He felt a tingle in his stomach. It wasn't the booze, that hadn't kicked in yet. This was something he had felt every now and again. Something that always came and went.

—I thought the shop owner was a woman. Sara.

—Sara was the daughter. The shop belonged to her mother, and Ahmet, her husband. Good man.

—You wouldn't happen to know where they went, now would you?

—Sorry. They just . . . disappeared.

George exhaled what little hope had sprung inside him and poured himself another glass of whiskey.

—*Zum Wohl!*

That one didn't burn as much going down. It wasn't the first time George tried to drink himself into oblivion. He knew what was coming: despair, followed by rage. A headache, bloody hands. George didn't care. He always enjoyed that first hour or so, when self-pity was stronger than self-loathing.

—His sister might know.

— . . .

—Ahmet's sister. Fata. She'd be over fifty by now but she might still be around.

—Fata. Do you know where she lives?

—Nah. Haven't seen her in years. Schöneberg, maybe. Fata Hassan is her name. Sorr—

The barkeep grabbed his throat and fell to the floor. It took a few seconds for George to realize he was holding a knife. His knife. George looked at himself in the bar mirror and got angry at the man staring back. He wanted to know more. He had questions his mouth was too numb to ask, and the man gargling on the ground wasn't answering them. He turned around to see who would, but the room spun the other way. He spotted half a dozen young people sitting in the corner. The floor tilted when he got up to approach them and sent him crashing against the wall. The people laughed at him as if it were his fault, as if he were impotent. George's knife hand started acting on its own. Blackout.

George was sitting at the youths' table. Their heads were missing. They all sat there, headless, taunting him. George grabbed each body, one by one, hoping to shake some sense into them. Blackout.

Guilt was for the weak, but George felt ashamed of what he had done. He tried to fix it, put these people's heads back where they belonged. He matched each one to a body as best he could, but the heads kept falling. George found some cocktail shakers to hold them in place. The whole process was tiring, and when he was done, George sat himself back at the bar for some rest. When he woke, the room had stopped spinning. He saw the scene he had created and decided it was probably best to leave.

The man sitting next to him was still facedown on the bar, but the puddle of drool had grown bigger and redder. George wiped his blade on the man's shirt and grabbed the whiskey bottle before stumbling out of the tavern. He cursed the blinding sun and headed to Schöneberg on foot, hoping the walk would sober him up faster than he was drinking.

The police stopped him midway. George's heartbeat went up a notch. He had spent his whole life chasing the traitors. There was nothing else. That was his life. It was his brothers' life, his father's. Every day felt exactly like the last, and for as long as George remembered, he had seen the world as pale and bleak.

Fighting was the only thing that really got his heart pumping, the one thing that reminded him he was still alive. When four police officers stood in front of him on Goebenstraße, he thought the ensuing battle would be the highlight of his day. He went for one last sip of whiskey, but the bottle was empty, and in a brief moment of lucidity, he remembered two words the dead barman had uttered: "Fata Hassan."

George got on his knees and thanked the police for stopping him.

—Oh thank God! I'm so glad to finally see someone. Can you help me find my way home? I've had *way* too much to drink and I'm afraid I'm completely lost.

The officers asked where home was, to which George replied that he hadn't found a place yet. He had just moved to Berlin and had been living with a friend for two days.

—Can you please take me to her place? I don't know where it is—Schöneberg, somewhere—but her name is Fata Hassan. Please help me.

The Tracker could be very charming, and after a brief stint at the police station, two Berlin police officers drove him to an apartment building on Freisinger Straße. George thanked the officers and entered the building. He found Fata Hassan's apartment and kicked her door in.

When Fata returned home from work that night, she found a man sleeping in her bed. She did not scream. Instead, she went to the kitchen and grabbed a knife. She returned to the bedroom to wake the stranger.

George woke not knowing where he was. He gathered he was in Germany when he heard Fata speak but remembered nothing of what had transpired earlier. It was only when she told him her last name that George realized who he was speaking with. He introduced himself as Sara's cousin, which brought a smile to Fata's face. Eager to meet a new member of the family, she made dinner for the both of them. George listened to Fata reminisce about her brother and his wife for hours. It was almost midnight when he finally asked where he could find Sara.

—America! They went to America. I don't know where. Ahmet said he couldn't tell me and I haven't heard from him since. But that's where you'll find your cousin.

George's head was still pounding, but he enjoyed the feeling of normalcy that came with a home-cooked meal. He was polite, did not strangle or stab his host. He thanked Fata for dinner and said he hoped they would meet again. He was almost out of the building when Fata ran after him.

—Wait! I have something to show you! I found this in the family album. You can have it if you want.

In her hand was a picture of a man, two women, and a child. On the back of it, a handwritten note said: "With my beloved wife, our daughter Sara and little Mi'a. 1931."

ACT III

18

Twilight Time

Germany surrendered the same day we arrived in Moscow. The highest-ranking asshole left alive signed the German Instrument of Surrender—good name for a piece of paper—and poof. Nazi Germany ceased to exist. Just like that.

I thought it would mean . . . more to me. I don't know what I thought. That it would put an end to all the suffering, restore my faith in humanity, something like that. I think they just ran out of people to kill. The dead are still dead, the burned still burned. The war in Europe is over but it rages on in the Pacific. More bombs, more death, more bodies floating in rivers.

They'll put some Nazi leaders on trial, but the rest of them aren't going anywhere. The policemen who shot families on the street. The baker who told the Gestapo his neighbor was a Jew. The kind people who stood by and did absolutely nothing. They're all there. I'm still here.

What I really hoped for was to feel like myself again. I thought it would erase what I've seen, what I've done. But you can't make the past go away. The war has smeared all of us, and those stains won't come off in our lifetimes.

Oh, and I fucking hate Russia. Mother said I would. Of course, she said it because she knew I'd want to decide that for myself. I thought: It can't be that bad. I'm sure I'll find something to like. New place, new friends. It'll keep my mind busy. Maybe I can stop thinking about what I did. Maybe I can stop thinking about Bad Saarow. I helped her pack. I didn't whine, not once. Now I can't say she didn't warn me.

She never said anything about moving into a haunted house. Our place was built at the end of the century. They call it "Art Nouveau." I doubt it was ever "nouveau." When electricity came along, they stapled the wires on the walls and ceilings and painted over them. The lights flicker whenever I walk by. I swear, we live with the spirit of the previous owner and he's just as pissed as I am about the water heater. My guess is he killed himself after staring at green walls for too long, that or the seizure-inducing roses on the kitchen wallpaper.

I barely understand why we had to leave. I sure as hell don't know why we had to come *here*. Mother said we're going to build rockets, but there had to be better places than this. The Soviets torched everything west of here to slow the Germans' advance, and the Germans burned it all again on the way out. There's nothing left. No farmland, no livestock. There's nothing to eat, anywhere. Moscow's just fog and *slyakot*, mud and melting snow taking over the city streets. The people are great, though, except one in seven is dead and the other six are famished.

It's the Soviets that defeated Hitler. For every American soldier who died, the Soviets lost eighty. We haven't met anyone here who didn't lose a close friend, a husband, a brother. They'll rebuild everything, of course, with slave labor: two million prisoners of war and just as many Soviet dissidents Stalin had arrested. No wonder these people are paranoid. This whole place is a prison without walls. And if you don't play nice, you get sent to the one *with* walls, and forced labor, and death. There's lots of death, and brainwashing. Millions of little brains being washed. School is bad enough, but the youth organizations are just . . . I'm a proud member of the Komsomol. We're the end of a long assembly line for perfect Soviet citizens. You start at seven—because why wait?—and join the Little Octobrists, then you graduate to the Young Pioneers at nine. They're like Girl Scouts.

Creepy, zombified propaganda-spewing Girl Scouts. Joining is voluntary, of course. You have a choice, unless you really want to go to school, get a better job, or not have your neighbors look at you funny, or not add a tenth circle to this fiery, everlasting hell. I volunteered. Mother said I had to.

19

Ac-cent-tchu-ate the Positive

I received another letter from Hsue-Shen.

My dear Sarah,
It is with a profound sense of irony that I have accepted a commission in the US Air Force. I cannot vote or marry but I can apparently hold the rank of colonel. The commission is only temporary. I shall travel to Germany to interrogate a group of rocket scientists who surrendered to American forces shortly before the Reich fell. Though their expertise would no doubt prove useful, I shudder at the prospect of welcoming anyone who enabled Hitler in the slightest manner.

I understand and respect my friend's reluctance. That is why I chose him. Von Braun's value is obvious, but that of those who were captured with him is not. Few people understand the science well enough to weigh their knowledge against their character. This entire endeavor is but a moral compromise, but if one is to make a deal with the devil, one should at least be able to negotiate the terms.

—MOTHER! THE WATER HEATER BROKE AGAIN!

—Then get out of the shower.

My daughter is having a difficult time adjusting to our new circumstances. She believed the war's end would be an end, but for her it is only the beginning. Cold water and stale bread are also not helping.

—I'm freezing! Oh, and there's definitely something moving inside my bedroom wall.

—It's only the wind, Mia.

—Seriously, Mother. What are we doing here?

—We are giving the Americans someone to compete against. We are going to build V-2s, then make even better rockets.

—Great! Why are we in Russia? Rocket scientists are in Germany, not here.

—Do you wish to go back?

—Fuck no!

—MIA!

—Sorry.

—Do you know where Wernher von Braun is at this very moment?

—Hmmm. It's the middle of the night in America, so I'd say in his bed.

—*Witzenhausen.* Von Braun is in Witzenhausen.

—That sounds suspiciously German.

—It is. The Americans have not deigned to debrief him yet. I had to pull some very reluctant strings in Washington to make sure they send someone.

—Are you telling me I went to Germany for nothing?

—I am telling you we need to put pressure on the Americans.

—How? Wherever he is, Mother, von Braun's not here. The Soviets may have been good at this before Stalin, before the purge, but they're so far behind now . . . We're not going to build rockets ourselves, Mother.

—Then I suggest you find someone who will.

—There's no one! The Soviets aren't up for this any more than the Americans were. It's the Germans that build rockets. That's why I went there in the first place.

—Get some Germans involved, then. The Americans will only take about half of the people you gave them. You left over twenty-five hundred people behind in Bleicherode, if I remember correctly, and a good third of the people working for von Braun never even left Peenemünde, which happens to be inside Soviet-occupied territory. There are plenty of people left with some knowledge of the V-2.

—I don't know, Mother. I mean, there are V-2 rockets out there already. They exist. What good is making one with a hammer and sickle on it?

—We are creating a race and the Soviets do not have anything to race with. It will take them years to get a working rocket. You can give them a V-2 in ten months.

—That seems *very* optimistic. I think it would ta—Wait a minute. *I* can?

—Yes, darling. You know enough. Give the Soviets a working V-2 and you will get the Americans' attention. Make it cross an ocean and I guarantee von Braun will get his own research center and all the resources he needs. Then you can race him higher and higher, all the way to the stars.

—Me. . . . What will *you* do?

—I will support you as best I can, of course. I also need to find old air.

—Old what?

—Air. I require air from the past. I need air from centuries ago, as far back as possible. I need . . . old air.

—That sounds fun. Do I dare ask why?

—No, Mia. You do not. I am too tired for science this evening. Tonight, you and I are carving.

—We are?

—We are performing the Maqlû.

—What's the Maqlû?

—It is an ancient ritual.

—I figured that part, Mother.

—*My* mother and I did it together, before you were born. We would sit on her bed. It was rare for her to let me inside her bedroom. We would light a candle on each of the nightstands,

106

barely enough light to see what was in front of us. In the winter, the draft of cold air from the window would make the flame waver. I tensed with every flicker. I think my mother enjoyed scaring me.

—What does it do?

—It was meant to protect against witchcraft, evil sorcerers.

—Don't tell me you believe in all that.

—I did at the beginning. Perhaps not, but I *wanted* to believe. I was much younger than you are now. There was a sense of danger to the ritual. It had the allure of the forbidden. Now I find it quite soothing. But enough talking. I will get what we need for the Maqlû. You get us some iced tea from the refrigerator.

—Fine.

—With some ice, please.

—I know! . . .

— . . . Thank you, Mia. Now take this block of wood and start carving.

—Carve it into what?

—The evil sorcerer. Anyone who wishes to harm you. I would suggest the Tracker.

—I don't know what he looks like.

—It is a piece of wood, Mia. A human shape will suffice. When we are done, we will drown it in ink, then crush it while we recite the incantations.

—We're making voodoo dolls. How exciting.

—Do not make fun of your mother. As I said, it is . . . soothing. You'll see.

— . . .

—Mia?

— . . .

—Mia! What are you doing? Stop staring at your tea and start carving.

—Look.

—No, Mia. I will not look at your tea.

—Not the tea, Mother, the ice.

—I have seen ice before. Now can we please—

—Closer, Mother! Bubbles!

Where is she going with this?

—I see there are small air b—

Air bubbles.

—Yes! Unless I'm mistaken, that's air that was trapped when the ice formed, air from whenever you made the ice. Yesterday, or last week.

—Old air. This . . . is . . .

—I know, Mother. Now all you need is to find old ice. Somewhere with lots of snow—Antarctica, maybe Greenland . . . If there is melting in the summer season . . .

—It would create a fresh layer of ice each year. Count the layers to date the ice. Like the—

—Like the rings on a tree. . . . Can I have my drink back now? I thought we had voodoo dolls to make.

—I'm sorry, Mia. This is just—

—I know, Mother. I know.

20

My Mama Don't Allow Me

I don't know how it's possible but my uniform is getting itchier with time. What do they make them with? Asbestos? These Komsomol meetings are a complete waste. I'm supposed to make rockets, not to reminisce about the great sacrifices placed on the altar of the Motherland in the name of freedom and independence. Seriously, who comes up with this nonsense?

Still, I have no idea how I'm supposed to speed up a rocket program that doesn't exist. I mean, there are a handful of Soviets working on different things, but none of them are where we need them to be if we're going against von Braun. Mother is right. We'll need some Germans to help, but which ones? Even if I knew, they'll need to work for someone, somewhere. I can probably get German scientists to build a German rocket, in Germany. That I can do—

—Nina?

But if we want the Soviets to race, we'll need some Soviets. We need a Soviet something to approve a Soviet program, a Soviet chief designer, Soviet money. I don't know how—

—You're Nina, aren't you?

Shit. I keep forgetting Nina's my name in this hellhole. Who wants to know? Oh, behind me. Another Komsomol. She's . . .

—I . . . Yes. I'm Nina.

—You're not from around here, are you?

She can talk. She stands out like . . . well, like a black girl in Moscow. Come to think of it, she's the only black person I've seen here. She's also taller than me. No one's ever taller than me. Where am I supposed to be from again? Oh yes.

—We're from Uzbekistan.

I have no idea if we look Uzbek or not. I've never met an Uzbek before but, apparently, neither have most people.

—Neat! Come with me. Quick!

What? Come with her where?

—Where are we going?

—Through here, behind the building. Hurry! We don't have much time.

She's . . . skipping along. I don't even know why I'm following her. This feels like a couple of ten-year-olds hiding from their parents. Are we hiding? Oh, she's stopping now. She's digging through her bag. A cigarette. She's lighting a cigarette.

—Isn't that against Komsomol principles?

Smoking, drinking, modern dancing. The marks of hooliganism and decadent fascism.

—I think we're allowed one vice. Just one.

She's handing me her cigarette.

I . . . I took it. What's wrong with me? I just took it from her hand. I couldn't say no. The tip is still wet from her lips. This feels . . . intimate, someh—WHOA! Head rush. Holy cow, that's rough. I'm doing my best not to—

cough *cough*

I feel . . . dizzy. She's smiling. Is she making fun of me? She hasn't stopped smiling since we got here. It's a beautiful smile. Childlike, careless. Now I'm self-conscious about everything. Is my face all red? How does her uniform fit her so well? I look like a fool in mine. Another drag.

. . .

So this is what smoking feels like. Light-headed and super awkward.

Why does she keep looking at me? She stares while she smiles. Few people can do that, look someone in the eyes for more than a second or two. Those who can do it with intent. They want submission. Not her. She just stares, with . . . insouciant abandon. I find it impossible not to look back, but I don't know what to do with myself. I'm fidgeting. Why am I fucking fidgeting?

—I have to go. See you next week?

What? No, don't leave. She's putting out her cigarette, skipping back the way we came.

—Wait! You never told me your name!

—I'm Billie! Bye, Nina!

Billie? I have so many questions. She's gone now. I wanted more. More of . . . something. Oh shit, I think I'm going to be sick.

21

Che Puro Ciel

—What was it like, Mother?

—What was what like?

—Hiroshima.

— . . . I don't know.

How could I? No one saw it. Those who did are dead or dying. The Americans did not televise the murder of countless civilians. Newspapers used words like "terror" and "devastation," but even a thousand words are not worth one picture. The only way Mia and I can experience the event is through science. We can do the math.

Come.

—Where are we going?

—Come with me!

—Outside? But it's raining!

—You will survive. Here. Look at the sky and choose a point about two thousand feet above your head. That's where it would have happened, where the bomb exploded.

—It didn't detonate on the ground?

—No. Up in the sky. Within . . . a millionth of a second, the temperature at that point reached tens of millions of degrees and vaporized what was left of the bomb. The expansion created a pressure wave, probably over a million pounds per square inch, moving outwards at . . . three thousand miles an hour, give or take. Now imagine a one-mile circle all around you. That is nine or ten blocks in every direction, from here to the Bolshoi. Somewhere between three and four hundred city blocks. About one second after the explosion, everything in that circle was hit by a wall of air moving at supersonic speed. Every building was ripped apart or toppled over. Bodies were squeezed like lemons, compressed with enough force to rupture most internal organs. The same circle was hit, almost instantaneously, with a lethal dose of neutrons and gamma rays.

—What does that do?

—It does not matter if you were inside that circle. Look up again. At the point of detonation, the air surrounding the weapon was bombarded with enough X-rays to form a ball of burning air many times brighter than the sun. Within ten seconds, that ball of fire had reached the edge of the one-mile circle, blowing burning debris and broken bodies at hundreds of miles per hour. Anyone who was still breathing was burned alive instantly. By then, the air blast would be two or three miles ahead, still moving incredibly fast. Then came the heat, visible and infrared light. It caused blindness, third-degree burns up to ten miles away, perhaps more. In about a minute, tens of thousands were dead or dying. Just as many were burned or injured.

—Hell on earth.

—A quick death for most. The ones who *did not* die will experience hell.

—Neutrons and gamma rays.

—Yes. Living cells will absorb the energy. If they absorb enough—

—It'll kill them.

—Not directly, no. If you were close enough for that to happen, the firestorm would have hit you first. But it will damage cells, enough to stop them from making proper copies of themselves. When the cells die their natural death, their imperfect offspring will not survive. The faster the cells reproduce, the more sensitive they are to radiation.

113

—So the brain—

—You figure it out, Mia.

She does not need to hear me say it. She knows enough to play it out in her head. Bone marrow will die first, but it will take a month before it causes severe internal bleeding or infection sets in. Epithelial cells in the intestinal tract will be next. Nausea, vomiting, diarrhea. Death will come faster, a couple of weeks. Nerve cells are slow to regenerate so they will die last, but with enough exposure, they will die. Seizures, convulsions. Dead in a day. Brain cells do not reproduce, so they will not be destroyed. Too bad. I would prefer not to be conscious for this.

—Mother?

—What is it, Mia?

—Did we do this?

— . . .

—Mother?

—No, Mia. That was not us. You are soaking wet. Go back inside and get rid of these clothes before you catch your death.

A white lie, perhaps. The truth is more complicated than yes or no. The work of thousands, tens of thousands, went into that project. A million small pieces of knowledge interlocked in just the right way. Some of the pieces were ours, undoubtedly, but we did not put the puzzle together. That will have to be enough.

—Aren't you coming in?

—I think I will stay a bit longer.

I like the rain. It's a new dawn. The age of gods is over. The era of man began when a neutron struck the nucleus of a uranium atom. The emperor did not just rule over Japan, he was a direct descendant of the sun goddess. A divine being was just cut to size by science. The last living god bowed to man. Nothing will ever be the same.

22

I'm on My Last Go-Round

—I don't know what's on your mind, Mia, but you need to focus. We have work to do.

I am focused, very focused. Just not on this.

—Yes, Mother. . . . Did you know hundreds of Afro-Americans came here during the thirties?

—They were recruited by the state, were they not?

—Yes. How do you know? Never mind that. Why would anyone want to move here, under Stalin?

—I can think of many reasons. Jim Crow laws, the Great Depression. I would surmise many were simply looking for an adventure. Is this about your new friend?

—My fr—Yes. Her father studied agriculture at Tuskegee University. He brought his family here to teach the Soviets new cultivation techniques.

—This is fascinating, Mia. Now can we—

—She was an actress. Kind of.

—Who was?

—My friend. Billie. She made a Soviet propaganda film about racism when she was eight.

—I would love to meet her someday, Mia. Can you please focus on the task at hand?

—I'm sorry, Mother. What can I do?

—I told you before. You need to start a research program, put a team together.

—But I don't know how! I don't even know who's in charge, here *or* in Germany.

—Don't worry, Mia. Neither do the Soviets. Right now, there are a handful of Russian scientists in Germany. In Bleicherode, where *you* were. Boris Chertok is running what they call Institut Rabe.

—Rabe. What does it mean?

—Some German acronym for rocket building, I suppose. Things are more complicated here in Moscow. They are still bickering over who should be in charge of the technology. NKAP—that's aviation—thinks it should be theirs. The People's Commissariat of Ammunition wants it, so does the People's Commissariat of Armament. Our man is with the Main Artillery Directorate, General Kuznetsov. He more or less single-handedly decided Rabe was under his command, and no one objected.

—You said "our man." We have a man?

—Yes, Mia. We do. For the time being, he believes he is working for a secret commission only Stalin knows about, but it will not last. You will need to make more permanent arrangements.

—A secret commission. You made it up?

—I did. We had nothing to blackmail Kuznetsov with, or anyone else here for that matter. I had to spend a fortune on a low-ranking government official just to create the paperwork. Fortunately, there are more commissions and committees here than anyone can remember. You first priority should be to find a suitable general, or a member of the Politburo.

I've watched Mother do it but I never turned anyone before. It's not that hard from what I've seen. Debt works best, especially the gambling kind. Ask for something illegal but harmless at first. Threaten and squeeze for more. Rinse. Repeat. Like most things, guilt doesn't last. Habituation is a horrible thing. We've done it a thousand times over generations, amassed file after file of everyone's dirty little secrets. Mother says we could overthrow governments if we wanted to. I don't know if that's true but we could sure run one with the money we're spending.

My grandmother had hundreds on the take. Scientists, government officials, a whole network of people gathering information for us. Some of it is pretty bad, but the most useful is usually petty crimes, love affairs. It's amazing how many people will end up selling state secrets because they couldn't keep it in their pants.

—Do we have enough money for this? I mean, we're still paying a ton of people.

—We have enough, Mia.

—How much?

—I have shown you the accounts, what documents we need to move money around.

That she did. Lots of paperwork. People can't hide money, they just can't. We have to make sure it comes from somewhere. Family trusts from long-lost relatives, research grants from some obscure foundation. Yuck.

—I know, but how much do we have?

—Difficult to say. Most of it we owe to the Eighty-Seven. They made a fortune in the Dutch East India Company. You can do the accounting. You should know where the money is.

Aaaaand. She wins. She knows how much I hate accounting.

—It's okay, Mother. You know about these things a lot more than I do.

—It was not a suggestion, Mia.

I really don't like where this conversation is going.

—Mother, what is going on? *You* do the accounting, *you* buy people, *you* get the Russians to build V-2s. Why me? Why not you? Why do *I* have to do all this?

—Because it is time, Mia.

—Time for what?

—It is time for you to have a child, time for us to be the One Hundred.

23

Gloomy Sunday

Fuck no! I know the rules. Mother and me plus one is three. There can never be three, not for long anyway.

She's my mother. I'm not ready for her to go. I'm not ready for *anything* without her. She's my protector, my guide. She shows me the path and I follow. It took a hundred generations to get us here. I'll mess that up in a week. I won't ruin everything because Mother is having a midlife crisis. We are the Ninety-Nine and I live in her world. I like it there. I trust her a hell of a lot more than I trust myself. I'm not . . . right. I still hear the dead in my sleep.

"Don't you want to know what happened in Bad Saarow?"

I'm a mess. I shouldn't be in charge of anything. I've been trying to run things for about five seconds and already the Allies are accusing the Soviets of breaching the agreements on the liquidation of the German war machine. They're right, we're not dismantling anything. We're building more rockets, German rockets the Americans already have, but at some point we'll want to work on new designs. If they send inspectors, they'll know what we're working on. They might know already. Russians are supervising but they aren't learning anything. We have a bunch of Germans trying to build a German rocket, in Germany. For the most part, they're all free to move around. Anyone could talk, defect. This was a bad idea from the start.

Mother knows it but she won't say. She wants me to figure it out for myself. I have, but it doesn't mean I'm any closer to a solution. The scientists here aren't up to the task, not even close. They were ahead of the game not that long ago, but Stalin has a way of ruining things. I wasn't ready for any of this. I need Mother. That's the one thing I know.

"It is time for you to have a child." I've never even had a *boyfriend*. I'm nineteen years old and I've never had sex! Does she think I don't want to? I want to. I want what every girl my age has. There's so much I've never experienced. I can calculate thrust coefficients with my eyes closed but I don't know what it's like to sleep next to someone, to feel their chest move with every breath, or how much heat two bodies can generate. Shit, I even crave the physics of it. I want someone to make me feel . . . normal. I want it with every fiber in my being, but I won't kill my mother for it. I won't watch her die, even if it's what she wants. I've seen enough death already. Fuck her. She can't die.

I wonder if she knows. I wonder if she thinks I've been with someone before. She gave me a diaphragm when I turned sixteen. Thanks, Mother! I had to ask a friend what it was. That was . . . embarrassing. She should have known I'd never use it. As if I'd trust her life to a piece of rubber. If there were a pill, maybe. For the longest time, I thought: She must know, she knows everything. Now I'm not so sure. She knows everything about us, but I don't know how much she knows about *me*. There *is* a me.

Does she know I'm seeing someone? I do my best to complain every time I leave for brainwash group, but I'm sure Mother senses I'm not as reluctant as I used to be. Billie—I love that name. She . . . She's not me. That's what drew me to her. She knows things I don't. She wants things I don't. I don't know what I want. I'm not . . . attracted to her, I think, not the way she is to me. I don't know. I've never felt those things, with anyone. Maybe that's what it feels like. I keep asking myself if I want to be her or be *with* her. I don't know if there's a difference.

She kissed me— *We* kissed once. I like the way she kisses. It'll never lead anywhere. Not here, not with me. Maybe that's why I let myself enjoy it. It's unsettling, in a good way. To be close to someone, to look at her and see something familiar and yet completely different, to look at a woman who's not me . . . I don't know what I'm doing or why I'm doing it, but I feel . . . unique when I'm with her. I feel good. I'm me. There *is* a me.

Maybe that's what bothers me most. Maybe it's not Mother I'm so afraid to lose.

I look at Mother and I see glimpses of myself, but some of it I don't recognize. I haven't lived enough yet. I've never seen myself her age, but she has. The flow of time is the river that separates us. It's a one-way mirror neither of us can put down, and I don't want to switch sides. Mother is *us*. She bears the weight of a hundred lifetimes. She's her and me, and everyone that came before us. She feels *their* pain, cries *their* sorrow. Mine, too. She knows what I think and feel, what I fear. She knows me better than I know myself. We are the Ninety-Nine.

I've seen myself pregnant before. I've had dreams about it, bad fucking dreams. I've seen Mother rip through my stomach and crawl up to my face. I've seen myself do it. Bloody, small versions of us, limbs bent and broken, speeding up my body like a spider. Each time, I bleed to death while my child whispers: "Ma. Ma." I'll die if I have a child. I know it. Not like that—I won't stop breathing. I'll still get up every morning—but I'll die. There won't be a me anymore.

Mother said it. She'll be born and I'll lose myself, instantly. One look at her, that's all it'll take. I'll see myself staring back and I'll know I'm on the wrong side of the mirror. I'll know that I was never me. I was her the whole time. I was always the Kibsu.

24

"Murder," He Says

—You're lucky. You might not always feel it. You might not feel it now. But you are. You have everything. A nice apartment—small, but cozy—in New York City. I like this place. I've been here two hours and I like it already. You're a—what is it you do again? You told me when we met. Oh yes. You're in family finance. I'll be honest, I have no idea what that means. I imagine it's a valuable service. You do whatever it is you do and people are better for it afterwards. I bet you're good at it, too! You must get some sense of accomplishment, some pride for what you do. There are bad days, of course. I'm sure you feel worthless at times, but overall you strike me as a happy person. Are you? Don't just stare at me. Nod or something.

Oh, you wish you were more. I understand. Everyone does. You wish you were . . . special. Well . . . Let me give you some advice, honey. Don't. You're not. You'll never be special. You're as ordinary as they come. You're the luckiest woman in the world.

Me and my brothers—did I tell you I have three brothers?—we're special. We've been told from birth how special we are. We're not like you, that's for sure. We're . . . stronger. We're—how do I put this in a way that's not insulting?—we're more . . . intelligent. I must sound so full of myself right now. Believe me, I'm not. I wish I were like you. I wish I were in family finance. But I'm not. I can't. You see, my brothers and I, we have a mission, a function. We were born with purpose. We're like medieval knights on a holy quest. Do you want to know what that quest is? What our GREAT mission is all about?

—Please, sir. Please don't kill me!

—Did you just call me sir? Sir was my father before we killed him. My name is Charles. Call me Charles. Seriously, I'm twenty-four years old, do I look like a sir to you? The use of honorific indicates distance. I felt quite the opposite. I know you were being polite but I felt a connection, like I could share things with you that I don't get to share with most people. . . . Now I forgot what I was saying. DAMN IT! Don't interrupt me again. I was telling you about our quest.

We . . . we're hunters. We hunt people. This is when I'm supposed to say they're bad people, that they deserve it. The truth is I've never met any of them. My father never met them, neither has *his* father. They have something, apparently, a machine that we want. Something that can save . . . more people than you can imagine. I've never seen it, of course. No one has. Maybe it doesn't exist. All I know is that these women left Germany and landed here, in New York. Only we won't find them in New York because that was thirteen fucking years ago. That's how we measure how close we are, not in distance, but in time. To be honest, thirteen years is as close as I ever got.

Do you understand what I'm saying? We spend our whole lives, every hour of every day, chasing people we've never met, looking for something we've never seen. It's been like that for . . . Do you know how amazing your life looks to me? What I wouldn't give for just one day of family finance? I envy you. I . . . *envy* you.

—Please! I don't want to die! PLEASE! HELP ME! HEEELP!

—Shhhh. You'll wake everyone. Now I'm going to have to gag you.

—NOOO! HMMM . . .

—Stop it! I don't want to kill you. Not like that. I'm not a maniac. I just want . . . I thought we were sharing . . . I wonder why they call this duck tape? It's green. Ducks aren't gr—

I'm sorry. I thought I heard something. . . . Why'd you have to scream? I can't see half your face anymore. I liked looking at your face. To be completely frank, I also find begging quite unbecoming. It makes you look—I don't know—*stupid* is the first word that comes to mind. I don't want to think of you that way. Don't be like them. They all beg. What do they expect? Sorry to have bothered you. I was going to kill you, but you said please, so . . . In this particular case, I'm willing to take some of the blame. I did use some rather graphic language earlier. I—

There. You must have heard that? I think there's someone at the door. I'll be right back. Don't go anywhere. That was a joke. I know, you're tied up. Not funny . . . I have redeeming qualities but I do lack a proper sense of humor. My whole family does.

Yep. There's someone at the door. He must have heard you. Now you've done it. I'm going to have to open the door and kill this fellow before he wakes up more neighbors and I have to kill them, too. You understand how bad this can get, don't you? It could turn into a vicious cycle, very vicious. Watch this.

What can I do for you, young man? There . . . it's done. Don't fight it. Now if you would please fall forward so I can close the door. Thank you.

This is really going to ruin the carpet. It's a shame. I could imagine myself living here. Did you see how quick that was? This man was alive—what? three seconds ago—and now he's not, or he soon won't be. I don't think he ever realized what was happening to him. Maybe he did. Who cares? He's dead. You did that. . . . Yes. I was instrumental in the man's demise, but you, you started that chain of events. Maybe his wife is waiting for him to come back, maybe his kids are. What do you think will happen if they come looking for him? All because of one scream. And for what? You don't seem particularly pleased. I know I'm not. Look at him! Was it worth it?

I realize this may seem somewhat cruel to you. I hope you find some comfort in knowing it wasn't a random act. I think you'll see what I was getting at very clearly in a few minutes. I've told you a bit about my life already, but there is something else I'm trying to explain to you, something I would rather not share with someone who's bound and gagged. Now if you want . . . If you want, I'll untie you and take this off your mouth so we can have a civilized conversation. Is that a yes? Very well then.

I'm so sorry. I didn't realize these were so tight. I'm going to rip this off quickly, it might sting a bit. Again, I apologize. Are you comfortable? Just nod. You're still in shock. I hope you're calm enough to listen to what I have to say. I'm not going to hurt you if you just listen.

—Please. Please don't hurt me.

—Isn't that what I just said? I just said: "I'm not going to hurt you if you just listen." Your answer to that is: "Please don't hurt me." You see how someone might interpret that as a sign that you *weren't* listening? Again, I'm willing to cut you some slack given these unusual circumstances, but you should really make an effort. Anyway, moving on. As I told you before, the life we live, it's . . . unrewarding. You're taken over by this . . . unbearable numbness is how I would describe it. Case in point: a minute ago, I killed a man and I got nothing out of it. I felt nothing. There were other factors at play, or course. It happened really fast. I didn't know the man. What matters is that I didn't feel a thing. I don't feel anything, except . . .

Look at you! You're terrified! It's beautiful to watch. I wish I could feel that. I would give anything to feel something this intense. You don't know how much I envy you at this moment, and while this may seem insignificant to you, that ounce of jealousy going through my veins is about as much feeling as I can hope for. Envying you is the highlight of my day. I thank you for that.

There are moments, like this one, where . . . I told you I thought we had a connection. Watching you lie in bed, scared beyond your wits, I developed a certain fondness for you. Have you ever had a dog? You don't need to answer, it doesn't matter. What I'm trying to say is that—Don't worry, this won't hurt a bit. Shhhhhh. See. I told you it would be painless. What I'm trying to say is that I'm going to watch you die, and when the life is gone from you, I might feel something other than envy. I wish you knew how much it would mean to me, how grateful I'd be if I could, even for a moment, feel remorse.

25

Songs My Mother Taught Me

—I'm not ready, Mother.

I know she is not. I saw the despair in Mia's face the moment I told her, but I did not need to see. I remember walking into our ship cabin like it was yesterday, the emptiness of it. The room was unremarkably tidy, my mother's clothes still hanging in the small closet. I still cannot say exactly what was odd about it. It felt . . . staged, artificial, the way your neighbor's house looks when they invite you over for the first time. Magazines angled just the right way, a tennis racket conveniently forgotten by the doorway, a book that was never read left open on the coffee table. I knew my mother was gone and that she would not come back. I knew I would never be the child again. *I* was not ready.

—I know.

—I need more time.

I did, too. There were no warnings, no signs. Mother did not leave any subtle hints, or they were too subtle, or I was not smart enough. All I know is that my world ended in that third-class cabin. There was nothing left. Only me and a bright-eyed child who did not know why her mother was crying. I should have known. I knew the rules. I knew there couldn't be three, but I still saw us as two. My mother. My daughter. I was just a spectator, the one taking the picture. It took some time before I felt like I could do anything on my own. I just went through the motions, making sure my daughter was fed and sheltered. In her own way, it was Mia who kept me going. I owe her my life. I owe her time.

—I understand, Mia. I will give you some time.

—How much time?

—I will give you . . . enough.

I can tell she was expecting more resistance. She probably had a whole speech prepared. I would not be surprised if she had spent the entire night memorizing it, weighing every word, fine-tuning her rhythm. I should have given her the satisfaction, but I do not want to lie to my daughter again.

—Okay.

She is smart. She got what she wanted out of this conversation. She has nothing to gain by talking, but everything to lose. Now let us see if I can get what *I* want.

—I will give you some time, but you will have to give me something in return.

—What?

—Quid pro quo. You have to be in charge. You have to take care of things.

—I thought I was.

She is, sometimes. She dips her toes into her new life but she won't dive in. She's a dilettante, a substitute teacher, the babysitter watching someone else's children.

—Not like that, Mia. I mean *really* take care of things. We have been in Moscow for nearly a year and the Russians have not made any real progress. Neither have the Americans. They are utterly convinced they have the ultimate weapon. Such shortsightedness. I want a race, Mia. I want them to build bigger and better rockets, not because they want to, but because the other one will if they don't. You need to speed things up. You need to get us there. *You* do. You must not rely on me anymore.

—What about you? What will you do?

—I *would* like to continue my mother's research before I go. I need to know if this planet has a future.

—Before you *go*? You say it like you're planning a vacation or something.

—In a way. You can help with my research if you want. I would love to spend more time with you. What I would *really* like is to see a man in space before I die. Can you do that for me, Mia? Can you make that happen?

—I'll try, Mother.

—You'll do more than that.

She will. She might not like what it means for her, but she *is* us. She has the will of her ancestors, their determination. A hundred life spans of refusing to give up is coursing through her veins. She may not be ready to accept it—she sees it as weakness—but it is *in* her. It has always been. She will follow her instincts. She will watch herself do things she never thought possible.

Right now, she is thinking about what she has to lose. Me, the person she thinks she is. But there is a part of her brain that craves all this. She is a Labrador who fell into a lake for the first time. Her instincts will kick in. At first, she will be surprised that she can swim at all. Soon, she will not want to get back to shore.

— . . .

Her brain is working overtime. I know that look too well. It starts with a feeling, not a thought. The urge to act, to do any-thing. Throwing paint at the canvas. Out of the chaos, a shape emerges. She cannot quite make out what it is, but she knows it is there, begging to be seen. She can either freeze, afraid of los-ing what little there is, or trust herself and throw more paint at it.

—Mia?

—I know what to do.

There it is. She is starting to believe.

—What?

—I know what to do, Mother, but you're not going to like it.

Of course I won't. I am losing my little girl. I am no more ready to lose her than she is to let me go. She is my daughter, a reminder of what I once was. I love watching her grow and slowly turn into us. Mostly, I love that she is trying not to, clinging to her sense of self at all costs. Resist, Mia. You *will* lose, but the fight is worth it. Those days will never come again.

—What am I not going to like, Mia?

—I have to go back to Germany.

26

You Gonna Miss Me When I'm Gone

She has that long scar on her left shoulder. Not straight like a cut. It twists and turns, like a river on a map.

—Billie, look at me! It's only for a few weeks.

—I don't want you to go.

I don't want to go either. That's not true. I do. I didn't tell Mother the whole reason why, but I do want to go. At least, I did an hour ago. Now I'm lying next to Billie and every bit of certainty has gone out the window. . . . All she had to do was turn her back to me and I feel like I'm already a thousand miles away.

—I have to.

—Why? You're not the only interpreter in Russia. Tell them to send someone else. Tell them you're sick.

—It doesn't work like that, Billie. You know it doesn't.

I meant that. Now that I got myself assigned there, it'd be really hard to say no. Stalin's pretty much removed that word from the vocabulary.

—You *want* to go. I can see it.

I don't know what this is. Jealousy? I look at her and I see . . . strength, independence. I marvel at it but I also worry that she doesn't care, that I can't reach her. I worry all the time. Now she's showing me an ounce of frailty and I can't feel anything but guilt for making her less than she is.

—Billie, I—

—Forget it. You want to go, so go.

—Billie! I care about you.

So much.

—Does your mother know you're here?

—What?

—Your mother. Did you tell her about me?

Touché. I don't know why that hurts, but it does. Guilt I can live with, but I wasn't ready for shame. What stings the most is how deliberate it was. This was *meant* to wound.

—Do you want me to leave?

Her face changed. That carefree grin of hers is gone. This is more restrained. A soft smile that barely dimples her cheeks. I don't think it's conscious, but part of her knows she went too far.

She's lifting the covers. She wants me to move closer. For a second or two, it felt like our roles were reversed, but it's over now. Billie's Billie, and I'm . . . unsettled, overconscious of everything. I feel the cold on my exposed shoulder. I feel my fingers tingling, the texture of her skin. I want her. I want to get closer and closer and never stop. Even with our bodies pressed against each other, I want . . . more.

—Where did you tell her you were going?

There was no tone here. She really wants to know.

—To my mother? To the library.

—The library!

—What's wrong with the library?

—Is that what I remind you of? A dusty old place full of forgotten things. I'm not that boring, am I?

That she is not.

—I love the library! It's full of adventure, mystery.

—Like me!

I . . . Why am I crying? I don't know what's wrong with me. This is what I wanted. Her hand running down my side. Her lips sending shivers down my thigh. But it's too much right now, or too little. I feel exposed like an open wound. I'm shaking like a fucking leaf.

—Stop.

—What's wrong, Nina?

—Nothing. I just . . .

I can't put it into words. I'm terrified. I'm scared of *everything*. Of what I am. Of leaving her. Of what Mother wants me to do, of what might come of it. I don't want who I was to end. I don't want this to end. I want this moment, now, to last, frozen like an ice sculpture. But it won't. It'll melt and disappear. Everything does.

—I don't want to lose you.

—Then don't!

I wish it were that simple.

—I'm afraid, Billie.

—Of what? What are you so afraid of, Nina?

—I'm afraid you'll grow tired of me.

—I will.

— . . .

—But not before I figure out what's in that big head of yours. And just like that, I'm not afraid anymore.

27

La Vie en Rose

1946

It hasn't been a year, but Germany is a different country. The bombs have stopped. The nightmare has ended, but it feels as though no one is fully awake. The Germans are in shock, stunned, stripped of who they were and everything that held their world together. It doesn't matter what they believed in, it's gone. They were promised the world and lost everything. Those who believed feel cheated, robbed by one man's stupidity. Those who didn't are defeated just the same. There's no prize for having been ashamed early.

The real healing won't begin until the occupation ends. Half the men are dead. The other half are crippled, hollow. Women will face the cold and famine like everyone else, but *their* war began when the fighting stopped. Allied soldiers defeated the men but they won't leave it at that. I hear the Red Army is the worst. War means rape—it always has—and this was the biggest war of all.

Me, well, the uniforms are different but the stares are the same. I'm scared shitless everywhere I go. I see shadows that aren't there, hear footsteps no one is taking. I tell myself I don't believe in the Tracker, but he is everywhere around me. He's not alone. Dieter, the SS. I see their faces everywhere, in everyone. I'm haunted by the ones I killed and the ones who would kill me.

I swear every waiter in this café was an SS officer. I'm only half imagining things. Most of them couldn't find a job anywhere but working tables. Breathe, Mia. Just do your job and get the hell out. If this is what it takes to keep my mother alive . . . I'll do what needs to be done. Send a man to space. Shit, I'll send *everyone* to space. There'll be no one left here but Mother and me. And Billie. I'll keep Billie. I wish she could see me now. I'm a different person when I'm around her. That's funny. I *am* a different person around her. I wonder what she'd think of me if she knew what I am. She'd probably run away screaming. Maybe not. Billie doesn't scare easy.

I can't think about her now. I have to focus, for real. I have some ideas, some designs I've been working on, but I need help. I need the Soviets, or von Braun. They'll get it done. I just have to . . . motivate them enough. Mother says Moscow will have nuclear weapons in a couple of years. They'll want a rocket to put it on. Point a hundred of those at the US, there's your motivation. I have another idea. If it works, it'll scare the hell out of the Americans. It'll put the fear of God into them. I want a Soviet threat hanging over their head, literally. I want—Oh, I think my date's here. Colonel Sergei Korolev.

—Over here, Colonel! Please, sit down.

God, I hate my accent in Russian. I sound . . . I don't know how I sound. Weird, mostly.

—I am here to meet with General Kuznetsov.

I might have mentioned the general. I'm not exactly at the top of the food chain in this Soviet mess. I'm not really *in* the food chain, or a citizen for that matter.

—I know, sir.

—Sergei.

—What?

—Call me Sergei. They made me a colonel so I could work in military installations, but I am not a soldier.

He doesn't look like one. Big eyes, big chin, with an even bigger grin stapled above it. He looks like a boxer, or a baseball player. He must be near forty, but it's like he forgot to grow out of his baby face. I like him. Even the way he carries himself is endearing. He seems . . . curious, not as pretentious as the others. Humble is a bit of a stretch, but he might not be as big an ass as the other geniuses I ran into.

—I apologize, sir. The general couldn't make it, but I can speak for him. Please sit, you and I can talk.

—Why would I talk to you? Who are you?

So much for that. Of all the people who could judge me, this one's a fucking criminal! He's a decorated genius criminal, but still. Someday, I swear, I'll have actual power and people will have to listen to me. It would be so much easier, not to mention faster, than this degrading show I have to put on every time. Here we go again. Puppy eyes.

—I'm terribly sorry, sir. My name is Nina.

—Your accent, it's—

I know. I know.

—I'm an English interpreter. I work in the Podlipki office. I realize you were expecting someone else. I know how frustrating that can be, but if you give me a few minutes of your time, I think you'll like what I have to say.

—I meant no disrespect, ma'am. It's just that you are not in uniform, and I cannot discuss what I am doing with a civilian. I could get in trouble.

Maybe not a dick. He's hard to size. He *is* handsome, though. Quite the flutter bum, actually. I don't know why I'm just noticing.

—Oh. I don't need you to tell me anything. I'm here to ask you if you'd like to be in charge of a rocket program.

Come on, Mia. You can do better than that. You sound like a traveling salesman. Would you like to buy an encyclopedia?

—What program?

—The . . . Your program. You'd have your own team. You'd run the research.

—I hate to be the bearer of bad news, Nina—can I call you Nina?—but no one is going to put me in charge of anything.

I am! I'm going to put him in charge because . . . Because I want to. Also because Stalin doesn't pay his people and I found someone at the Politburo who owes a shit ton of money to the Russian mafia. Maybe I need to rephrase that.

—What if they did?

— . . .

He's just staring at me, smiling. Is he thinking or is he flirting with me? Still staring. This is awkward.

—Sir?

—Why me?

—The work you did at the Jet Propulsion Research Institute was phenomenal. You're . . . *good*. That's why.

He is good, but I picked him because he wants to go to space.

—There were plenty of smart people at the research institute, plenty who were not arrested for treason. What makes you think they would like my help, or that I would want to help them?

—You're here, sir, extracting German technology.

—They did not leave me a choice. All I want now is to go home to my family.

—Well, you have a choice now. This is your choice.

Except I really need you to do what I want. It's like a choice, but with fewer options.

—Do you know what they did to me? What the government did to me?

—I know enough.

He and most of his colleagues were arrested during the Great Purge. They said he was slowing down work at the research institute. Stalin labeled them "members of an anti-Soviet counterrevolutionary organization." Korolev was tortured for days until he "confessed." The charges against him were eventually reduced to sabotage. He got a new trial. Only he didn't know. He was already on his way to the gulag. He went to a gold-mine prison with six hundred people. Six months later, when they found him, there weren't even two hundred of them left. Now he has to work for the people who did that to him.

—I'm not sure you do. Look.

—EWWWWW. GROSS!

Shit. I can't believe I said that out loud, but the man just handed me all his teeth! Seriously, who does that?

—I—

—I'm so sorry, sir, I didn't mean that. I just—Who did that to you?

—Scurvy did that to me.

—Oh. I thought—

—Yes. The torture was bad but not as bad as the cold.

—I'm terribly sorry for what you went through, Colonel. I am.

—Sergei, remember? You do not have to be sorry, you did not do anything. But if this is my choice like you say, then my answer is no. I do not want to build weapons for them anymore.

Oh, no. I could be curling up under the covers with Billie right now but I'm here, doing this. Time for a speech.

—I . . . I think you're lying, sir. I'm sorry. I do. I think you love science more than anything else. You send things up on a world designed to keep them down. I think you'd build rockets in your backyard if the government didn't want your help. Regardless, I think you'll want to see *this* through.

—See what through?

—Space. We're going to space.

—Ha! You are funny, young lady. No one cares about space. No one. What people want is to make bombs. Always more bombs, until we all vanish without a trace.

He's a pessimist. He seems happy, though. A happy pessimist. I don't know why but I like that. Expect the worst in people and you'll never be disappointed, I guess. Maybe that's happiness.

—*You* do. You care.

— . . .

—I know you, sir, a bit. I know you've read *The Problem of Space Travel* by Potočnik. You've talked about it. I know you've thought about going up there, what it would mean, what it would

137

take. Yes, they'll want you to build missiles, but the rockets are the same. There's also something special I'd like you to work on. I want to send something up there. I want to send it up and not have it come down. You can do that, can't you?

—You said I.

—What?

—You said *I* want to send something up there. *I* don't want it to come down. *I*, not they, not we.

Oops. I might have gotten carried away a little. Am I in trouble? No. I don't think so. This is the one good thing about not being a white man. It won't be hard to convince him I'm just a spectator in all this.

—I don't know what you mean.

—Who are you?

If I could answer that question, I probably wouldn't be here talking to him.

—I told you, my name is Nina. I'm an—

—An interpreter, I know.

—It doesn't matter who I am, sir. Pretend I don't exist. But if you say yes, you'll have your own department. They'll want a working V-2 before they let you build anything new—they have no imagination—but you can use any of the German scientists to get it done. Then the fun begins.

—I could use any of them?

—Any of them. You can have Gröttrup. You can have his entire team if you want. All you have to do is say yes.

— . . .

—Please say yes.

—No.

—NO?

—No. I am sorry. You *are* right. I love this with all my heart, but not as much as I love my family. I have put them through enough already. When they let me out of prison last year, I had not seen my wife in five years. I have been away from my daughter for most of her life. Like I said, I will do what they want me to do but I am not staying in Germany. I will go back to Moscow, back to my family.

—That won't be a problem, sir. You can see your daughter—Natalya, is it?—every day. You can see your wife. You can take her to work.

—I will not bring them here. They have a life at home.

—Of course not, we'll do everything in Moscow.

Almost. I'll set them up on Gorodomlya Island, about a hundred miles northwest. They'll be part of a new research institute I'm getting our man at the Politburo to create. Everything will be in one place, close to home.

—In Russia? But the Germans are here, in Germany. That is . . . why they are called Germans.

—You let me worry about that, sir. All you have to do is say yes.

Time to get ourselves some Germans.

28

It's a Good Day

Hmmm. That beer is good. I've earned it, even if Mother will be mad. I can hear her already: "Mia! Did you kidnap seven thousand people?" It does sound kind of bad when you put it like that. I'll admit, what I did was a little radical, but she said herself we couldn't keep things the way they were. I had to do *something*. That was something. It was *really* something.

Technically, I didn't kidnap anyone. We asked them to come to Moscow. I even wrote them a note. "As the works in which you are employed are being transferred to the USSR, you and your entire family will have to be ready to leave for the USSR. You and your family will entrain in passenger coaches. The freight car is available for your household chattels. Soldiers will assist you in loading. You will receive a new contract after your arrival in the USSR. Conditions under the contract will be the same that apply to skilled workers in the USSR. For the time being, your contract will be to work in the Soviet Union for five years. You will be provided with food and clothing for the journey which you must expect to last three or four weeks."

Okay, we weren't really asking, but you can't just *ask* thousands of people if they want to move to the Soviet Union. Some of them are bound to be less than enthusiastic about the prospect of living under Stalin. I was. So maybe it wasn't the most voluntary thing ever. We told them they were being mobilized. At gunpoint, yes, but kidnapping is throwing someone in the back of a van. These people packed their things. They brought their books with them, photos, even furniture. I mean, in theory, they could have said no. I don't think they'd have shot anyone.

We had to get them all at the same time before the word could spread, so we did it in the middle of the night. We let them pack their belongings. Some even took their pets with them. It's *definitely* not kidnapping if your pet comes along. I don't know why I'm justifying myself. Mother wanted me to be in charge, that's what I came up with. If she doesn't like it, *she* can take care of things.

It wasn't even that many people, around twenty-two hundred engineers. But their families came with them, so . . . more. Oh, who am I kidding, it was fucking spectacular! A hundred trains. A hundred! Moving von Braun's people looked like a small-town parade compared to this.

Calm down, Mia. It's a good plan. The Russians won't trust anyone with new technology, especially not the Germans. We use German scientists to get the knowledge they have now, but we don't give them any new information or let them in on new projects. In a few years, their knowledge will be outdated and they won't pose a threat to anyone. They can go home, no one will care. I'm saving their lives, really. Okay, maybe not. Still a good plan.

Mother, well, she'll get over it. Unless she finds out how much money I spent and who I spent it with. She told me that the Russian mafia had this "code," that they would never work with government. Well, that's changing now, and this guy at the Politburo owed them a lot of money. Like *a lot* a lot. He doesn't anymore. He just doesn't know.

All in all, I think I did pretty well. I got myself a rocket program, a research bureau full of German engineers, and I even have someone to run it. Oh, and I didn't get killed, by the Tracker or anyone else. I think I earned myself a beer.

One beer. Then I'll go. . . . I'm nervous all of a sudden. I tried not to think about it. I told Mother I had to come. I told Billie. Hell, I tried to tell myself, but let's face it, I could have done all this from Moscow. *This* is why I wanted to come. I don't leave Berlin until tomorrow, and Bad Saarow is only an hour away.

29

As Time Goes By

I don't remember ever being here. I feel like I'm in a brochure. Beautiful lake. Birds chirping on cue. Even the sun's angled just right. Everyone's smiling, all the time. It's like they put something in the water. It's gorgeous. I just feel really . . . out of place. I also wish I knew what I was looking for.

"I didn't think you'd come back, not after what happened in Bad Saarow."

Something happened here, only I don't know what that something is. I just hope it was newsworthy or I'll have spent the day digging through the local paper's archives for nothing. I *have* hope. I mean, the bar for newsworthiness is . . . low. Heavyweight champion Max Schmeling at the local golf club. Plans for a miniature train. Oh, the town choir won some kind of prize.

This is interesting, sort of. A list of people who didn't donate any money after One-Pot Sunday. Families were encouraged to cook a "one-pot meal" on Sundays during the fall and donate the money they saved for charity work. Hitler's party took credit for it. Happy Nazi charity work, and if you didn't give, they shamed you in the local newspaper.

Kuchen contest. I could use some cake right about now.

Memorial service for the victims of the . . . something-camp tragedy. "A ceremony was held on Sunday honoring the two young girls who lost their lives at the Glücklich Entenküken summer camp."

. . . A few days by the lake. It's beautiful out here.

"Ten-year-olds Gisela Mayer and Renate Neuman were brutally murdered . . ."

I'm dizzy.

". . . brutally murdered by another campmate on September 16 . . ."

Renate. I remember that name but that can't be it. I wasn't here. Renate. Blue eyes. Angel face.

I'll cut you up, you little bitch.

No . . . This isn't real.

All dressed up in her little white dress.

She's calling me names. "Stinky Gypsy! Stinky Gypsy! My mother says Gypsies shouldn't be allowed at camp!" They're all calling me names. "Where'd you get that necklace? You stole it, didn't you?"

My necklace. The one I'm wearing right now. They're pulling at it. "Criminal! Stinky Gypsy stole a necklace!" The chain broke. She took it. Renate's holding it over my head. "Give it back! Give it back!"

None of this happened. This is a dream. My dream. I can make it what I want.

A few days by the lake. It's beautiful out here. Mother's dropping me off. She looks so young. We'll go boating, maybe some fishing. She'll . . . "Stinky Gypsy stole a necklace!" NO WAIT! Where are you going? Give it back! The bathroom. They're all laughing. She . . . She dropped it in the toilet. Wake up, Mia!

"The perpetrator, a seven-year-old child, was found covered in blood, the carving knife still in her hand."

The knife.

I'm in the kitchen . . . I'm hiding in the meat locker trying to cool down. They found me. They drag me out. They throw some cabbage at me. Renate pours milk on my head. The milk is cold but I'm burning inside. The fever's so loud I can't hear their screams anymore. The knife rack is on the counter.

I'll cut you up, you little bitch.

This isn't real.

White dress. Cold milk. Knife.

I grab it with both hands.

This is a dream. My dream. I can do what I want.

Blue eyes. Angel face.

I want this dream to end! I want to wake up now!

I put the knife to her chest. She winces as the tip of the blade digs in. I push harder.

MAKE IT STOP!

. . .

She puts both hands on the wound to stop the bleeding. She's looking at me in disbelief, still not sure if this is real or not. Someone pushes me and I fall on top of her.

. . .

"No one knows what prompted this tragedy. When questioned by the police, the child had no recollection of the event."

Give me back my necklace!

White dress. Cold milk.

Her friend tries to stop me. I swing at her neck.

Screaming. Arms around my chest, my neck. I can't move. I'm on the floor, wrapped in grown-up arms.

"The child had no recollection of the event."

. . .

. . .

"I didn't think you'd come back, not after what happened in Bad Saarow."

ENTR'ACTE

Rule #6: There Can Never Be Three for Too Long

890 BC

Young Varkida lost her first child when the Tracker's army slaughtered her village. She heard the dogs rip her daughter to shreds as she ran for the river. A week later, she came across a caravan and chose to travel east with them to the steppes. A small group of people constantly moving would be hard to find. It also provided a modicum of protection. Varkida needed a daughter, and she quickly found a suitable progenitor among the merchants.

Varkida was the seventh of her kind. She feared the Tracker, the Rādi Kibsi. She knew that someday more like them would come and kill everyone. Her task was to save a few, to take them away before it was too late. Varkida dreamed of ships that could traverse the heavens, of a million wonders her mother had described but that she would not live to see.

Varkida studied the sky almost every night. One evening, she left the caravan to track a star that hid behind a hill. It was late by the time she came back, and she made nothing of the silence. It had been a long day, she thought, everyone must be tired. She had ventured far enough, she had not heard the horde attacking. She had not heard the screams of the people the Tracker had tortured. She found a pile of torsos in the middle of camp. All the arms and legs were arranged around it like sun rays. She thought of running, but the Tracker had left no one alive and was unlikely to come back. Camp, as gruesome as it was, was the safest place to spend the night.

The next day she awoke to the sound of horses. She immediately recognized the small tribe of nomadic warriors whose path they had crossed a few days earlier. The caravan members called them the Arimaspi. Varkida noticed how nearly half of them were women. Even the sight of two dozen arrows pointing at her head could not dampen Varkida's fascination with the intruders. Their double-curved bows were a lot shorter than Varkida's. Their small size meant they could be raised without hitting the horse's back. They had a much shorter draw and could be fired quickly while riding. The horses were short-legged with a large head, rugged animals perfectly adapted to the extreme temperatures. Varkida had never seen mounted warriors. For nearly two thousand years, the people of the steppes had been breeding horses and using them as livestock, but their use in warfare was usually limited to pulling chariots. Everything about these people was designed for speed and mobility. Ride fast, shoot fast.

The archers did not release their arrows. Perhaps they did not see Varkida as a threat. Perhaps her pregnancy was beginning to show. Varkida asked if she could ride with them and offered the caravan horses as tribute. A few months later, Varkida gave birth to not one, but two beautiful daughters.

A year after the twins were born, she was asked to take a husband. She chose the best archer of the group, a seventeen-year-old man, a year younger than her. Each warrior carried a bow and an *akīnakah*, a short blade, halfway between sword and dagger. Handling sharp objects came naturally to the Kibsu, but a father who mastered the bow would be beneficial for the girls. Varkida gave birth twice more in the first three years of marriage.

The four girls grew up together among the horses. The twins were supposed to look like each other, but by the time their youngest sister was eight years old, they were all mirror images of their mother. Different clothes and hairstyles could no longer hide the obvious, and the tribe members grew to believe that mystical creatures were living among them. Fearing punishment from the goddess Tabiti, the tribe exiled Varkida and her four daughters.

Varkida feared for her children, but the five Kibsu thrived on their own. The girls were accomplished riders. Each was given a foal as a pet. Horse and woman had grown up together and their connection was palpable. The girl's father had also served his purpose. All five women were quick with the bow, which Varkida had greatly improved over the years. Their weapons were more precise and powerful than all, and the twins, even by Kibsu standards, were absolutely deadly with a blade.

They were attacked by another small tribe a few months after their exile. The Kibsu were outnumbered but made short work of the enemy. The survivors surrendered and begged to join the Kibsu tribe. Varkida saw the men and women kneeling before her. She drew her bow and quickly shot every man through the heart. She then turned to the women and told them they had found a new home.

The tribe's reputation grew with their ranks. They were fast and fearless. Men did not dare stand against them, and women often left their own tribes to join them. Varkida had an army. Everyone from the Black Sea to Lake Baikal soon feared the wrath of the *hama-zan*.

The Kibsu had not encountered the Tracker for many years, but Varkida vowed to be ready when the time came. The enemy was ruthless, and she would respond in kind. The rules of the tribe were simple. Everyone would be fed and clothed but receive no wages. Those who wished to share the spoils of victory had to offer the head of a slain enemy as tribute. All could visit a neighboring tribe where they could have sex and return. If they became pregnant and gave birth to a girl, she would join the tribe and be cared for. A boy meant either leaving the tribe or leaving the child with the father. When they turned sixteen, Varkida gave the twins permission to have a child of their own.

A decade later, the seven Kibsu led over six hundred women against the Zhou army at Haojing.

Upon their return, they learned of a Thracian incursion into the steppes. The Thracians were known as warlike, brutal, but the accounts of these killings left everyone but the Kibsu transfixed with terror. People skinned alive, bathed in oil and set on fire, children left crying among the corpses with their eyes gouged out. This, Varkida thought, had to be the Tracker.

That evening, the tribe sacrificed a horse to the gods. The horse's forelegs were tied together. Varkida stroked its head a few times before pulling on the rope to take it down. She tied another rope around the animal's neck, placed a stick of wood under the rope, and started turning. The crude tourniquet cut the air and blood flow to the horse's head, and it died without putting up a fight. Varkida flayed off the skin of its belly, and her daughters and granddaughters joined in to cut off the flesh before boiling it. They drank the wine, burned the *kanab*, and the tribe's chanting flowed through the steppes until the sun came up.

After a day of rest, the women mounted their horses and rode west towards the enemy. Five days later, they spotted the Thracian encampment near the Volga River. None of the women had ever seen an army this size. Silence spread through the tribe like rain in drylands, and four of Varkida's riders turned and ran in fear. Varkida spotted three horse-drawn wagons and a tent forming a square on the south end of the encampment. She used the space between them as a unit of measurement. The crowd occupied an L-shaped area of roughly twelve by five wagon squares for the longer rectangle and two by four squares for the smaller one. She counted the number of people in her square and multiplied by sixty-eight. Twenty-two hundred men would soon be trying to kill them, give or take a hundred or two.

Varkida noticed that the Thracians were gathered in groups. This was no army, she realized. That horde was a collection of small tribes hastily put together for a single purpose. These people had never fought or trained together. They had likely met only a few days ago. The *hama-zan* would not be facing a disciplined cohesive unit, but dozens of small groups acting somewhat independently. The enemy peltasts carried a wicker shield but favored mobility over armor. They could handle a sword but their weapon of choice was the javelin. Varkida had seen Thracians before and knew of their tactics. They were skirmishers. They would rush towards their enemy, hurl their weapons at them, and retreat. They would repeat the cycle, thinning the enemy forces one volley at a time.

Varkida's strategy was similar, but her tribe was highly disciplined. They had trained together for most of their lives and could anticipate one another. She knew that many of the men they were facing had never seen cavalry, let alone fought against it. Varkida would strike first, but she knew that surprise was fleeting. They had to destroy the enemy's will to fight. Shock and awe were crucial, especially while so broadly outnumbered. She had her troops form a single line over a mile wide, and they sprinted towards the encampment. They held their bows steady. They did not scream or yell but instead let the sound of their horses drum fear into the hearts of the enemy. Two hundred meters from camp, they released their first arrows. Rushing at twelve meters per second, they would enter the range of the enemy javelins in under twelve seconds. Each archer fired a second and third arrow before turning around. Varkida did not need to signal her troops. The sight of her horse raising its head and shifting its weight to the rear was enough. The Thracians moved forward, but the women had learned to shoot from behind, turning their bodies and guiding their horses with their legs. Twelve seconds later, the Kibsu's army was again two hundred meters away, and three thousand arrows had rained on the Thracians. Everyone stopped to regroup, and they launched another attack, then another. Each time, the Thracians ran forward as much as they could to get away from the river.

The women's bow cases, or *gorytos*, could hold about seventy-five arrows and were still more than half full after six assaults. By then, a third of the Thracians were dead and their tribes had begun to spread out. Varkida looked at the other Kibsu. Her daughters and granddaughters did not acknowledge, nor did they need to. Within seconds, seven units of eighty women or so were storming towards the enemy.

The Thracians braced themselves for three more salvos and lowered their shields to run forward, but this time the horses kept coming. Unprepared for the onslaught, few had time to throw or even raise their javelins, and the riders easily broke through their lines while firing arrows at close range. The women never stopped. Each unit regrouped almost instantly and rode towards the next target the Kibsu leading them had chosen. The Thracians had never seen that sort of discipline. The women flew around them like swarms of bees, their arrows always on target. Two minutes after the battle began, the *gorytos* were empty and the women were on their feet, blades drawn. They all screamed at once and rushed towards the men nearest them. All the discipline they had shown on their horses made way for pure rage. One of the twins broke her sword inside a man's skull. Bare-handed, she then approached a young peltast holding a javelin. He extended his weapon to keep her from coming, but the Kibsu kept walking. She didn't stop when the javelin pierced her shoulder. She didn't stop when it came out the back. She walked through it all the way to the man's hands, grabbed the sword from his belt, and cut his throat. The next javelin came from the air and lodged itself inside her skull. She never felt it. Her daughter also died, moments later, when a battle-ax struck her neck. Two hundred women died on the battlefield that day. None of the Thracians lived. The handful that were left standing dropped their weapons and ran, but they did not make it far. One by one, the women's swords silenced the screams and the pleas for mercy. There was no bounty to be shared, but by nightfall the head of every man had been offered to Varkida as tribute.

As the sun set and the tribe headed back east, Varkida turned and saw the horror they had left behind. Thousands of headless corpses lay in a sea of red. A mound of heads broke the sky. *Her* heads, she thought. They were given to her. She got off her horse and vomited what was left of her soul. At that moment, Varkida understood that she and the Tracker were the same. She knew who it was they were saving people from.

Varkida looked at her daughters and granddaughters and realized what she had done. She began as one, but they were now five. If each of the girls did the same, the Kibsu would soon be twenty-one, then eighty-five. In two hundred years, there could be sixteen million of her. Another two hundred and—she did not know if the planet could hold that many.

Varkida ordered a celebration to honor the fallen. The women drank and smoked and shared stories of the dead. When the night was winding down, she retired to her hut with her family. She told them about the future and her plan to change it. She told them they could not fight like the Tracker or they would become him. They had to be better. Varkida told her eldest daughter it was time for her to lead, and to teach *her* daughter to abide by the principles she had set. She gave them a set of rules they should live by and made everyone recite them a dozen times.

> Preserve the knowledge.
> Survive at all costs.
> Don't draw attention to yourself.
> Don't leave a trace.
> Fear the Tracker.
> Always run, never fight.
> There can never be three for too long.

The Kibsu would live, she said, but they would live as mother and daughter. One daughter, never more. She prepared an infusion from *haumala* plants she had gathered herself. She poured three cups, kept one for herself, and handed one to each of her youngest. The family held hands for a few minutes before they drank the hot liquid. They all knew what would happen next. They had used this poison on their enemies before. One by one, their muscles would seize until paralysis spread to the heart and lungs. Varkida hoped it would be painless. Before her breathing stopped, Varkida asked the eldest to lean forward. She took off the necklace her mother had given her and placed it around her daughter's neck before whispering in her ear.

—You are the Eight now. . . . Take them to the stars, before we come and kill them all.

ACT IV

30

Nature Boy

1949

Dear Sarah,

It has been almost two years since I last heard from you. I can only hope your silence is not the result of indisposition and that you are in good health and spirits.

There is so much to tell, I do not know where to begin. After three years on the East Coast, I am returning to Caltech. While I greatly enjoyed teaching at MIT, I missed the hands-on thrills of rocketry and the camaraderie I had only found in California. I could not pass up the opportunity to work with Professor von Kármán again. They honored me with his former title and I am now the Robert H. Goddard Professor of Jet Propulsion. I have also been named director of the Guggenheim Jet Propulsion Center.

I was recently gifted another title, one I accepted with more trepidation. My wife Ying gave birth to a beautiful boy last October. We have named him Yucon. My son was born here and, with great encouragement from my colleagues at Caltech, I have recently mailed in our application for citizenship.

While I welcome this new life as an American family, I fear for the safety of my Chinese one. My father-in-law is a Kuomintang official and it has become clear that the civil war that has plagued China for so long will soon end in a communist victory.

Perhaps it is my inexperience as a father that is showing,

perhaps it is the uncertainty about the world my child will live in, but I find the weight of responsibility somewhat difficult to bear. My son is but a fragile new life and already he has inherited a thousand years of baggage. His life will be shaped by choices he did not make. He will face problems others created for him and be judged for their actions before his. I did not create the injustice my son will face but I chose to bring him into a world that is filled with it. His presence brings me more hope than I dared imagine, and a hefty dose of guilt I did not expect.

I do not wish to burden you with the complaints of a fearful parent. It is, all things considered, a time of joy for us and I hope it is one for you as well.

Sincerely, your friend,
Hsue-Shen Tsien

31

Still a Fool

Whatever I am, wherever *we* are, I know we weren't always the prey.

I keep telling myself I didn't know but it's a lie. I blocked those memories, somehow, but I knew. It's in me. It starts with a tingling, hair standing on end. Heightened senses. Everything becomes clearer, crisper. There's a monster inside me. I keep it caged up but it's there, constantly clawing at the walls. I thought I could control it, tame the beast. I thought I was stronger than *it* but I was wrong. It won't fetch or heel.

For months I thought it was just me, what I am, but I look around now and I see it in everyone. Every time someone cuts the line at the store, every time people bump shoulders in a crowd. They can control it most times, but their first instinct is violence, hatred. Deep down, people are built to kill, exterminate.

Now they can do it on an even bigger scale. The Russians have the bomb. They nuked a small village this morning. They built it in the middle of nowhere, Kazakhstan. It had houses, a store, even a little bridge. They watched their fake little town burn when the nuclear device exploded. First Lightning, they called it. Lavrentiy Beria was in charge, Stalin's right-hand man. Basically, anything really bad, Beria handles. Stalin's absolute priority after the war was to get that weapon. He has it now. It's what we wanted, but having Beria in charge makes my skin crawl. This monster had twenty-two *thousand* Polish prisoners executed in 1940. Soldier, civilian, priest even, it didn't matter.

Beria had them all shot and piled the corpses in mass graves. He did the same to ten thousand Georgian nationalists before the war. They gave him a medal for it.

I heard the scientists on his nuclear project were told in advance of their reward or punishment based on today's outcome. Get the Order of Lenin if it goes boom, life in a gulag if it doesn't. Beria loves his gulags. He's the one who got most of them built. Those who played a more critical role would get higher honors or a bullet in the head. Lots of smart people here breathed a sigh of relief when that village was vaporized today.

I bet you things are a little more tense on the other side of the Atlantic. The balance of power moved a hell of a lot in one day. The Americans finally closed their concentration camps for Japanese-Americans. Just watch. They'll fill them up with communists before the decade's over. Got to have someone to hate, even if it's your own people.

It's all I see. Hatred, pain, ugliness. I can't work. I can't think. The truth is I don't think I *should* be working, or thinking, or breathing. I go through the motions every day. I watch Korolev stumble and fail but I can't bring myself to help. I want no part in this, or anything else.

Stalin, Beria. These are the good guys, the people who defeated Hitler. These are the people we're supposed to save. Fuck no. Let this world burn, and me with it.

32

East of the Sun (and West of the Moon)

1950

They arrested him. Former "Red Squads" accused Hsue-Shen of being a member of a "subversive organization." He was questioned by the FBI before he decided to take his family to Shanghai. They seized his belongings, which, they said, contained classified materials, and they put him in jail. His friends got him out, but he is now under house arrest. His security clearance was revoked, his application for citizenship denied. His son isn't even two. His daughter is four months old. It doesn't matter where these children grow up now, they will be strangers everywhere. Discarded by their own country, mistrusted wherever they go.

They said he was a member of the Communist Party. The accusation is preposterous; his family served the opposing side. They said he attended "meetings." I am certain he has. Social gatherings of liberal scholars, reinventing the world over a gin and tonic. Not exactly a plot to "spread communism" and overthrow the government. Common sense rarely prevails in the face of paranoia, but this is completely asinine.

I hardly recognize the world anymore. My daughter is running from her duty. Her mind is troubled, and I cannot blame her for it. It would be difficult, with the evidence at hand, to reach a different conclusion. The world as it is does not beg saving.

I watch Mia suffer and I wish I could make it stop. I feel the guilt Hsue-Shen spoke of. I thrusted my daughter into a life she did not choose, as my mother did with me. We were never asked to be who we are. Whatever choice we made, it happened long before Mia was born. Perhaps I should have let her make it again.

I know now why my grandmother hid her climate research from everyone. I know why she did not tell a soul. She was ashamed. She did not fear that our efforts were in vain if the planet was doomed. She would have shared that thought, like my mother did. She *hoped* the planet was dying. She was looking for a way out. Something was eating away at her soul, and she was desperate to rationalize it, one carbon measurement at a time. She wanted to stop. She did not want her daughter, her granddaughter to carry our burden. She wanted to live, and for her child to have a normal life.

It should have been obvious. I chose not to see her failings because I did not want to face mine. I will not betray all that came before me, but I do share my grandmother's sentiment. I, too, would very much like to live, for Mia to pursue happiness in any way she wants. I wish I could die of old age and watch my granddaughter grow. I wish we were someone else.

33

I'm Gonna Dig Myself a Hole

1951

—Korolev left a message for you. He said your presence is requested at State Central Range No. 4.

Mia barely spends time with Korolev anymore. I doubt she realizes how much he—the entire program—is struggling. Korolev misses her—he says so loudly and often—but he does not know *what* he is missing. He longs for Nina the interpreter, not the scientist with an IQ forty points above his. I can hardly blame him; he doesn't know that person exists. He has only seen glimpses of what she can do.

—Tell him I can't go. I can't handle Kapustin Yar right now.

—Who is Kapustin Yar?

—It's not a who, Mother, it's a place. Total shitville. Too hot or too cold. Getting supplies, materials, getting anything there is a nightmare. We can't even drink the water. I hate it.

—I would assume the living conditions have improved since your last visit. Besides, you will not be there that long.

—You don't understand. It's so cold, the launch troops are drinking the rocket fuel to stay warm. When the snow melted in the spring, they found a dead soldier, frozen like a Popsicle. They didn't even know he was missing. Hell, they found a whole herd of horses. The *horses* froze to death, Mother.

—Korolev needs you, Mia.

I do not know how to reach her. I thought the work might bring her back but there is too much anger and hate inside her.

She is angry at the world for being what it is. She hates me for hiding the truth. She hates herself with infinite conviction.

—No he doesn't. Korolev only wants to go back because that's where he kissed me for the first time.

—What?

—Yes. We had our first successful launch with the R-1. Out of the blue, Korolev pours me a glass of champagne, says, "To the stars!" and kisses me. I should have slapped him.

—Mia! People will think—

—Oh, Mother. *Everyone* thinks Korolev and I are having an affair. His *wife* thinks we're having an affair. She served him with divorce papers last year. He said he wanted to save his marriage. Good luck with that. Anyway, tell the soon-to-be-divorcé chief designer that he can find someone else. Tell him I'm allergic to cats.

—You are not, but what does that have to do with anything?

—That place is hell? Even the mice know it. There are snakes everywhere and it gets super cold at night. We put this nice and cozy insulation over the R-1 wiring and the mice moved in. Then they ate the wires because, why not? So yes, we bring cats every time we go up there to keep the mice from destroying the rockets.

Four, almost five years of work and this is what we are left with.

—Mia. I know you still hate me, but the Soviets—

—I don't hate you, Mother. I hate myself.

—Do you think there is a difference? Can I finish what I was saying now?

—Yes.

—The Soviets will never get anywhere without your help.

—They have the R-1, the R-2.

—The R-1 is an imperfect copy. And no, they most definitely do not have the R-2. Twelve test launches, Mia. Twelve. All of them failures. That is the longest test series on record and they could not hit their target once. They will fail without you. You also need to publish what little work you have done so that others can build on it.

—I can do it later.

—Get someone to publish your findings. Trust me, you do not want to spend a decade teaching your daughter about things she could teach herself at the library. Spread your rocket knowledge far and wide and your child will only have to learn about rockets.

—It's not as bad as you think, Mother. They're making progress. Korolev is working on the R-3 and—

—Mia, you need to wake up. The R-1 has a range of two hundred and eighty kilometers and it barely works. Now they want to hit three thousand. Korolev is ambitious—I will give him as much—but the R-3 is a gigantic quagmire. New technologies, new propellants, new problems. It is quicksand, Mia. It will be the end of Korolev's bureau if you do not step in.

—We're doing what we can.

—*You* are not doing anything, Mia. You stare at the clouds for hours on end while *they* do what they can. Unfortunately, what they can is not enough.

—I'm not ready, Mother. Tell him I can't.

—I told him you were indisposed. He did not seem to care. He said nothing about bringing cats, but he did mention two dogs. Derik and . . .

—No! Not the dogs! I thought they were running a second test series on the R-2!

—He spoke of five launches in one month. How do you know the dogs?

—It's Dezik, not Derik, and Tsygan. I feed *all* the dogs, Mother. They'll use them to study the effects of space travel.

—Which would suggest they are thinking about sending a man up soon. This should be cause for celebration, should it not?

—No! Tsygan is the sweetest thing, Mother. She just wants her belly scratched, not to get blasted a hundred kilometers into the sky.

—Presumably, the objective is to bring the dogs back alive.

—There's a parachute.

—You see . . . How do they not run out of air?

—They have a little pressure suit with a bubble helmet. But something will go wrong, Mother. Something always does. The parachute won't deploy. The rocket will explode. Korolev is going to kill those dogs.

—Then you should go and make sure that does not happen. Go for the dogs, Mia. Go for Korolev, or yourself. Whatever the reason, you cannot spend the rest of your life hiding from everyone.

—I don't—

—I need to show you something. Wait here one moment.

. . .

You have asked me what we were many times before and I did not have an answer for you. Here. Look at this picture.

—It's a fish, Mother. I don't know what we are but I'm pretty sure we're not fish.

—It is called the Amazon molly. It was discovered in 1932 in—

—In the Amazon.

—No, Mia. In Texas. It gets its name for the way it breeds. The female molly—they are all female—finds a—

—All females? How's that possible?

—That is what I am trying to explain. They are named after the Amazons of Greek mythology. In most versions of the myth, the women warriors would visit a neighboring tribe and have sex with them before returning home. They would keep only their female offspring and either kill or abandon the males in the woods.

—So this fish of yours kills its male babies?

—No, it does not need to. The Amazon molly finds a male from a species that resembles it, and tricks it into believing it found a mate of its own kind.

—They have sex?

—I do not know the specifics of their mating ritual. I do know they need sperm from the male fish to trigger the development of the embryo. Do you remember when we talked about genes?

—Pea plants.

—Yes. Pea plants. What makes the Amazon molly so special is that none of the genes from the male fish are passed on to the offspring. Only the mother's genes are. All of them. The babies get *everything* from their mother.

—Everything. You mean, like us?

—I do not know if it is *exactly* like us, but yes.

—They're all the same fish?

—I suppose it depends on your definition of "same." . . .

—Shit. We're fish. Why are you showing me this, Mother? Is that supposed to make me feel better?

—Yes, it is. What I am trying to tell you, Mia, is that the world is vast and full of strange things. Just because something is strange does not mean it should not exist. You feel different. You *are* different, Mia, *we* are. That does not mean you have no place in this universe. I cannot tell you what you are, but I can say with *absolute certainty* that you belong here as much as everything else.

34

Unforgettable

—I'm tired, Nina. I'm tired of this.

I'm surprised Billie stuck with me this long. I've been distant, cold. I need her but I can't stand her being close to me. I can't look her in the eyes; it reminds me of what I am. I stay awake every time I spend the night because I'm afraid I'll hurt her in my sleep. I just lie there and stare at her bookshelves. She's read *A Hero of Our Time* again. It's not shelved where it used to be.

—It's okay, Billie. I'll leave.

—I don't want you to leave! I want you to talk to me.

— . . .

What would I say? Hey, I killed some thirty people. Want to play chess?

—You're hurting, Nina. I can see that. You're in pain and I want to help you, but you won't let me.

—I don't need your help.

—You need *someone's* help. I love you, Nina. I love you with all my heart, but you won't let me do that either. I can't just sit and watch you suffer from a distance. I can't do that. You need to let me in.

She's right. I won't let her. She doesn't know me. She's never seen what's inside. What she loves, what she thinks I am, it's a lie. If she saw . . .

—It's probably best if we stop seeing each other.

—Fuck you, Nina!

There. Anger I can relate to. This is real. I deserve that.

168

She . . . I don't know exactly what she deserves but I know it's better than this, better than me.

—I can't give you what you want, Billie. I can't share everything that's in my head. I don't want it in my head. I sure as shit don't want it in yours. *I'm* making you unhappy. I can see that. You said you can't do it. I understand.

—Fuck you!

—Billie, I—

—I never said I didn't want to. I said I *can't*! As in it's too hard! I see you suffering and I suffer *with* you. I watch you drown and I'm gasping for air. You and I, we're . . . I'm not giving up on you, Nina. I don't give a rat's ass if that's what you want.

—Why?

—Because you don't do that, you pudding-head! You never give up on the people you love. When the storm comes, you hold on to them and you don't let go. Do you hear me, Nina? You don't let go.

I *am* the storm. She should get as far away from me as she can.

—You have to.

— . . .

She's . . . getting out of the house. This is her place. I should be the one leaving.

—Billie, wait! Where are you going?

— . . .

She left the door open.

—Billie!

—Come!

—I—Let me just get my shoes. . . .

—Who needs shoes?

Neither of us, apparently. She's sprinting. This is true Billie. I want her to run away, she makes me run after her. I *am* running, barefoot in the middle of the night. I want her. It's me I can't stand.

She's getting away. The streetlamps aren't working but the

moon's so full we can almost touch it. Faster. We aren't the only ones who can't rest. I see cars across the Moskva, silhouettes in dimly lit windows. Moscow's ill-behaved, it only pretends to sleep. This feels good, somehow. The pavement's still warm, but the faster I run, the more I feel the night breeze blowing in. She's going for the bridge.

Faster. My heart is stomping louder than the city. It's not the running, it's me gaining on her. Hunting. She's slowing down in the middle of the bridge. Full stop. This is where she wants me. She's . . .

—Billie, DON'T!

She can't hear or she won't listen. She's climbing over the guardrail.

—Catch me before I fall!

She's crazy. She's across the rail now, leaning over water. I need to run faster.

—Stop it, Billie! You'll kill yourself!

—Not if you catch me first!

No! She let go of one hand. She's dangling sideways, arms spread like an angel. She's gonna fucking kill herself.

I'm almost there. Her hand is slipping, or she's letting it slip. Her fingers are stretching. I won't make it in time. I—

—FOR FUCK'S SAKE, BILLIE! ARE YOU CRAZY?

I caught her, barely. She's still leaning back but I've got her arm. I've got her.

—I knew you'd catch me.

—Billie, don't you ever pull a prank l—

—It's okay, Nina.

—No it's not. You—

—Shhhh. You're hurting my wrist now.

She's climbing back over. Her wrist's all red. I squeezed it with all I had.

—You're insane, you know that?

—Maybe. But I knew you'd catch me. And when *you* fall, I'll be there to catch *you*. Whatever it is, it doesn't matter, Nina. Give me your hand and I'll catch you.

—Billie, I—

—I'll catch you. I swear. All you have to do is give me your hand. Now say you believe me.

I'm not going to cry.

—I want to.

I want to believe her. I want it so bad I feel my heart will explode, but I won't cry. It's bad enough I'm barefoot on a bridge at 4:00 A.M., I won't cry on top o—

—Stop crying, Nina. We look like a couple of fools already.

—I hate you.

—I know. Now let's go home and get some sleep before you leave.

—I'll be back in a month. If you change your mind, I'll—

—I won't change my mind. Now you go to this place, this Kapustin Yar, and you find yourself.

—There's nothing there to find.

—Then we'll keep looking together. Either way I'm not going anywhere. I'm here, Nina. I'm here now and I'll be here when you get back.

35

Pink Champagne

The smell of rocket fuel's so strong it scratches at your throat. Somehow I feel better out here than I did at home. It might be the booze. Maybe I just really like things bleak and lifeless. Kapustin Yar is three hundred and sixty degrees of nothing, an endless sea of dead grass and dirt roads. Our little island is made of steel and concrete. There's nothing fragile here. We can't hurt anyone but ourselves.

—Hands on your desk, Sergei.

—One kiss. Then I swear I will get back to work.

Korolev is a child. He's a charming, intelligent child, but he has all the maturity of a five-year-old.

—No! You have a rocket to launch, Mr. Chief Designer. Remember? Also, you look like a goldfish when you do that.

—It will work! We reinforced the nose cone so it does not overheat. *You* gave us the idea to fix the guidance system. How do you know about accelerometers, anyway?

I usually make sure my ideas come through other people, but there aren't any right now. Also, that takes time and we don't have much of that either. I just need a vague excuse for not being a complete idiot.

—I told you, my father liked to tinker. I spent hours watching him. And we didn't fix anything, we just reduced the vibrations so the thing could work. It might not. The accelerometer could be bad to begin with.

—It did just fine in the horizontal test. It will work! Trust me! There is no point in worrying about it now.

I don't trust him. Well, I do. I just don't trust the other eleven million people involved in building that rocket. He's right about one thing, though. There isn't much more we can do from here.

—I hope it works. I don't think you can afford many more of these failed launches.

—Have dinner with me tonight.

—I'm serious, Sergei! You need to be more careful.

—Careful how? My wife is not going to divorce me twice.

—Not about me, you nitwit. You speak of space rockets in front of everyone, orbiting satellites—

—I thought that is what we were doing. You said yourself—

—I know what I said, but Stalin wants missiles. You need to give him that first or you'll get a visit from Beria and the secret police.

—They will get their missiles. The R-2 will work. Then we will build the R-3.

—The R-2 is too small, and even if you built the R-3, it still won't cross the Atlantic. You know that's the only thing Stalin is interested in.

—I will be fine.

—You keep saying that, but you know how Beria thinks. If you're not adding to the might of the Soviet empire, then you must be trying to sabotage it. You of all people should know what they're capable of.

He thinks he might lose his job, but Beria's a madman. Korolev won't survive another stint in the gulag. He definitely won't survive a firing squad.

—You are worried about me.

—I'm worried about the program.

— . . . Nah! You are worried about me.

Fine. I like him. I keep telling myself it's the work, but there's something endearing about Korolev. He's like a puppy. He also builds rockets for a living. Life around him—I don't know—I don't hate myself as much when I'm with him.

—You keep telling yourself that.

—I will. So? Dinner?

—Just dinner.

—Cross my heart. We will talk shop. I will tell you about that paper from Tikhonravov. He has some fascinating ideas.

Oh, good. He's read it. "On the Possibility of Achieving First Cosmic Velocity and Creating an Artificial Satellite with the Aid of a Multi-Stage Missile Using the Current Level of Technology." Mouthful. Mother said I had to publish, and Tikhonravov is my voice in all this while I play Nina the interpreter. He works in another bureau, NII-4. I thought it best to keep some distance. I'm paying him, of course, but he is brilliant. His next paper is called "Flight to the Moon." I don't think anyone here will pay attention, but the Americans will think that's what the Soviets are working on. Hopefully.

—Okay. Dinner. But on one condition.

—There I was hoping my mere presence might be enough.

—Send the German scientists back home. You're not using their ideas anyway. You're paying them to play cards all day.

—End of the year. I will send them all home. I promise. Seven o'clock in the office?

—Seven thirty. And I'm not sleeping with you.

—I said cross my heart! Why not, by the way?

—You are still a married man, Mr. Korolev. And I'm a woman of virtue, not some able Grable you can just—

—Forget I asked. I will see you tonight. I want to check on the dogs before I leave.

—Poor dogs. I still hate you for that, by the way.

—I know.

—Good. Just making sure.

36

How High the Moon

—I can't believe Korolev proposed. What's wrong with men? Did he really think I'd say yes? Ooooh, we fixed the guidance system. Yes, *Glavny Konstruktor*. I'd love to marry you!

Here, Tsygan. Let's get you out of that cage.

Mother, I have something to show you!

— . . .

Three successful launches in a row. I'll admit, it was exciting. Saber-some-champagne exciting, not propose-out-of-the-blue. What kind of person does that?

—Next thing you know he'll want me to cook his meals, wash his clothes. Fat chance, dog killer. Right, Tsygan? It's okay. The bad man is gone now. You can look around. This is your new home.

Mother, I'm back! Where are you?

— . . .

It's good to be home. I'm glad I went, though. Mother was right. I must be as crazy as Korolev, but being in the middle of nowhere shooting dogs into the sky is as close to normal as I've felt since I came back from Germany.

—Mo—

—Mia?

—Yes! I'm in the kitchen.

—Who are you talking to? I can hear you blab—Is that a dog?

—Very perceptive, Mother. This is Tsygan. Tsygan, meet Sarah, your . . . grandmother.

—I think not.

—Mother, you won't believe what Korolev did in—

—Not now, Mia. I think you better sit down.

—What is it? No, not the shoes, Tsygan.

—Sit, Mia.

—You're making me nervous now. Just tell me!

—Your girlfriend has been arrested.

My heart stopped. Too much to unpack here.

—Who?

I didn't know what else to say. I just need a second to get myself back together.

—Billie. They arrested her.

—For what? What did she do?

—You know why, Mia. I do not think you are the only one she was close to.

Shit. This is bad. This country wasn't made for people like her. I just need to know that she's fine. I need her to be fine.

—Wha-what did they do to her? Where is she?

—In a psychiatric clinic. Her mother put her there.

No, not this. Anything but this. Billie won't survive in a cage. Is this my fault? Did someone see us? I hate myself for making this about me, but I can't handle this being my fault. I've hurt her enough already.

—How long?

—A day or two after you left. She's been there a whole month.

37

Moanin' at Midnight

My daughter would not take no for an answer. The clinic is quite small. Hopefully everyone is sound asleep and we can sneak in and out. Mia is angry. She does not understand. Billie's mother was smart to have her committed. She can either be mentally ill or a decadent fascist conspiring against the state. Neither are pleasant but she would not survive the latter. She would be in the gulag already if she were a man. Homosexuality is a crime for them. Women get arrested for plotting against the government, or they are "reeducated."

—Through here, Mia. This window is open.

Part of me is glad we came. What goes on in these places is inhuman. I have heard of ice-pick lobotomies performed in the US. Place a sharp pointy object, like an ice pick, underneath the eyelid and drive the point through the bone and into the brain with a small hammer. This is a more "gentle" clinic. They will not punch holes in Billie's brain, but she will wish she were dead nonetheless. I wonder if her mother knows what they will do to her.

—Mother! Are you coming?

I am. I should not be, but I am. From the outside, we could only see light in one of the rooms up front. This must be where the nurse on duty is working. This corridor is empty. I hope the guards are not making their rounds.

—Patient rooms are on the second floor, Mia.

—I know.

She is upset. I sympathize, but we should not be here. Do not draw attention to yourself. I told her not to come. I *ordered* her. It was foolish of me but I thought she might do what I asked. This is the second time Mia has disobeyed me, but it is the first time she has done it to my face. I suppose I should be glad it lasted this long, but nothing good can come from this escapade. They do not allow visitors during treatment. Even if they did, it would be bad for Mia to be seen with Billie. There is also a distinct possibility Mia will not get the reaction she wants. Either way, there is nothing we can do for that woman.

—Here, Mother. She's in here.

The door is locked. They will not let them out of their room. I wish Mia would be satisfied seeing her through the window, but I know my daugh—Strike that. I never knew she could pick a lock. She is good.

—Go, Mia. Talk to her so we can leave.

—I'm not leaving without her.

I do not remember ever being this stubborn. I must have been.

—Mia! You have not thought this through. Just get inside and talk to her.

—Stay here, Mother.

I hope Mia gets some satisfaction out of this, a modicum of closure. I hope Billie is capable of having a conversation. Mia does not understand what goes on within these walls. There is no telling what kind of mental state Billie is in, what drugs she is on or what they are doing to her. I can only guess.

[*I don't want you here! GET OUT, NINA!*]

This was a bad idea from the start.

—Mia, you need to keep her quiet.

—I just—

[*GET OUT!*]

—Listen to me carefully, Mia. You need to keep her quiet

178

before the situation escalates. Do you understand what I am trying to tell you?

—I know! I'm trying!

She believes the old Billie will surface if she is able to calm down. I fear she might be out of reach.

—Mia! They use psychotropic drugs to make subjects more suggestible. Billie could be having hallucinations. She might not even know if this is real or not.

She might have spent the last month vomiting all day. They give patients nausea-inducing drugs and make them watch homoerotic pictures while they lie in their vomit or feces. She would have received shock therapy, electric current applied to her hands or genitalia while being shown photos of naked women. Masturbatory reconditioning. These "treatments" may not change anyone's sexual preferences in the end, but they will do a number on their mind. Mia should know that.

[GET OUT! GET OUT! HEEEELP! SOMEONE GET HER OUT OF HERE!]

—Stop it Billie, please!

Too late. I hear footsteps in the stairwell. A guard. Medium build, about my height. Baton in hand, no firearm. I see one exit behind me, one behind him. He is coming this way.

[What's going on here?]

—Good evening, sir. My daughter and I are visiting our cousin.

[There are no visitors. How did you get in here?]

It was worth trying but we broke in in the middle of the night. It will take more than a story.

—We were just leaving. Take this envelope, sir—take it—and let us agree that we were never here.

I had a feeling we might need to bribe our way in or out. It is the one constant in this country now. People are underpaid if they are paid at all. He saw what is in the envelope. If he were going to do anything, he would have done it by now. He will pretend to think about it, either to convince me I was lucky he took my money, or to convince himself he has some moral character left. Now. He just slid the envelope inside his shirt pocket.

[I SAID GET OUT!]

Shhhh! The guard is entering the room. I know why. If she keeps screaming and someone else comes . . . He does not need the complication any more than we do. He could lose his job, or the money he took from me.

[You ladies need to go now. And you, will you shut up already?!]

Mia is just standing there. She is waiting for a happy ending but none is forthcoming.

[HEEEEELP!]

[I told you to shut. Your. Mouth!]

He put his baton on Billie's throat. She cannot protect herself. Her arms and legs are tied to the bed. I do not think Mia will—

—MIA, NO!

Open-hand strike to the throat. I did not see it coming. Neither did he. This is what I was afraid of. This is why I came. The guard is on the floor clawing for air. She must have crushed his trachea. I could open up his throat before he asphyxiates, but the money will not be enough. He will talk. Will Billie?

Mia is still waiting for the person she knows and loves. That person is likely gone, and Mia just killed someone right in front of her.

—MOTHER, BEHIND YOU!

AAHGHH! I think my arm is broken. Another guard. I did not hear him approach over his colleague's gargling. Assess, Sarah. His baton is in my right hand. I grabbed it without thinking. Push him against the wall and strike with the forehead . . . I broke his nose. He will focus on that while I snap his collarbone.

There is a nurse standing atop the stairs. She was looking at me. She froze, but fight-or-flee will kick in soon. Here it is. Flee.

I must catch her before she calls for help and this gets out of control.

Faster. I should land midway through the stair leg if I jump over the rail. Ugh. I twisted an ankle but I am three feet behind her. Close enough to lunge forward.

She hit the concrete floor hard. I have her in a choke hold.

—Do not resist, ma'am, you will only make it worse.

We lie a few inches from the doorway, but no one can see us. If the noise did not alert anyone, this should be the end of it.

I hope Mia has Billie under control. I will find out when this nurse stops moving. Brain hypoxia will begin five minutes after the blood flow is stopped, but I am exerting over a hundred pounds of pressure on her neck. If her vertebrae are not severely damaged, enough blood vessels will rupture when crushed against her spine. Another thirty seconds should suffice.

I must remember to wipe down anything we touched. The window frame, the door handles. The police do not have our prints, but Mia and Billie were close. They were in youth group together. Zero degrees of separation. It will not take a genius to—

—Let's go, Mother.

What is Mia doing here?

—Mia, you should be upstairs. Wipe our prints. Keep Billie quiet.

—We need to go.

I do not have the courage to tell her what needs to be done. We cannot leave a witness anymore, not after we killed three people. Mia will never forgive me, but that is something I must learn to live with. Do not draw attention to yourself. I broke the rule and I will pay the price. I will send Mia home and take care of Billie myself. I only wish they could say goodbye.

—Mia, we cannot leave just yet. There is—

—Mother! It's done. Let's go.

She knew. That look on her face. It is not resilience, or the knowledge that it had to be done. She is . . . angry. Is she angry at me? Perhaps Billie did not give her the recognition she wanted. Mia loved and she was not loved back. She felt vulnerable. That is not what we do best. It could be something else entirely, but it does not matter anymore. The nurse is dead. It is time for us to leave.

38

Hey, Good Lookin'

I'm proud of you, Son.

That's what he said. Those were his last words. What an idiot. His brother, Uncle Hans, he knew better. Hans didn't go easy. My brothers and I had to chase him down. It took us almost a year to catch up to him. He called us dimwits before we slit his throat. He always called us dimwits, but I think he meant it more that time. He said: "You fools have no idea what the hell you're doing." Back then, I thought he was just a coward. Now I think he might have been on to something.

I was always proud to be the eldest. I thought that made me—I don't know—more me than my brothers. I worshiped my dad as a kid, and being allowed children sounded like quite a gas. Damn. I don't wish our life on anyone, but when my son was born, I kind of looked forward to teaching him what I know.

Ha! The little buggers can't do anything when they're born. They don't even speak. I mean, I knew all that going in, but I didn't realize I'd be twiddling my thumbs for years while a tiny me makes spit bubbles and shits himself all day. I also didn't realize he'd spend all his time with his mother, which meant *I'd* have to spend time with his mother. I must have not done a very good job at that, because she took the kid and ran after two years.

I had it all worked out. I wasn't gonna kill her. I wasn't even gonna yell. We'd both admit to our wrongs and start anew. It was all in my head, but I honestly thought it would work, and I was even a little proud of myself. She took a bunch of pills and drove her car right off a cliff. What kind of sick person does that to a child? I barely knew the kid but he was one of us. He didn't deserve that. I took it hard. There was some drinking, some unfortunate incidents. I had to move a couple of times. It doesn't really matter, what matters is that I wasted five years and I don't even have *one* son, let alone four.

Now Charles and Leonard are in Washington. Lord knows what William is doing. And I'm here, thirty-four years old, trying to sway the ladies. I had plenty of hunt left in me when I retired. I still do. I'm sure my brothers would say the same, but I was good at this. I hated every moment but I had instinct. They wouldn't be in America right now if it weren't for me. I found that photograph. Me. Thousands of years we didn't know what the traitors looked like, until I came along. We might have found them already if I'd gone with them.

That made me think. If my son were still alive, I'd show him things, teach him about our ways, but really, there isn't *that* much to teach. Find the traitors, get the device, save the world. There. I could show him how to fight, whatever, but I couldn't teach him what it meant to have spent an entire lifetime chasing after someone, the connection you develop, the intimacy. I *know* these women. No kid of mine will know them as much as I do, not until they reach my age and then, bam. Start all over again. I love tradition as much as the next guy, and I get how we don't want to reproduce like rabbits, but this system of ours is really lossy. What a waste.

I dream of our world at night, I see its moons traverse the red sky, but I know now what I see can't be real. I've only heard my father describe a place he'd never seen for himself. We're playing telephone. Our dreams get garbled with every generation. Colors get diluted, details are erased. We lose a bit of who we are every time we're born. We're watered down like cheap drinks.

When the children I don't have are old enough and they come to kill us, what will I say? "I'm proud of you, Son"? Fat chance. I'll tell them: "You dimwits have no idea what the hell you're doing."

I need a drink.

39

Hymne à l'Amour

—You lied to me, Mia!

She lied and I did not see it. She said it was done. I do not know what upsets me most, Mia's deception, or that I cannot read my own daughter anymore.

—I had to! You would have killed her. I couldn't let you do that.

Mia has killed before. It nearly destroyed her, but she did what had to be done. She followed the rules. How can I leave three thousand years of work and sacrifice in her hands if she will risk it all for one person?

—I trusted you, Mia! What you did put us both in danger. Billie could have told them everything. I am still not sure why she did not. We could have been arrested, executed. Or sent to die in a mine somewhere. Billie could have had us *both* killed. She still can.

—She didn't! I knew she wouldn't.

—How could you know? She was screaming for you to leave!

—I think . . .

—What do you think? That you were being selfish? Dishonest?

—I think she didn't want me to see her that way.

—Mia, she—

—She gave me her hand! My hand was on the bed and she . . . She put her hand in mine.

—That is not good enough, Mia. You put your feelings ahead

of everything we hold dear. We cannot take that kind of risk. If both of us were to die, it would mean—

—You would have done the same thing.

— . . .

—You would have let her live if you'd been in my place. You would have, Mother, or everything you told me about us is a lie. We're the same, aren't we?

Is that what upsets me so much? That I have it in me to risk it all on someone? That I would give up everything we worked for? I think of those who came before me, of my mother, and all I see is strength. Would they have sacrificed everything for the person they loved? Survive at all costs. That is the rule. That is the only reason I am here, the only reason Mia lives. We are the Kibsu. We survive. Is it really Mia I am upset about? I have felt my own conviction waver ever since we moved to Russia. Have we lost our way, or have we always been weaker than I thought?

—Perhaps, Mia. Perhaps I would have, but it does not make it right.

—Why are we here, Mother?

—Here where? I do not understand.

—Why do we do what we do?

A rhetorical question if there was ever one.

—You know the answer, Mia.

—Take them to the stars, I know. But that's *what* we do. I'm asking you why?

—Before Evil comes and kills them all. We do what we do to protect people.

—From what? Who will come? What Evil?

—Where is this all coming from, Mia! What are you trying to tell me?

—Who's coming? It's not the Tracker. He's been here all along if he exists at all. More people like him?

—Mia, it is—

—Answer me.

—I assume it is people like him, yes.

—People like us?

My daughter thinks we are monsters, like the Tracker. Perhaps we are . . . related to him, like sun and moon, day and night.

—Does it matter?

—No, it doesn't. What I'm trying to say is that this is all about *them*. Take *them* to the stars. We're not going, Mother. We're doing it for *them*. Not *us*.

—I do not see how this has anything to do w—

—Then if we can't trust a single one of them, if they're all so fucking aw—

—Watch your tongue, Mi—

—If they're so *fucking* awful, all of them, that we can't believe in the ones we love, what's the point? Tell me, Mother. Why are we doing all this if they're not worth our love, or our trust? You want me to lead us. You want us to be the One Hundred. I'll do it, I will, but I have to know why. It has to mean something.

Now I understand what Mia was doing. She was saving one life to give meaning to another. This was my doing in some way. I asked her to take charge. I asked her to pursue a goal she did not set, for a purpose she did not believe in. Letting Billie live was . . . science. We are creatures of facts and empirical evidence. We trust what can be proven or observed. She was asked to believe in something she could not see, and so she devised the only experiment she could think of to prove its existence. She took a leap of faith.

I wonder how many of us did the same. How many times throughout history did we need proof that our path was righteous, that the goals we pursued were worthy of the effort? I imagine that moment would come with a new generation, or the promise of one. It is one thing to extend the self for a nebulous purpose. It is another to ask your child to spend a lifetime doing the same. Perhaps this is how our entire journey began, with a leap of faith in someone.

ENTR'ACTE

Rule #2: Survive at All Costs

AD 921

At the young age of twenty-six, al-Muqtadir bi-llāh had been
the Abbasid caliph for as many years as he had not. Though he
would rule the caliphate for over a quarter century, al-Muqtadir
bi-llāh showed little or no interest in the affairs of government,
leaving most decisions to his viziers and members of his harem,
including his mother. The caliph was thus unaware that the
king of Volga Bulgaria, who had converted to Islam, had asked
for his assistance in establishing a proper Muslim kingdom. He
was also unaware that he had agreed to the king's demand and
sent a delegation from Baghdad.

Among the small group forming the diplomatic mission were
Ahmad Ibn Fadlan, who served as secretary to the ambassador,
and the Sixty-Five, one of his many servants. She—her name
was Nabia—was good with numbers and proved a valuable asset
when matters of trade or taxation were at hand. Ibn Fadlan was
kind, and Nabia was thankful for the opportunity to live among
men and travel to foreign lands. She had read the ahadith stories of fierce Muslim women warriors, of the women poets and
rebels, but a lot had changed in the last century. Slave or not,
Abbasid women were now kept behind closed doors, treated as
objects of pleasure to be possessed or traded.

From the Caspian Sea, the mission made its way up the
Volga River through the Khazar Khaganate. Relations between
the Khazars and the Abbasids were cordial at the time, and all
hoped for an uneventful journey. On the seventh morning, the

Sixty-Five spotted a silhouette on the riverbank ahead of them and woke her master. It wasn't a Khazar. The man didn't wear a tunic, nothing but a cloak covering half his body. He was holding an ax in one hand and his penis in the other, peeing in the river. The boat drew closer, but the man didn't turn or hide, showing no sign of modesty. Nabia's master told her he was Rusiyyah, a Viking. They ruled all of Kievan Rus' to the north and west and had been using the Volga as a trade route for over a century. They sold goods and slaves to the Abbasids and often traveled all the way to Baghdad. Neither Nabia nor her master had ever seen one up close.

When the man was done peeing, he gestured to them to come ashore. The Vikings wanted to trade.

Nabia was well traveled and her master thought she might prove useful in bargaining. They made their way to the small camp the Vikings had set up next to their ship. The camp was filthy by Abbasid standards, but it was the Vikings' physique that struck them. In the middle of camp, a man was having intercourse with one of his slaves out in the open. Nabia and her master tried their best not to stare, but both were aroused by the scene. In his journals, Ibn Fadlan would write: "I have never seen bodies as nearly perfect as theirs. As tall as palm trees, fair and reddish."

The Abbasids had nothing to trade with. The riches they were carrying were meant for the king of Volga Bulgaria. The Vikings also had very little to offer: a couple of slaves, some fur and honey.

Nabia was taller than most, and she stood with unusual confidence. She was unique. The leader of the Viking party thought something unique would make for a proper tribute to his earl, and he asked to buy her for a handful of coins. He did not take kindly to Ibn Fadlan's refusal but reluctantly added one of their slaves to the offer. A slave for a slave, plus what was already a fair price for a slave. Ibn Fadlan knew that another no would amount to an insult. The Vikings could easily slaughter all of them and leave with whatever they wanted, or simply take Nabia. There was little anyone could do to stop them. It was certainly better to leave with something than with nothing, but Ibn Fadlan reminded himself the Vikings had made a very generous offer, and when he waved Nabia goodbye from the deck of his boat, he did so with pride and a smile.

The Viking ship followed for more than a day. It was not until they split that Nabia fully realized what was happening to her. She sat up front with every man to her back. Each carried an ax or a blade, and the scars on their arms and legs were a stark reminder that the Norsemen had seen battle before. Their ships were fast and agile. The Kibsu were never good swimmers. She could neither fight nor flee and chose to rest as best she could for whatever came next.

They arrived in Novgorod a few days later. She was presented to the earl during a visit from Igor of Kiev, son of Oleg, descendant of the great Rurik and supreme ruler of the Rus'. Igor looked into Nabia's eyes and saw something he had not seen before. It wasn't defiance, or the hatred he had seen so many times. She looked at him as her equal. And so, instead of spending her days milking cows serving the earl of Novgorod, Nabia got back on a ship and took the Oka River all the way to Kiev. Igor's wife had died, and his infant son needed a mother. The Sixty-Five needed a daughter, and while her consent was not necessary, she embarked on that voyage willingly.

The wedding was a wild and chaotic event. Neither of the newlyweds remembered much of it. Life in Kiev was better than what she expected. The Vikings, for all their brutality, were genuine and honest. They showed a profound sense of community. The city was lively, and Olga—that was the name she had taken—felt at home almost instantly. She adored Sviatoslav, her adoptive son, and grew to love her husband almost as much. Viking women enjoyed quite a bit of freedom. They could own property. They ran the affairs of the house as they saw fit. *Konnungar* and earl women also shared their husbands' power and privilege. If Igor were to die, Olga would rule until their son was old enough to reign.

Come spring, Olga gave birth to a beautiful daughter, Hilde. "She has her mother's eyes," said Igor when he saw her for the first time. As pleased as he was, what Igor needed was another heir, and while holding his daughter for the first time, he told Olga she would soon give him a boy. Seven slaves were strangled and stabbed to ensure the gods' goodwill. Olga knew the rules—the Kibsu come in twos, not threes—but she chose to be a wife and mother first, Kibsu second. Hilde might not survive winter, and she convinced herself another daughter was a good insurance policy.

Hilde did survive to see her sister born. Brynhild *also* had her mother's eyes. She and her sister had their mother's cheeks, her smile, her everything. Igor did not have another son. Hilde was reminding him of his wife a bit more every day. Brynhild reminded him of both. Igor tried his best to see something of himself in his girls. They were bold, fearless. Olga hoped that would be enough. She knew full well it was time to leave, but she chose not to. She loved her husband and could not fathom leaving her son behind.

When Sviatoslav was six, Igor was killed while collecting tribute from the Drevlians. After they captured him, they bent two birch trees, tied one to each of his legs, and watched Igor tear in half as they released the trees. Olga thought this might be the work of the Tracker, but she did not care. There would be no running. The Drevlians sent emissaries to Kiev to tell Olga of her husband's death. They asked that she return with them to marry their prince and settle peace between their people. Olga thanked them for their offer and said she would welcome them to her court the next day. She had her people carry the emissaries inside their boats as if they were palanquins, and dropped them inside a trench she had dug during the night. All of Kiev watched as the messengers were buried alive.

Their death did little to quench Olga's thirst for revenge. She requested the Drevlians send a proper diplomatic party so that she could return with them and meet the prince with distinction. The Drevlians sent a group of noblemen, whom she received with the highest honors. While they were bathing, Olga locked the doors and set the bathhouse on fire.

She sent a second message to the Drevlians and asked that they prepare a feast on the site of her husband's death so that she might mourn him properly before marrying the prince. They did. Mead flowed profusely that night, and when Olga felt she had mourned enough, she and her party slaughtered the five thousand Drevlians who had gathered with them. Olga returned home to prepare an army and kill anyone left alive. The Drevlians knew better than to fight the Rus' again, and they retreated behind their walls. Olga did not want a siege to drag on for years, and she offered to leave if the Drevlians simply gave her pigeons and sparrows as tribute. The Drevlians were suspicious but thought they had nothing to lose by answering such a small request. Olga wrapped some sulfur inside small strips of cloth and attached one to each of the bird's feet before lighting them on fire. The scared birds returned to their nests at once and set the city ablaze.

When the Vikings returned home, Olga told her children their father had been avenged, but when she approached Sviatoslav to hug him, the boy cowered in fear. Consumed as she was with wrath, she failed to notice that her son had watched her through it all. He had seen her drink blood and slaughter children his age. The boy's mother had died. All that remained was a monster. Olga could not bear to see herself through her son's eyes. She took a small ship and headed south with her two daughters.

Wife and mother first, Kibsu second. Olga had bet it all on

a man and a boy, and she had lost both of them. She had lost her family, her home, and most of herself. Olga had broken the rules, and it had caught up with her. She fought when she should have run. She stayed when she should have gone. She had *two* daughters. That night, Olga held Hilde for hours, until she fell asleep in her arms. When Hilde was dead, her mother kissed her on the head and gave her body to the Dnieper. Olga had broken the rules, and she had paid the price. She had lost the will to live, but she would not dare break the rules again. Survive at all costs.

Mother and daughter changed their names. Don't leave a trace. Olga became Eurybia, goddess of the sea. She arrived in Athens a month later with her daughter Zosime, the survivor.

ACT V

40

You Belong to Me

1952

Nights are getting colder. I should have brought a scarf. Here it is again. Big armored Packard limousine. It's the third time I've seen it since I left Korolev's house. Whoever it is, it's someone important. Tinted windows. I can't see who's inside, but the car slows down every time it drives by. I'm pretty sure it's me they're looking at. I'll take the long way home. No way I'm walking the alley by myself.

It could be nothing, but with the day I had, my guess is it's more bad news. Korolev and I had a fight. I told him we should scrap the R-3 project altogether. That didn't go well. I had to throw some math at him and, well . . . He doesn't like it when I'm smarter. Makes him feel . . . I don't know how it makes him feel. All I know is he was mad. It might have something to do with that marriage proposal. He said I owe him an answer. *Owe.* What's the hurry? Oh, yeah. I told him I won't sleep with anyone before I tie the knot. Anyway, he can find someone else if he doesn't like it. It's also not my fault his rocket's a mess. Glushko built a nineteen-burner engine for the R-3, but the mixing chamber is too big to survive the pressure. He says he's solved the problem, but I don't want to build another engine for a rocket that won't cross the ocean. If we're going to do this thing, we're going to do it right. I want to go straight for the prize and build an intercontinental ballistic missile. A short-range missile is just that, a missile. It can't be used for anything but killing people. I want to build something that will get us to space. I want to build the perfect rocket.

Where the hell is everyone? Another car slowing down. Black sedan this time. Looks a hell of a lot like the secret police. Oh shit, this one's stopping. Two men getting out. They're . . . Yep. They're secret police all right. I hate the MGB. There's an alley behind me twelve meters to the right. It's too far. I'd need to slow them down first.

—You need to come with us.

They're both large and heavy. It's intimidating but it usually means slow and clumsy. I could push one on the other, duck behind cars, and make the alley before they draw.

—Who? Me? This must be a mistake.

Forward might be better. I've got high heels. Push one down, kick him in the eye. Take his weapon. I can probably puncture a kidney with a hard kick.

—It's no mistake, ma'am. Just get in the car.

Could it be because of the clinic? Maybe Billie talked. I need to decide now. . . . Pistols are holstered, straps are on. Shoulders are relaxed. Whatever they want, they don't see me as a threat. There's no point in taking them on now.

—I'm coming.

I'll reassess in the car. I'll fare better in there anyway. Confined space, limited freedom of movement. Holsters aren't made for sitting. Drawing is awkward when you sit. They put me in the middle, one man on each side. The doors are unlocked, so I could push one out if need be. We're moving now, but where to? I guess I can just ask.

—Where are we going?

—Just sit back and relax, ma'am.

Of course. I'll relax. Who doesn't like being driven to an unknown location by the secret police? One of them is pouring himself a drink. *He's* relaxing, that's for s—Oh, he's handing it to me. I guess he was pouring *me* a drink. This is crazy. I don't know what's going on but, clearly, I'm not getting arrested.

I wonder how far we're going. I hope it's nearby, because neither of these guys is the talking type. It'll be a long— EWWWWW. Warm vodka. A whole juice glass of it. For once, I agree with Mother. I don't think I should be drinking this. Then again, I could be on my way to a firing squad. I'll have one more sip.

Music would be good. . . . Anything. . . .

Shit. I forgot about dinner. Billie probably spent the whole day cooking. She'll have to eat alone. I hope she doesn't stare at the clock while our food's getting cold. Not that it makes a difference, Billie can't cook to save her life, but I like it when she tries. I know she does it for me. She couldn't care less about everyday things. I wish I were like her, but I need a bit of normal in my life.

I think this is it. We're pulling into a driveway. It's a big house. *Big* big. Here's the limousine I saw earlier. This has to be a party official, a general maybe. This whole place screams: "Look at me! I'm important!" What the hell am I doing here?

—You can get out now, ma'am.

Hand on my back. I could turn fast and break his arm, shoot the other one and take the car. This might be my last chance. He's guiding me towards the door. I'll play along. At this point, I'm more curious than scared. I have to know who went through all this trouble just to meet me.

It could be someone saw me with Korolev and wants to know what he's working on. Maybe someone from another bureau. Glushko? It's no secret he and Korolev aren't fans of each other. Maybe it's one of the Germans. There are only a handful left, but Korolev doesn't trust them. He's had them working on rockets that will never be built. He'll cherry-pick a few things from their designs, but that's about as much as they can hope to contribute. I'm not sure any of them has enough pull with the party higher-ups, though. Maybe Gröttrup. He must know someone. He lives in a villa outside of Moscow. This could be it for all I know. Everyone else sleeps in crowded barracks. "Communal apartments," they call them. Has a nice ring to it.

—This way, please.

Again with the hand on my back. I don't like being touched, especially by MGB goons.

We're inside. This is not Gröttrup's. I've met his wife, and whoever lives here isn't married. I've only seen the lobby but I know a man decorated this place, an insecure one at that. Ostentatious doesn't even begin to cover it. Is that a fucking Fabergé egg? Seriously, who puts that in a lobby? Someone who thinks it'll look great next to medieval armor, I suppose. There is so much ugly here, it feels like a yard sale for stupidly rich people.

We're walking now. They're taking me to another room, the dining room. Not as crowded as the entrance, but more pretentious if that's even possible. This room is meant for guests. I bet whoever lives here never set foot in here alone. Goon number one is pulling out a chair for me. Goon number two is pouring me some wine. These guys really want me drinking. Nice glass, though. I can still run, but I really want to know whose house this is. The table is set for two. White porcelain with gold trim. I suppose all I have to do is wait. Ewww, that wine. I really shouldn't be drinking. . . . Anyone who serves this to guests has to be evil.

The Tracker. What if it's him? I doubt the devil lives in the suburbs, but why not? He . . . wants to see me before he kills me. He'll torture me until I give up Mother. Stop it, Mia. This is stupid. There's no— Oh, someone's coming.

. . . Beria? Lavrentiy Fucking Beria? Now I know why the MGB is here. He doesn't run the agency anymore, but he is the—what's that stupid title again?—Curator of the Organs of State Security. He's not the Tracker, that's for sure. Mother said they're stronger than us. Beria's an . . . emaciated little rat. What could he possibly want with me? Is he after Korolev? I'll know soon enough. He's sitting down.

—How do you like the wine?

He's waving the goons away. Whatever he needs to discuss, he wants it to be private.

—It's very good, sir.

Worst thing I ever drank. Warm vodka was better than this.

—Château Trotanoy. A '45. The soil in the region consists almost exclusively of black clay.

How la-di-da. Now I know who decorated the house.

—I did not know that, sir. Thank you.

—I'm terribly sorry. I forgot to introduce myself. Do you know who I am?

—Yes, sir. I do. It's an honor to meet the deputy chairman.

—Oh, please. Call me Lavrentiy. We're amongst friends here.

Friends? He's been drinking more than me if he thinks we could ever be friends. This man kills and tortures for a living.

—I couldn't possibly, sir.

They're bringing us food now. The secret police are bringing me food. Why? This house is so big, I know he has staff. Why aren't *they* serving us? What is this thing? Is this a fucking *bisque*?

—Please. Eat.

It smells fine but I'm too nervous to eat. Anyway, I'm not sharing a meal with this man. I just want to know why I'm here and get the hell out.

—I'm sorry, sir. I don't know if I'm coming down with something or if I'm just very tired but I seem to have lost my appetite.

—Are you sure? I had the chef prepare his veal blanquette for us. It is absolutely divine.

—Please send the chef my apologies.

—I will. Shall we get on to business, then?

Finally.

—Yes. Please.

He's getting up. He's thanking the MGB officers. I guess they're not coming with us. There's a large double door ahead of us. That's where he's taking me.

—After you.

It's his office. It's oddly empty. There's a large wooden desk—dark wood; it's actually pretty—but not much else. A rug, a couple of chairs. A red sofa, velvet. There's something odd about this room. It's the walls. There are no books here, no bookshelves. There's nothing on any of the walls. They're all padded. Red velvet with crystal buttons. The man loves his velvet. He even put some on the inside of the doors. Speaking of, he just closed them.

—You should get comfortable.

Comf—I'm sorry, what? Did I say that out loud? No, I didn't. I meant to, though. This is . . .

The walls. Now I know what's bugging me about the walls. The padding isn't decoration. It's soundproofing. Beria is taking his jacket off.

—I should go.

—When I say so.

Whoa. So *this* is his thing? He prowls the streets at night. He brings girls to his home, wines them and dines them, then he rapes them in his soundproof office. I thought this had something to do with Korolev, with my work. I bet this asshole doesn't even know who I am.

—Let me go now or I'll call for help.

—Oh dear. Scream, or not. It doesn't matter. You are in my power now. So think about that and behave accordingl—

Fuck.

What did I do? I didn't think. My hand just . . . flew. One right hook to the jaw and Beria crumpled to the floor like a wet towel. I'm glad I knocked that little rat's lights out but I'm in trouble now, serious trouble.

It's getting hot in here. Think, Mia. Beria's not going to stay unconscious forever. The right move is to kill this piece of shit, him and everyone in here. Survive at all costs. We can be out of Russia by morning. That's what I should do, but I won't. I don't want to kill anyone anymore, not unless I have to. I'll lose everything. Billie. My research. I'll lose myself.

Don't draw attention to yourself. That's also a rule. . . . Assassinating the highest-ranking military officer in the Soviet Union is probably not the best way to keep a low profile. Beria will be mad but he'll get over it. I mean, the man has other fish to fry. I can continue my work, see my project through to the end. I can see Billie. That's the plan. The little rat gets to live. I get to walk out the front door, hopefully.

Here we go. Open the office doors, no one's here. That corridor seemed much shorter when I came in. I'll trace my steps back. I don't want to get lost in the house and walk in on an MGB poker game. . . . Dining room is clear. . . .

One of the goons is in the lobby. Smile, Mia. Big smile. He's not doing anything. I think this might just w—He's reaching for something! There's nowhere to run but the way I came in, nothing to duck behind. Flowers? He's handing me a bouquet. Why on earth would he give me a bouquet?

Consent? Any girl who walks out of here is a threat to Beria. But if they accept a bouquet, it will be that much harder for them to claim it wasn't consensual. All right, I'll take your stupid flowers.

—Thank you for the bouquet.

More smiling. He's opening the door for me. I wonder what happens if you refuse to t—

—IT'S NOT A BOUQUET! IT'S A WREATH! MAY IT ROT ON YOUR GRAVE!

Shit. That was Beria. I need to not be here right now. The MGB asshole is closing the door. I guess he's not afraid to turn his back on an unarmed girl. Bad call. He's only five feet away but that should be enough to get some momentum. Elbow up.

Slam his face into the door. Bam! Left arm around his neck, grab his pistol with the right.

Where's Beria? Good. He ran when he saw me grab the gun. Deep breath. I'm burning hot but I'm in control. Take a couple of steps back and open the door. Let's see what's out there.

One more MGB at the bottom of the steps. One reading in the car. I'll use the guard I'm choke-holding as a shield. He's getting harder to move, he must be coming about. I'm pushing against his back as hard as I can. I can't see a thing now but we should hit the stairs right about . . .

TAK

TAK

Gunshots. Shit. My human shield just took two to the chest. He'll go limp soon and I can't shoot back while I'm holding him. This asshole must weigh close to two hundred pounds. I need to cover some distance before I drop him. Damn, he's heavy! PUSH, MIA! PUSH!

Guard number two is right beside me now, raising his gun hand. His arm is thirty degrees ahead of me, but he'll aim for my chest before he pulls the trigger. I have a smaller arc to cover if I aim for his foot.

TAK

His hand dropped. His whole body's bending in pain. The foot is a complex machine: twenty-six bones, loads of muscles and ligaments. A hundred things send pain signals at once when a piece of metal shatters them at the speed of sound. I've got the tip of my gun on his head.

TAK

So much for not killing anyone. Where is the last one? Is he still in the car? No, the car door's open. Where the hell is he? To hell with him, I'll just take the car. . . .

Crap. The keys are gone. I can't leave on foot; we're in the middle of nowhere. They'll have two hundred men combing through these woods in twenty minutes. The good news is he doesn't have a gun or he'd have used it by now. I'll put my head to the ground, see if he's hiding anywhere.

Oh yeah, I see your ugly black boots behind the limo, asshole. You better have the keys on you or I—Wait . . . I don't need his keys. The limo keys are in a bowl in the lobby. He's closer to the door but he won't see me until I run by him. RUN!

Now he sees me. The door's still open but he's . . . right behind me. Up the stairs and—

—AAAAAGH!

He's got me by the hair! I'm in midair staring at the ceiling. This is going to hurt.

The gun! I dropped it when I hit the ground. Where is it? Ugh. Asshole stepped on my hand. GET UP, MIA!

He's found the gun. He's on one knee, picking it up. Fight or flee? He'll shoot me in the back if I go for the door. The suit of armor! That ugly thing is holding a sword. I just hope that thing's real. Yes. The sword weighs about four pounds. The center of percussion should be about two feet from the hilt. If I swing hard enough, it should remove a head. The gun's in his hand now. One! Big! SWING!

Gotcha. . . .

Beria's back at the end of the corridor, staring at his headless henchman on the ground. Do I kill him now? I'll never see Billie again if we have to leave Moscow. Screw him. I'm not giving up everything I care about for this jerk. I'll just throw the sword down and give him a nice wiggly hand wave.

I've got the keys. Time to go.

41

Night Train

I shouldn't have told Mother. I should have just kept my mouth shut and went on with my life. Best I can do now is stare at the window, eat my cereal and *Butterbrot* while she tells me we have to move.

—We have to move, Mia.

Here we go.

— . . .

—We have to pack our things and get out of Russia. Tonight.

I probably can't ignore her all morning. Deep breath.

—I'm not going anywhere, Mother. Not after all the work I put in. And we need milk. This one's gone bad.

—Perhaps I need to remind you of recent events. You just killed three people, inside the house of Stalin's right-hand man. You did it right in front of him, and you let him live.

—I let him live *precisely* so we wouldn't have to move! That was the whole point.

—You are not thinking straight.

Maybe not. But I'm still not going anywhere.

—He doesn't know who I am, Mother. He's the only one who's seen my face. What's he going to do? Knock on every door in Moscow himself on the off chance I'll open the door? Besides, what would he arrest me for? I don't think Beria will want to draw attention to his extracurricular activities.

—I think you gravely underestimate the lengths to which a man will go to reclaim his pride.

—Oh, Mother. That's what he does all day, every day. He'll arrest a couple more people, torture them a little longer. If that doesn't do it, he'll find himself a revolution he can crush. Trust me, he'll be back to his old self in no time.

—I will not take that chance, Mia, not with the Tracker closing in on us. We have to move.

This again.

—Enough about the Tracker, Mother! He's . . .

—He is what? A myth? Do you truly believe our ancestors were killed by a figment of their imagination?

—No, Mother. I don't. But I won't give up everything because of him. I'm sorry. Fuck him.

—MIA! The Tracker will slaughter us if he gets the chance.

—So will any number of people. There's evil everywhere, plenty of it. World War II is barely over and they're at it again in Korea. Five years, Mother. That's how long they waited before sending more people to die for nothing. Sixty million dead wasn't enough, apparently.

—I under—

—Seriously! I just left the house of a man who ordered hundreds of thousands of people killed. Lord knows how many he sent to their grave himself. As if being a mass murderer and a sadist wasn't bad enough, it turns out he moonlights as a serial rapist. Just tell me, Mother, how bad can this fucking Tracker be?

—Mia—

—I'm not running from him, or Beria, or anyone else.

This is the first time I have something that remotely resembles a life. I'm not giving that up for this man or any other. Enough.

42

Thinking and Drinking

—What can I get you, hon?

—Do you have any tea?

—Tea? Look at the sign, dear. What does it say?

—It says . . . all patrons must be twenty-one or older.

—Not that sign, dummy. The big bright one. This is a bar, not a tearoom.

—I'm sorry, I never drink before noon.

—Well, that's sad. But seeing as you're my only customer, how about a soda? . . . Yes? Come on, my treat. You can't leave a lady alone in a bar, now can you? I'm Sue, by the way.

—You can call me Charles.

—What brings you to the city?

—How do you know I'm not from here?

—Oh, hon. That's very cute. Do you mind handing me that knife over there. I have to cut these lemons before people come in. . . . Thank you. Seriously, why are you in Washington?

—I'm looking for someone.

—You're not chasing after a girl, are you?

—Two, as a matter of fact. They lived around here not that long ago.

—Maybe I know them.

—Sarah and Mia Freed.

—Doesn't ring a bell. Sorry.

—They might have changed their names.

—Hmmm. That sounds to me like maybe they don't want to be found.

—Oh, we'll find them. My brothers and I are getting close.

—That's . . . kind of creepy. But none of my business. Let's talk about something else. How many brothers do you have?

—Three.

—And they're all here with you?

—My brother Leonard is. George—he's the eldest—is in Europe, probably drunk. Billy, the cadet, was just arrested in Chicago.

—Oh no! What did he do?

—Burglary. Someone saw him breaking in. Billy ran, but he didn't get far. Some off-duty cop dropped three flowerpots on his head from two floors above.

—Seriously? You're pulling my leg. That's the craziest thing I've heard in my life. I'm sorry about your brother, though. I'm sure he'll get out soon.

—He won't. George said we should leave him behind.

—I don't know how they do things in Chicago, but here, they won't keep you long just for a break-in. Either way, you can't just abandon your brother. Family's forever, right?

—They say he killed three people.

—Oh my God.

—They worked on him for six days straight before he signed a confession. I think someone else had confessed before him but they didn't care.

—These cops. They'll pin anything on anyone. . . . They beat it out of him, didn't they?

—They drugged him, too, but Billy wouldn't have talked if he didn't want to. I think he wants us to leave him there.

—Why would anyone want to stay in jail?

—It's not . . . this.

—What's that supposed to mean?

—How can I put this? You've seen parents screaming at their kids during a Little League game? The same parents that make their five-year-old practice four hours a day instead of playing with their friends. Our life is kind of like that. Some kids just can't handle the pressure. Besides, Billy was always—I'm not sure how to say it—different. Our mother died giving birth to him. Father raised him by himself, the way *he* wanted. It was . . . difficult for Billy.

—Wait. Did he do it?

—One of the women Billy confessed to killing was shot in the head. That's not Billy. He was always afraid of guns.

—If he didn't do it, he can recant, can't he? He can say they forced him to talk.

—There's another woman that was dismembered. They found her head in a sewer, her torso in a storm drain. They kept finding body parts for weeks.

—That's hor—

—I thought: Now there's my Billy! He carved our dog into pieces when he was seven, tried to put him back together afterwards when he saw we were angry. Billy likes to chop things up. Speaking of, you cut yourself. . . . Your finger's bleeding.

—It's nothing. . . . I think you should leave now.

—Leave? No, I can't leave you like that. Let me see. That's a pretty deep cut. Run some cold water on it before you put a bandage on.

—I'm fine. I really think you should go.

—I can smell the blood from here. . . . That's what set Billy off, every time. He was always so calm, ice-cold. Even as a kid, people picked on him, pushed him around. Billy was bigger than other kids his age but he never did anything, never fought back. If there was blood, though, a scrape, a small cut, anything red, Billy would just lose it. I saw him pound on someone twice his size until the man had no face left. Father said it was the smell of iron. I always thought it was the blood, you know, the symbolics of it, but it's a physical reaction to whatever chemical is released when your skin touches metal. We didn't believe it, so we experimented on our little brother. Sure enough, if you rubbed Billy's hand on silverware long enough or had him count a jar of pennies, he'd start throwing things around.

—Please go, sir. Leave, before I call someone.

—You know, I don't think I've ever told anyone about Billy, or my father. I don't open up a lot around people. I'm not sure why. Somehow I feel comfortable talking to you. It's like we have a connection.

43

Blue Moon

I thought I would have a ton of data from ice core samples by now. We funded a research project in Copenhagen, but it is taking longer than I thought. I see now that I am not as patient as I used to be. I want to know if the level of carbon dioxide slowly increased over millennia, or suddenly, presumably with the advent of industrialization. I thought all I needed was to measure CO_2 concentration from different time periods. Getting air from the past seemed hard enough, but Dansgaard—the man spending the money in Copenhagen—said I also need to know the temperature at the time. It makes sense. If I am to explore the correlation between climate and carbon dioxide levels, I would need to know both.

Thanks to Mia, I know how to find old air, but it does not come with a weather report. Yet I believe the answer might still be found in that ice cube tray. I was so focused on the air bubbles—if I got old ice, I would have old air—I forgot I would also have ice. Perhaps the frozen water has something to say about the temperature.

There are only so many things one can look at. Water is just hydrogen and oxygen, but both of these come in different flavors. Hydrogen has a heavier cousin called deuterium. The same is true of oxygen. There is hefty O out in the world with two extra neutrons. It takes more energy, more heat, to evaporate water that contains heavy isotopes. It should therefore rain more of it in warm weather, less when it is cold. If that is true, counting the heavy oxygen in the ice core samples would allow us to calculate temperatures in the past. More would mean warmer, fewer would mean cooler. Dansgaard is following that theory. Unfortunately, it will take months, maybe years, before we find out if it works. I require something new to keep my mind occupied.

Truth be told, all I can think about is Beria. That monster tried to rape my daughter. Mia wants me to let it go, but I cannot. She should have killed him when she had the chance. We should have moved. I understand why she did not want to. She is in love. She and Korolev are making real progress for the first time. What I fail to understand is why I did not force her to leave.

Of all the people who saw her face that night, Beria is the only one still breathing. He does not know her name—he never thought to ask. There is no reason for Beria to visit Korolev, at least for now. That was, more or less, the extent of my daughter's argument. It is flawed in so many ways. Beria prowls the same streets she walks on every day. It is only a matter of time before he runs into my daughter again. And yet we stayed. We broke the rules.

I could not bring myself to rob my daughter of what she loves. I put her happiness ahead of our survival and I should be ashamed but all I feel now is anger. I watch the sun set and I think of Beria telling his chauffeur he wants to go for a ride. I dream of the girls he lured to his home and I wake up screaming. Mia let her girlfriend live because she needed her faith in humanity restored. Now it is my turn to search for solace. I do not believe in a moral universe, but even *I* need to feel some semblance of justice. I need to restore some cosmic order.

44

Hound Dog

—No, Nina. Tikhonravov's packet design is better.

Korolev is stubborn as a mule. I should be flattered; it was my design. Two rockets with giant tanks strapped around a third, all of them sharing fuel. Drop the side rockets when they're empty. Like the milk churns on that bicycle I rode downhill in the Bavarian Alps.

—Sergei! You're not listening.

It was a good design, but I had the government commission a study to figure out exactly how much we could extend the range by dropping parts of the rocket during flight. One of the researchers there really ran with it and came up with a smarter version of what I had. I like it. It's robust, elegant.

—You are right. I am not listening.

—It's still the same! Only simpler. Remember how much trouble we're having with the R-3? Simpler is better, Sergei. Pumping fuel between rockets will be a mess, you know that. This way, we'll have four boosters, each with its own fuel. We jettison them when we're done. It's the same thing! Except it's lighter, easier to build, and it won't break every twenty minutes.

—You said "we" again.

—I guess I did.

—If the rockets are carrying their own fuel, why not put the second stage on top of the first, like the Americans are doing?

Oh, that thing. The US stuck a smaller rocket on top of a

German V-2. It failed a bunch of times, but it went pretty high when it worked.

—You mean Bumper?

—No! The ferry rocket!

Ha! So that's what it is. This is funny. There was a symposium on space travel in New York City, and *Collier's* magazine covered it. "Man Will Conquer Space Soon." Twenty-eight color pages full of the craziest ideas. Von Braun must have turned on the charm, because most of them are his. There's a circular space station, and this *insane* three-stage rocket straight out of a pulp magazine. It was meant to make the average Joe excited about space, but I see it turned into a dick-measuring contest for a certain Soviet chief designer.

—That was a magazine, Sergei. It's not real. If we put our boosters *around* the main engine instead, we can ignite them at the same time, on the ground. You know, where there's *air?* That way we won't have to worry about lighting a fire way up there in near vacuum.

—I still think—

—Four bullet-shaped boosters, Sergei. Four! It'll be so badass. Like some souped-up space hot rod with *four. hundred. tons.* of thrust.

— . . .

Aaaaaand I win. That's the upside of working with a five-year-old. I'll admit, I kind of feel like a kid myself. This whole project, it's . . . It fits. All of it fits together perfectly.

—We're going to need a bunch of tiny rockets for steering that hot rod. Did you ask Glushko?

—His answer was a resounding no. "It would be *impossible* to control a rocket by such thrusters."

—*Someone else* will make the tiny rockets, then. Your Glushko impression was spot-on, by the way.

—Thank you, Nina. You only have to make the most mundane thing sound like a presidential address. Try it.

—It would be *impossible*—Hahaha. I can't.

—We make a good team. Don't we?

—I think so.

I know so. I'm good at math, physics. He's good at the real world. People. Getting things done, knowing what everyone can and can't do. He's a dreamer, *and* a realist. It's a rare thing to have both. I can draw a combustion chamber—I see it in my head, clear as day—but I don't see the men bending sheet metal to get the nozzle just right. He does. He sees them tired on a Friday, with a sick kid or marriage problems. These rockets, what we're building, they're part science, lots of math, but they're also giant, clunky metal machines. They're made of steel, sweat and tears, late hours at the shop because you don't want to face whatever's waiting for you at home. Korolev gets that and I admire him for it.

—I know how much that rocket means to you, Nina, but it will not come cheap. I truly hope we can get the project approved.

—Now you're the one who said "we." Just tell them it will drop a five-ton thermonuclear warhead in the middle of Chicago. They'll be all smiles.

—Like you are now?

I *am* smiling. That rocket will put a man in space. I know it. Why is he staring again?

—Stop looking at me that way!

—You are going to break that chain if you keep twisting it.

My necklace. I didn't even notice I was playing with it. His fault. I get nervous when people stare. He knows, too. That's why he does it.

—Then stop looking at me like I have something in my teeth.

—Maybe you do. Did your mother give you that necklace? It looks old.

—It's been in the family for a while.

—Is it worth anything?

—I don't think so. I thought it was a garnet.

—I can have someone look at it if you want. Oh, before I forget, I am having drinks with Mishin and his wife tonight. Would you like to join us?

—Thank you but I can't. Not tonight.

I wish I could, but I told Billie we'd meet after work. I want to see her, but I love these get-togethers. Turning colleagues into friends. I see these people's math every day, their brains put to paper, but I know almost nothing about them. I suppose what I like most is that it makes me feel like a normal person for a few hours.

45

All Night Long

I'm waiting for it. I don't know what it is, but she'll ask me something in the next minute or so. Billie asks for things right after we have sex, and now she has that look.

—It's the third time you've spent the night this week. Anything you want to tell me?

It must be something big if she's tiptoeing around it.

—Not really. Mother works late every night these days. I hate being alone in that house.

—So that's why you're here. I feel so special.

—You should! You're amazing, and special, and smart. And special, did I mention special?

—You could spend the night at your man's.

Shit. So this is what we're doing. Why now? She's known about Korolev for a while, but she never made it an issue. I know *she* sees other people. What does she want?

—Billie, we talked about this.

—I know! I know! I'm not being jealous. I'm just . . . How long has it been since he proposed?

—Billie! No! I don't want to fight!

—We're not fighting! How long?

We're not fighting. That's good to know. It still sounds like a trap, though. It sure as hell *feels* like a trap.

—I don't know. A little over a year. Why?

One smile and I walked right into it. I deserve whatever comes next.

—I think you should say yes.

I didn't see that one coming. It'll take more than an orgasm to make me agree to *that*. What the hell is wrong with her? Did I say that out loud? No, I didn't.

—Billie! What the hell is wrong with you?

—You should! I know you like him.

—I like him, but I don't *like him* like him. I want to be with you!

—But you also want to be with him. It's okay. I get it.

What is there to get? Yes, I like him. He's brilliant. He's moderately romantic and most of the time he makes me feel like a regular human being. I like that, but I'm not going to lose *Billie* for it.

—No you don't. I said I want to be with you. I choose you! I. CHOOSE. YOU!

—Shhh. You'll wake up the neighbors. It's not a choice, Mia. You're not going to marry me. You can't. We have to hide to see each other. You can marry *him*.

—But I want to see *you*.

—Then see me! Why is this so hard to understand? I must not be saying it right. I don't *own* you, Mia. I don't want to. You say you want to see me, so see me. No one's stopping you. But I know you also want some sort of normal life, at least a part of you does. Holding hands in public. Dinner with the neighbors, that sort of thing. You'll never get that with me, not here. Get it with him.

I love that woman with every fiber in my being. I look at people, couples, and all I see is selfishness. People stick together for how it makes them feel. Keeping the other happy is just a way to make it last. Not her. She sees me.

—It doesn't bother you?

—Why would it bother me? Those are different things. A steak is great if you're hungry but it doesn't do you much good if you're cold. You need a jacket. Get yourself a jacket.

—Billie, I don't—Wait. Are you a steak in this story?

—All right, bad example. My point is I'm not jealous of your doctor, or the person who fixes your car. I want you to be healthy and have a working car. I want you to get married because I want you to be happy.

—What about you?

—I can be the sultry mistress. I know things have been . . . difficult at times but I can still be sultry, can't I? Please say yes, even if it's a lie.

—Like a movie star.

—Thank you.

—You do know that I love you, don't you?

—You keep coming back, so I kind of figured as much.

—Good . . .

Billie?

—What?

—We never talked about that night.

—What night?

—You know what night, Billie. You know what I did.

—You came for me. You risked your life for me, Nina. No one's ever done that. I was falling and you caught me. Everything else . . . it doesn't matter.

46

Songs and Dances of Death: Lullaby

I wanted to cut his throat, but this had to look like an accident, death by bad luck or natural causes. I had to know his routine: what he ate, where he ate, whom he ate with. I followed him. I set up camp in the thicket behind his house. On the first night, Beria brought home another girl—she could not have been more than eighteen. I saw her walk out of the house with her bouquet of flowers, full of hate and shame.

I followed her. It felt wrong, but I followed her. It took two days before I found the nerve to approach her in a café. Her name is Natalia. She is a student, though she misses school a lot to help her ailing mother. She had never met Beria before that night. She did not know he was the one who had her father arrested and sent to the gulag. When he took her to his office, he promised her he would set her father free. The next day, she asked the secret police when her father would be released. They told her he had died weeks before. Beria must have known. He had her arrested a week later. I do not know if she is alive or not. If she is, she will die alone in a cell somewhere.

Last week, Beria brought home another one. There was nothing special about her, nothing to set her apart from all the others. Except this one never left. I waited all night for her to come out, then I waited all day. Then I waited all night again. Finally, two MGB officers came out the back door carrying a large bag. They got a pair of shovels out of the shed and started digging in the yard. He killed her.

I killed her, too. I was a coward, looking for excuses. I was afraid and I let more people suffer. More people who will live with the guilt. More people who will convince themselves they did something to deserve this. I should have killed Beria the moment Mia came home that night. I should have reached inside his chest, plucked his heart out, and had him watch as it came to a stop.

Beria will die. He will feel his insides break apart and know it is the end.

I know how. The government just approved a new blood thinner called warfarin. Warfarin is also very good at killing rats, which seems fitting. In large enough doses, it will cause severe internal bleeding, including a hemorrhagic stroke. If the circumstances of his death are not suspect, a less than zealous doctor should conclude that a stroke did Beria in. The question then becomes: How do I get someone to ingest large amounts of warfarin?

I cannot force-feed it to him, he has to consume it willingly. Wine would be perfect—it is dark and strong enough to mask the taste of just about anything—but Beria opens a bottle for each of his victims. I do not want to be responsible for another woman's death. Fortunately, for me at least, Beria keeps the good wine for himself. What he serves his guests as pricy Bordeaux is actually plonk from Ukraine. When he is alone and not destroying lives, he has a penchant for Saperavi wines from Georgia.

That is it. I will lace a case of his favorite with warfarin and send it to him as a gift. With any luck, he will be dead within the week.

47

Jock-A-Mo

1953

I have to tell Mia. There is no way to know if I am responsible or not but I cannot hide this from my daughter. I just need to find the words.

—What are you working on, Mia?

—The perfect rocket.

—*Perfect* is a strong word.

—Oh, it has plenty of flaws. I just think they're the right ones.

—How so?

—It'll have a range of nine thousand kilometers. As it is, it will carry a payload of over six thousand pounds, but I think I can get it to ten. That means we can put a manned capsule on top of it and send people into space.

—Or a very large nuclear warhead.

—That's how we get the development approved. It's also going to be over a hundred feet long and weigh close to three hundred metric tons. The launchpad for it will need to be gigantic, *insanely* expensive. The engine runs on kerosene and supercooled liquid oxygen. It'll take a long time to set up, and they won't be able to keep it on standby for long before the fuel starts eating at the seals.

—Those are serious limitations, Mia.

—YES! What I'm designing isn't a viable weapons system at all. It can't be used as a deterrent because it won't stay on alert for more than a day. The launchpads will cost so much, they'll never build more than a handful of them. This thing . . . well, it will be completely obsolete as a missile by the time we build it. Its only future is as a space vehicle. It's sturdy, powerful. You could base a whole space program on it.

—What do you call it?

—Semyorka.

—Seven. How poetic. I am proud of you, Mia, always. I am grateful for all that you are doing.

—You can thank Stalin for dying. Khrushchev is a smart man. He and Korolev get along for now. That's the only reason we were able to drop the R-3 for good.

Now is probably a good a time to tell her. . . . Somehow it feels as if our roles were reversed. I am the child about to confess I broke a vase.

—Wonderful. Speaking of Stalin's demise, I—

—You what?

— . . . Are you aware that Lavrentiy Beria died yesterday?

—Yeah. The little rat went to his knees and begged for mercy. I heard they had to stuff a rag into his mouth to stop the wailing before they shot him.

—Indeed. You should know that I tried to kill him last year.

—Mother, no! We talked about this. If I wanted him gone, I would have killed him myself.

—I know, but—

—There's no but. You said it yourself. We kill to survive, like every other living thing. We don't hunt people.

—I did not hunt . . . I gave him a dozen bottles of Georgian wine laced with rat poison. Warfarin.

—Mother!

—It did not work.

—That's not the point!

—I know, the point is . . .

—You mean there's more?

—Perhaps. . . . I did not give it a thought when they announced Stalin's death in March. The papers said he watched a movie at the Kremlin on that Saturday with Khrushchev, Malenkov, Bulganin, and Beria. They all went to the dacha afterwards and drank all night. Stalin had a stroke. They found him in a coma the next morning. Four days later, he was dead. End of story.

—So?

—So I never saw the autopsy report but I heard they also found intestinal bleeding, which is not all that common with a stroke.

—I don't like where this is going.

—It could be nothing.

—Or . . .

—A hefty dose of warfarin *would* account for both the stroke and the intestinal bleeding. Many things would, really, but perhaps Beria brought a bottle as a gift that night and Stalin had a nightcap before going to bed. I heard Georgian wines were a favorite of his.

—You fucking killed Stalin?!

—Language, Mia. And no. I mean . . . there is a very remote possibility that I did, but perhaps Beria found out the wine I sent him was poisoned and he gave it to Stalin on purpose. They say that after Stalin died, he bragged to members of the Politburo that he had done it and saved them all.

—A remote possibility?

—Very remote.

—You fucking killed Stalin!

—I did not.

—You keep telling yourself that. I've got to go, Mother. Korolev and I are having dinner with friends.

Mia is not nearly as mad as I thought she would be. I do not know why this surprises me. It was always I who thought the rules could not be bent. Mia chose her own path. She wanted a normal life, and I wanted it for her. We broke every rule to get her there. She will not condemn me for breaking one more. My daughter is happy. She has a husband, a lover. She is passionate about her work, and we are making great progress towards our goal.

I did not think this was something we could have. Perhaps I, too, could have the life I want, see my granddaughter born and watch her become us one day at a time. I could tend a garden, do the small things other people do while they watch the years go by. I would love to grow old. None of us ever have.

48

Earth Angel

1954

Shit. I'm late for lunch. Billie's going to give me a mouthful. Where the hell is it?!

—Sergei! Did you see my necklace?

Where did I go? Nowhere. I was here all day yesterday. I took it off the night before. I remember that.

—SERGEI!

—WHAT? WHAT?

—My necklace! Have you seen it?

—Green jacket. I am coming.

—Your dress uniform? Wh—Oh there you are. What's my necklace doing in—

—I took it to an expert like we had talked about. Get dressed!

—I *am* dressed. I have to go. Why are you out of breath?

He's sweating like he just ran a marathon.

—I ran downstairs. I—

—You ran—

—I meant you should put on a dress. I will open some champagne.

—It's eleven, Sergei.

I think my husband is broken.

—That is perfect, because at ten forty-five, the USSR Council of Ministers officially approved our draft for the R-7 intercontinental ballistic missile.

—They said yes?

—You have your rocket, Nina. You did it. Whoa! No! You are too heavy!

I don't want to let go and let him see me crying. I worked— We worked so hard on this. It's . . .

—It's your project, Sergei. *You* did it.

—Nina, I do not know exactly why you agreed to marry me but I—

—I—

—Let me talk. But I hope . . . I like to believe it was in part because you think of me as a fairly intelligent human being. I see you working, Nina, always. You jot down equations on napkins when I am not looking. My office is full of them. I pick them up from the trash can when you leave. When the car windows get foggy, I see the math you last did with your finger and I cannot understand the half of it.

—Sergei, that's—

—I am not an idiot, Nina. I read all those papers. Unlike you, I actually *know* Mikhail Tikhonravov, personally. He is a smart man but he could not write a coherent sentence to save his life. He also cannot do what you do. No one can. I do not ask because I assume you would say something if you wanted to. That and you make me look incredibly smart. The rest of us helped when we could but this is your rocket, even if you and I are the only ones who know it. You did an amazing thing, Mrs. Korolev. I think you should celebrate, and I would be honored if you let me celebrate with you.

I absolutely adore this man, but this is so not helping with the crying. I suppose if I'm going to sob like a child, I might as well do it over champagne. I'm a couple of days late, but one glass can't hurt, can it?

—I'll get the glasses. You said you had someone look at my necklace?

—I did.

I hate it when he does that.

— . . . And?!

—He could not tell me anything about the metal, but the gem in the middle comes from a meteorite. Fitting, don't you think? You dream of sending things into outer space and you are wearing a piece of it.

—He said it was a piece of meteorite?

—Well, not exactly. He said that mineral was not from Earth. It had to come from somewhere, right?

Shit.

49

Mr. Sandman

I better hold on to something. I can't feel my fingers it's so cold
up here. I don't know why I agreed to this. Well, I know why.
Korol—My husband asked me to and I said yes. I must be losing my mind, like the last manager did. They wouldn't tell the
excavation crew what they were building. They told them it was
a "stadium." Typical Russian nonsense, we're in Nowhere, Kazakhstan. Their surveys said there was nothing but sand here,
but they hit some heavy clay right from the start and they fell
behind. The generals in Moscow were quick to blame the manager, a kid from the Academy of Military Engineering. He went
crazy, literally. He's in a mental institution now. Maybe that's
where I should be. Instead I'm . . . fighting the wind a hundred
and fifty feet above ground, watching tiny people below pour
concrete into a giant hole.

We have to work through winter now if we're going to make it
in time. The pad itself is a forty-meter-square block of concrete,
about the width of a football field, so they'll be pouring for a
while. Still, that's where my rocket will launch from. I'm here
to inspect the gigantic steel platform hanging above it. Me. My
husband is scared of heights. I told him it was ironic, building
rockets, scared of heights. He doesn't get it. Russian humor is its
own thing.

I wanted to use the alone time to think. Hard to do in thirty-
mile-an-hour winds. I haven't told anyone yet but I'm beginning

to show. I'm not sure I'm ready. I could wait. There are places that take care of this sort of thing. There's so much to do still. I don't know if I can do all of it and raise a—WHOA! Big gust of wind!

If the R-7 flies like it's supposed to *twice*, we can go ahead with my satellite project. I'm sure there'll be some setbacks, but we'll get it done in a year or two. I can't wait to—Shit. That truck will hit the power line if it keeps backing up. I need someone with a radio.

—You! Hand me that walkie-talkie, will you?

— . . .

Nothing. I guess he didn't hear.

—Hey! Can you hand me your radio?

He's not in uniform. I wonder—I've never seen him before but there's something—

—Hello, Nina!

—Fuuuuuu—

UGH! Straight kick to the stomach. I can't breathe. I'm in midair, falling backwards. I'm staring at the sky, but I know there's no platform beneath me. A hundred-and-fifty-foot drop. I'll hit the ground at seventy miles an hour. Inelastic collision with a concrete slab. At that speed, even I won't survive.

 . . .

 . . .

Sharp pain. I should have hit concrete by now. I haven't. I stopped. I . . . There's a . . .

There's a piece of rebar sticking out of me. I don't— There's a fucking steel rod coming out of my stomach. I impaled myself midway down on the platform frame.

I have to stay conscious. I'm dangling in midair eighty feet above ground. I need to get down.

Both hands around the steel rod, I can pull . . . myself . . . up.

—AAAAHHHHH!

I can't. It's no use. They'll need to take me down but I'll be long dead by then.

That's not how I imagined it would end. It doesn't matter, I suppose. I wonder what kind of mother I'd have been.

It's getting dark. It won't be long now.

50

The Great Pretender

My dear Sarah,

I am writing to tell you that I am returning to China.

I have spent the last five years under house arrest, scheduled for a deportation that would never come. They would not let me stay because of what I am, and they would not let me leave because of what I know. I was denied access to sensitive information but permitted to teach. My colleagues tried to convince me that it would all work out and, for a while, I even believed them.

I wanted to stay. I wanted to build a life in America but they found a document from the American Communist Party with my name on it. They accused me of lying about who I was and what I believed in. It took me two years to realize they were right. I had been lying all along, though it was me and not the government I had been deceiving.

I convinced myself I could belong, that I could be as American as anyone else. All it took was hard work, the belief in life, liberty, and the pursuit of happiness. I realized how wrong I was when the prosecutors asked me where my allegiance lies. What they really wanted to know is whether I would build weapons to kill my people.

We cannot change who we are. I am Chinese. I wanted to be American. I believed I could be both, but they showed me time and time again that there is no such thing in these United States. I chose not to listen and I lied to myself. I *pretended I could be something I'm not and everyone I loved paid the price.*

I do not know what the future holds for me back home. I may be imprisoned or executed, but if I am, at least I will die knowing who I am.

Sincerely,
Your friend,
Qian Xuesen

ENTR'ACTE

Rule #1: Preserve the Knowledge

825 BC

King Shalmaneser III of Assyria invaded Anatolia to expand his empire. One by one, the states fell, but the small kingdom of Quwê refused to surrender. Perhaps it was the sense of pride she found in Quwê that attracted Ishtar, the tenth woman to call herself the Kibsu.

Ishtar's mother had been killed on their way to their new home. The Tracker had ambushed them, and her mother stayed behind to ensure Ishtar and her daughter Nourah got away. The Tracker tortured Ishtar's mother for days hoping to lure Ishtar back into reach. Ishtar covered her daughter's ears until the screams faded into silence.

Ishtar had learned everything there was to know about horses from her mother. Horses had taken her from Scythia to Anatolia. Breeding those same horses would put a roof over her head and feed her family. When Nourah was five, King Jehu of Israel sent emissaries to Quwê to procure some horses for himself and his family. The king's envoy spent days examining every mount in the capital. When it was all over, he settled on five stallions and two mares from Ishtar's stable. The king paid a premium price for his horses, and that one trade would change their lives forever.

That evening, Ishtar prepared a sumptuous meal: fish with her garlic sauce, *maza*, asparagus. She even bought some figs, Nourah's favorite. Mother and daughter ate together, and for a brief moment, Nourah felt like a princess.

The next morning, Nourah was awoken by a voice she did not know. There was a man standing next to her bed. Nourah flinched, thinking this might be the one who killed her grandmother, the one they called Rādi Kibsi. The man smiled and told her she had nothing to fear from him, that they had met the day before when he examined their horses.

Nourah asked where her mother was. The king's envoy said she was gone and would not come back. He explained that all the money from the horses had been returned to him. In exchange he promised to take care of Nourah as his own. Nourah ran outside and screamed her mother's name. She screamed and screamed until she couldn't. Lost and hopeless, she packed her small belongings and sat in one of the chariots next to a father she did not know. She did not look back as the caravan left Quwê, never to return.

A few miles north, Ishtar cried herself into oblivion. She woke alone at sunset and prepared a fire. Ishtar looked to the stars and begged the dead for forgiveness.

—I have betrayed you, Mother. I have broken my promise. I have abandoned our ways and forsaken my blood. I do not expect absolution, for I would not offer it in your place. What I did, I did for my child. What comes of my soul is irrelevant. My daughter knows nothing of our past. I have not told her where we came from and why. She will never hear our stories, for that knowledge is a death sentence and my child is innocent. I have seen our blood spilled, our homes burned. I have heard our screams. Our ways have brought us pain and death and I refuse to watch my daughter suffer for a promise she did not make. I will not force her into a life of fear and violence. I will not deprive my daughter of the peace she deserves and guilt her into doing the same to her child. The cycle ends now. I have betrayed nine generations of us to save the next hundred. I give my life for my daughter's, as you have done for me. We are the Kibsu. We are the Ten, and we shall be the last.

When the fire went out, Ishtar had taken with her all the knowledge she possessed.

Nourah spent only a few years with her adoptive father. The king's envoy died of consumption when she was ten. He had made her feel at home as best he could, but Nourah never stopped longing for her past. Every night, she rocked herself to sleep reciting the rules her grandmother had taught her. Nourah buried the man she had spent half her life with and rode her horse back to where they first met.

She bred horses in Quwê, as her mother had done before her. She met a man, had a child of her own. Nourah looked at the infant and knew that she was more than a mother. She was the eleventh. The eleventh of what, she did not know for certain, but she was part of something larger than herself. She was one and many, and neither she nor her daughter would ever be alone. Nourah spent her nights studying the sky. She lived a quiet life, careful not to draw attention to herself. When her daughter was of age, Nourah gave her all that she had to give: the necklace her mother had left her, and a handful of rules that had guided her home when she was lost and alone.

ACT VI

51

Death of an Angel

1956

She's gone. I still feel it. It's hard to describe. It's not . . . It's not anything. Just nothing where there once was something. I never heard her, but she was there. Her little heart thumping in the background, always, like the refrigerator motor. One of a thousand sounds you don't notice until they're gone. It's quiet now. Deafening silence.

I thought I was dying. I was. I was bleeding out. I can't say that I wanted to die, but I had . . . accepted it. Everything went dark, and I waited. For something, anything. I never believed in the afterlife, that my soul would somehow outlive my body, but part of me expected something more. Maybe my life flashing before my eyes would have been enough. I don't know, but I really wanted it. It wasn't for me. I wanted there to be more for her. My child never lived. I wanted death to be . . . worthwhile, somehow. I remember being angry about it. I welcomed death and it disappointed me.

They sent two men down with ropes to get me. They patched me up as best they could, then drove me to the nearest city with a decent hospital. It was three hours away, enough time for Korolev to learn about what happened and call Mother. He said I'd lost a lot of blood and he needed to know my blood type. Korolev saved me. In the shape I was in, a transfusion would have killed me. Mother told him I had a rare hereditary condition and she was the only one I could get blood from. He told the hospital to wait and had her flown in. I can still see Mother's face when

I woke up in that hospital bed. I asked if Billie knew and she didn't answer. That's when it hit me. They had my blood. The room was covered in it. Mother had already set it up. A body from the morgue. A fire. Don't leave a trace. I died that night, in fucking Kazakhstan. We were on a plane by morning.

Now . . . Now I just hurt. My insides are still throbbing. I feel pain when I sit or stand. Regular pain, I can handle. I've felt it before. A knife wound, a broken toe. That pain is familiar. The other pain is the one I can't stand. I keep touching myself. I feel my stomach without thinking and I remember that she's gone.

I lost a husband. Korolev went to my funeral, said his good-byes to a closed casket. He buried me. I lost my work. We were so close, I could almost touch it. There are so many things we could have done with Stalin out of the way. Moscow hadn't changed, really, but the air was filled with such promise. Hope is a powerful thing, and it's beautiful to watch. I won't see it. I lost that, too.

I lost Billie. I'll never see her face again, never watch her staring at me with that . . . undecided look. She said she didn't know what to make of me, but it ran both ways. I think that's what I miss the most, the uncertainty, the eternal discovery. I miss those brief moments of understanding, glimpses of the unknown. I miss *me* with her, our noses getting in the way, the way our bodies interlocked, the contrast of our skin. Do we truly care for people, for their empirical selves, or do we care for how we experience them? Is this a universal question or is this also about me? Whatever it is, I want more. I want to run my finger down her spine again. I want to bury my face in her hair and hide in that warm darkness for a long minute. It felt like the safest place on Earth. . . . I want to know how she got that scar. She wouldn't say.

I don't know why but I keep thinking she'd like California. It's warm, for starters. Billie never liked the cold. I don't think she'd ever seen the ocean. To me, LA feels . . . unreal. Everything is bright and colorful. I feel . . . so gray.

I hurt of anger. I should be sad—I am—but mostly I'm angry. I'm mad at myself, mad at the whole world. There's so much anger it feels like I'm drowning, and I can't stop it. I can't make it end. I'm here. It happened. I can't change any of it even if I can't bear another minute of my own existence. I'm helpless, impotent.

I'm not the only one hurting. Mother won't say but I know she took it hard. She feels responsible. She shouldn't. She warned me that evil was coming. I chose not to listen. This is all on me.

Back in Moscow, there were these crooked houses across from Billie's. They were old—both were built at the turn of the eighteenth century. Whoever owned them clearly didn't have the money or the will to fix them, and they were slowly falling apart. Their foundations were sinking, and both houses would have collapsed, should have, really, if not for the fact that they were leaning on each other in just the right way. Billie said they had been like that for decades. That is what we are, Mother and I, two broken things in a complete state of disrepair, leaning on one another. We keep each other alive. For now that will have to be enough.

52

Little Bitty Pretty One

Life magazine, October 21, 1957

RUSSIA'S SATELLITE, A DAZZLING
NEW SIGHT IN THE HEAVENS
THE FEAT THAT SHOOK THE EARTH

A glittering metallic pinpoint of light streaking across the predawn sky last week gave the U.S. its first look at Soviet Russia's great feat, the artificial moon Sputnik. After the satellite's first hundred or so orbital trips around Earth. Americans were settling into uneasy familiarity with the unarguable fact that Russia's moon was passing over them four to six times a day. In fact, there were three satellites girding Earth—Sputnik, a section of the launching rocket, and its nose cone. The famous "beep beep" from Sputnik's radio turned into a steadier squeal for varying periods. Scientists and lay spotters went sleepless to track the little satellite's travels with all the equipment they had or could throw together.

All the tracking fervor and growing familiarity with Sputnik did nothing to soothe Americans' shock at the original announcement of the Soviet breakthrough into space. It was becoming all too apparent Russian scientists are as good as any in the world—or better. . . .

. . . Russia promised shortly to launch a second satellite twice as big as Sputnik. Even without this, Americans knew that for a long time they would have ample reminder of Soviet scientific excellence whirling through their previously inviolate sky.

—I can see it, Mia! How did you do this?

—How did I do what?

—Make it visible?

—I didn't do anything, Mother. The sun has to be really low for us to see it, but it's just . . . there.

—This is fascinating.

—It's just a ball, Mother.

—What does it do?

—Beep-beep.

—I do not under—

—That's what it does. It sends radio signals. We can listen to it at home if you want.

—What else does it do?

—Nothing else. It's a silver ball that goes beep-beep.

WHY DID U.S. LOSE THE RACE? CRITICS SPEAK UP

SEN. GEORGE SMATHERS (D.): "Government ineptness, smugness have produced false sense of security. The President says we aren't competing with Russia on satellites. But we cannot afford to be second best; the stakes are our survival."

HARRY STINE, a rocketeer fired from Martin Co. for speaking out: "Russia listens to men with vision. But we lost five years because no one would heed rocket men. We're a smug, arrogant people who just sat dumb, fat and happy, underestimating Russia."

—Who knows, Mia? Perhaps that silver ball will spin its way into the collective consciousness and get people thinking about space. Regardless, there is a machine orbiting Earth and my daughter put it there. You should be proud of yourself.

—I suppose I am.

—You have lost a lot, Mia, but that does not take away from what you have accomplished. That rocket of yours will put a man in space.

—You really think so?

—I know it.

—I *really* wanted to see it launch.

—Close your eyes and see it now. Watch your rocket soar. Hear it growl as it plays its tug-of-war with Earth. I am there with you, all of us are. A hundred generations are watching. This is as high as we have ever gone, as close to the stars as we have ever been.

WE ARE SERIOUS, BUT WITH SMILES

U.S. reaction to Sputnik, which is Russian for "fellow traveler," took many forms. To calm customers' nerves bartenders concocted Sputnik cocktails with vodka as the base. . . .

Underneath the levity the U.S. was plainly worried. President Eisenhower said, in reassurance, that the U.S. satellite would be better scientifically than Sputnik. But Sputnik proved that there were great military, as well as scientific, advances in the U.S.S.R. Getting their heavy satellite up meant that Russia had developed a more powerful rocket than any the U.S. has yet fired and substantiated Soviet claims of success with an intercontinental missile.

53

Great Balls of Fire

—I've never seen anything like it. I've seen plenty of launch failures, but this was epic. The rocket eked its way a few inches from the ground, and then it gave up and went down in a blaze of national humiliation.

Rockets are the last thing I want to think about, but this was national television. The American response to Sputnik. I had to watch.

—That was your doing, Mia.

—What are you talking about? I didn't blow up their rocket. They did that all by themselves.

—But you did. The Americans were so stunned by your satellite, they rushed to launch anything of their own. They chose a rocket that was not ready. This was supposed to be a test, but they were stupid enough to add a small satellite to the payload. The press was all over it.

—I'm sure it had something to do with Korolev doubling down and sending a dog up there.

—Perhaps. That seemed cruel, if I may say so.

He barely waited a month before launching another satellite. That one did more than beep-beep. It had actual instruments. And a dog.

—Let's not talk about dogs, Mother.

—We could not take Tsygan with us, Mia. We have discussed this a thousand times.

I don't know why I'm still mad, but I am. That was two years ago, but I still imagine her waiting by the door. Poor thing.

—I said let's not talk about it.

—The point I was trying to make is that this . . . catastrophe works to our advantage. The *New York Times* is calling it a "blow to US prestige."

—Ha! That wasn't a blow, Mother, that was twenty thousand pounds of American pride going up in flames.

—"Spectators on nearby beaches gasped in awe and dismay as the orange blaze seethed up against a clear blue sky. Within seconds of the outburst, the flame changed to brown-black smoke. This spread into a crudely shaped mass that rapidly dissipated in the morning breeze." There is a certain elegance to the prose.

—I've read it. I almost feel bad for the guy in charge. He said something about it being a success.

—He did. "'It was a real successful operation in terms of keeping things running smoothly. Toward the close and a little later, this rocket was flying. It wasn't a long flight—but it was flying.'"

—Ouch.

—This is my personal favorite: "There was some doubt that the disaster ought to be technically described as an explosion. He substituted 'rapid burning.'"

—It *was* rapid. That was the biggest ball of fire I've ever seen in my life! The press has some interesting names for it. Flopnik, Kaputnik, Oopsnik.

—Your rocket has given us the race we wanted.

I think Mother is exaggerating, but I'm glad if this means rocket science becomes more than a military contest.

—Do you think they'll give von Braun his chance now that the Vanguard failed?

—They already have. The Vanguard launchpad was severely damaged and it is the only one they have. They are going to use his Jupiter-C rocket to send their satellite up. Von Braun promised the army he could launch in sixty days. They gave him ninety.

—Ninety days! That's nuts!

—He could use some assistance.

—From me? I don't—

—It is time, Mia.

—I'm sorry, Mother. I can't.

I wish I could. I just . . . Mother wants me to move on. She wants me to have another child. I don't know that I can do either. My insides were ripped to shreds when I fell off that platform. Mother said we've always been fast healers. Maybe. We did survive a lot worse, if we are to believe our journals. Lost limbs, punctured hearts. The Thirty-Three had her right leg replaced with a metal one, as I recall. She rode a horse with it.

Even if I could get pregnant, I don't know that I want to. My daughter's dead. I won't . . . *replace* her. Besides, I can't lose Mother now, trade her life for another. I can't be responsible for her life, or my child's, or the lives of a hundred fucking more of us. I don't know if this is mourning, but whatever it is, I'm not done yet.

54

Milord

—They're building rockets, Leonard.

—Who is?

—Oh, Brother. You do realize it was a launch platform you kicked the daughter off, don't you?

—I didn't think she'd fall off the damn thing! I just meant to knock her out.

—We have had this discussion many times, Leonard. I am not having it again. I was merely pointing out it was a launch platform you FUCKING KICKED HER OFF!

—I know what it was!

—Good. Hence, they're building rockets.

—The daughter was working there. That doesn't mean they—

—Oh, but it does. It most certainly does.

—The girl is dead, Charles. Her mother could be a chef for all we know.

—Think, Leonard. They lived in Germany before the war. Name one thing that the Germans were good at?

—Beer? Automobiles?

—I found out the daughter was in Bleicherode in '45. Do you know who else was in Bleicherode in '45? Rocket scientists, hundreds of them. Care to guess where some of these people ended up after the war?

—Rus—

—Bingo. Do you realize what that means, Leonard?

—What?

—It means they are trying to leave!

—Leave where?

—It doesn't matter!

—I don't know, Charles. That seems a bit—

—Why else would they be working on rockets? I think they want to get off this rock and leave us behind with these . . . apes. We'll never find the device if they do.

—Maybe.

—What do you mean maybe?

—I mean I don't know! All I know is the daughter's dead. She's not going anywhere. Call me crazy, but I don't think the mother's going to build a fucking spaceship all by herself.

—Not now, she won't. But that is how we'll find her. She will go where the rockets are.

—She's alone, Charles. If it were me, I'd find the smallest shithole in the middle of nowhere. I think—

—Don't think. Just pack up your things. You're coming with me.

—What? I thought—

—What did I just say about thinking? Don't make me repeat myself.

—Fine. Where are we going?

—The land of the free, Brother. We are going to the land of the free.

—America? We were just there!

—We were, but they weren't. That's . . . kind of a big deal when you think about it. As I recall, the goal is to be in the same place, at the same time. Now, when we find the mother, you have to promise me you won't kill her before she talks like you did with the daughter.

—I told you I didn't—

—Just tell me you won't kill her, Leonard.

—I won't. I swear.

—Good. I would hate to have to hurt you, my brother.

—Charles?

—Yes.

—What then?

—You mean after we find the device? We call home.

—Then what?

—Then they come, if it's not too late. Our people have a home.

—What happens to us?

—There is no us. Us was one man three thousand years before we were born and he got beat by a girl. You and I are cheap copies of something that wasn't that great to begin with. You do what you want, Brother. I'll buy myself a boat, drink plenty of wine, and wait to die, like we should have a long time ago.

55

Come On, Let's Go

Mia did it. It took thirteen years, lots of eviscerated American pride, and a dead dog flying over our heads, but mankind is heading to space. Von Braun launched Explorer I as promised using the Redstone rocket he built for the army. The air force built the Atlas, the Titan, and the Thor. Those rockets have become more than weapons, much more. Eisenhower passed the National Aeronautics and Space Act in September and handed control over all nonmilitary activity in space to a new agency. Science for science's sake. One of the first missions they approved is to orbit a manned spacecraft around Earth. Von Braun thinks he can do it first. Good for him. I know Korolev is pursuing the same goal. Whoever wins, I will get my wish. I will see a man in space before . . .

—You should hurry, Mia. It is almost noon.

—Noon? JPL is twenty minutes away!

—I know, but you don't want to be late for your interview.

—Fine, Mother. I'm going. I'm going.

—You never told me what the job was, by the way.

—The ad was for a computer.

—Mathematics, really?

—They have these giant IBM machines that can do thousands of calculations per second, but no one trusts them. They want *human* computers to double-check everything. I'm supposed to perform trajectory computations for rocket launches by hand. It's a far cry from the work I was doing with Korolev, but there's a certain purity in numbers you don't get with a clunky engine. Oh, and no degree required.

—You can have all the degrees you want, Mia.

—I gave myself two, but I think that just means women can apply. It's peacetime, Mother. They won't give someone like me an engineering job, even with the ridiculous résumé I gave myself. It's okay. I like math.

She can do the work. I am more worried about a tap on the shoulder from von Braun. I can picture his face. Lili? What are you doing here? I suppose she can call in sick whenever he visits. He works in Alabama, so that should not be too often.

—Do you know what you'll be working on?

—They didn't tell me. I think I might work on the Ranger program. I could help send something to the moon. Wouldn't that be great?

—Do you think you can beat the Soviets to it?

—Not a chance. They came *this* close to the moon in January already and they have another launch in September. They'll get there long before the Americans, but I need to work on something and we don't know anyone at NASA to start something new.

—Not yet, but we will. I only meant you should not waste your skills on something others are doing already.

—I like math, Mother. To be honest, I'm just happy to get out of the house. What about you? What are you going to do?

—I have my research. They just drilled a new three-hundred-meter ice core in Antarctica. There will be lots of data to look at.

—Who did? Your Danish guy?

—No, the US Army.

—You don't even know these people, Mother. There is *zero* data for you to look at. What are you not telling me?

I cannot bring myself to say it. It is not her judgment I dread, it is for her that I wish for a new life. I fear the verdict of the

254

dead, a jury of ninety-eight of my peers. What would my sentence be if my mother were alive? What would she have done if I had fallen to near death? I thought my daughter was gone. I thought I had lost her and it nearly killed me. I will not go through that pain again.

Take them to the stars. . . . We have taken them this far. We have done our part. They can take themselves the rest of the way.

56

Wonderful World

1960

—You don't need my permission to do anything, Mia. I just want you to think it through before you come to a decision.

—Mother, I know! At some point, we'll need to make calculations even I can't do. I really have a knack for programming these things, Mother!

—They are making computers better and better already. I am only asking if this is the best use of your time.

—They're also making them bigger and bigger. The air force has a new guidance computer for the Titan. Do you want to know how big it is?

—I assume it is very large.

I know nothing of computers. I really want to put an end to this conversation. I feel a hundred years old at the moment.

—It takes about three hundred square feet of floor space. The whole thing weighs twenty-one thousand pounds.

That *is* heavy, for anything. Mia has a point. We are in the infant stages of space exploration, but someday, when people leave Earth's orbit, they will need to determine a ship's position, calculate trajectories, et cetera, et cetera. They will need machines that can perform these calculations in an instant, and preferably not the size of a small apartment.

—I trust you, Mia. I was only asking.

I know I am looking for ways to justify myself, but if this "programming" proves useful to space exploration, then we are not truly abandoning our past if we make a new life for ourselves.

Mia working on computers would also serve my personal interests, if I decide to pursue my research. Information is coming faster and faster, from everywhere. Telescopes are more powerful than ever. We have even observed greenhouse effects on Venus, raising the atmospheric temperature above the boiling point of water. In Russia, Mikhail Budyko proposed a physical model of Earth's heat input and output. Groundbreaking work. He helped turn climatology from educated guesswork to quantitative science. His work will pave the way for complex, increasingly accurate models of Earth's atmosphere, but we will not get there with the machines we have today. Computing power is the cornerstone of this war, and if Mia wants to help speed up the process, who am I to stand in her way?

I think I know how we could find out how much of Earth's CO_2 comes from burning fossil fuel. I just need—

—Mother! You seem so . . . distant.

—I am sorry, Mia. I was . . . absorbed in somewhat self-congratulatory thought.

—No rule against being happy. Are you? Happy?

—I am . . . working on it. There are moments when I . . .

—Mother?

—There is a man standing outside.

—What do you mean, standing?

—He is staring at our house.

—Let me see. . . . It's him, Mother! That's the man who tried to kill me.

—Run, Mia. Run.

57

Will You Love Me Tomorrow

Where am I? This is our kitchen. I . . .

We ran out the back door. I was hit in the face with . . . There was another man, the same man. I believe Mia made it out.

Pain. What did he do—

—You're a hard one to catch, Sarah.

Here he is, sitting in front of me on another kitchen chair. I have never met him but I know who he is. All my life, I have been taught to fear this man.

My hand hurts. Throbbing pain. I can't . . . move. My legs are tied to the chair. My hands are roped behind my back.

—What did you do to me?

—Oh, that. I cut your little finger off while you were out. You don't mind, do you? I thought I'd save you some pain for the first one.

Did he? He must have. I can't feel it at all. Just pain. Blood should be gushing out but it is not. He must have cauterized it somehow. Whatever this is, he wants it to last.

—What is it you want?

—What do I want? Oh, you're funny, Sarah. Is that even your real name? Maybe I should have said— What was it you used to call yourselves again? The Kibsu? Do you still do that?

A genuine smile. He seems . . . happy. So much so he can barely contain himself. Too many things running through his head. Kill me. Talk to me. Torture me.

—This is a mistake. I am not who you think I am. Now please, sir, just untie me.

—More humor. I love that. I'll never understand why you held on to that Babylonian crap. Sounds so . . . melodramatic. I mean, do you say it with a deep, deep voice? WE. ARE. THE KIBSUUU! . . . No? Never mind. I'm sorry, that was rude. I apologize. I don't know you. I shouldn't make fun. If you're the Kibsu, what does that make me?

Blood rushing to every organ. I can feel my heartbeat in my neck. Three thousand years of instinct kicking in.

—Like I said, I—

—Stop wasting my time, Sarah, or I'll cut your whole fucking hand off.

Fear the Tracker. Always run, never fight. I've said the words so many times. But I can't run. I need to get my legs free.

—We call you the Tracker.

If I can get him to lean closer, I can knee the table through his windpipe.

—Like a hunter?

—Like a dog.

—Oh, that was uncalled for. You should really stop struggling, Sarah. You're not getting out of these ropes.

He is right. I am not going anywhere. . . . So this is how I die. Cut to pieces by the devil himself. It does not matter. Mia is safe. We will endure.

—Why not kill me now and get it over with?

—Kill you? What makes you think I want to kill you? Is it the finger? I would have cut your head off if I wanted to kill you. It's not the finger, is it? It's because of the Tracker thing? Am I the bad guy? The monster in your bedtime stories? I am. That stings. You really need new stories, Sarah. I'm not what you think I am. . . . We are . . . very much alike, you and I.

—I am nothing like you.

—Are you sure? I mean do you even know *what* you are? You have to know you're not one of them. Right? Yes, you do. Do you think you're different from me, too? Well, you're not. This isn't a zoo, honey. There aren't fifty kinds of animals. There's them, and there's us. I don't know why you would pretend otherwise. Frankly, I find it kind of insulting.

—You're a killer.

—Sure I am. So are you. Do you know how we find you? Every time. It's always the same. We look for the dead. Mass killings, unexplained deaths. Two dead guards and a nurse in Moscow. Was that you or did your daughter do that? I thought she was dead, by the way, before she ran past me. Good for her. Anyway, it doesn't matter which of you did it. You're a mass murderer, Sarah. You leave bodies behind like breadcrumbs. Don't take this the wrong way. I don't care. They're cockroaches, all of them. But don't pretend you and I are different.

—Why are you chasing us?

—No. No. No. That's not how this works. I ask the questions. And every time I'm not satisfied with your answer, I take a piece of you. A souvenir, you understand?

—What do you want to know?

—So many things, I don't even know where to start! Do you remember me?

—What?

I do not understand. He knows we have never met.

—I'll take that as a no. I'm sorry, that was a stupid question. Of course you don't remember me. It's just . . . I thought it might be different with you. I'm born . . . I'm a male—you can see that, obviously. What I mean is I need . . . someone, to be born. I come out of a woman. One of *them*. It's disgusting, but necessary. You . . . There's only you.

If he wants to kill me, he can do it whenever he wants. Why waste time talking to me? He seems genuinely curious. He does not know.

— . . .

—Oh, forget it. I thought you might remember things, that's all. Things from before. But you don't. Moving on. Where did you hide the device?

—What device?

I should not talk, but this I need to know. We have always assumed they were chasing us for sport. I thought they were just evil. I am certain they are, but if there is a deeper motivation behind it, I must find out what it is. I need to know what we keep dying for.

—Really? Oh, don't tell me you have a stupid ancient name for it. The wimbo, the kuplah, the amagonnagivittoya. Just tell me where you hid it and I will let you go. I swear. We'll leave you alone and never bother you again if that's what you want.

— . . .

—I guess not. Now you can't say I didn't warn you. I thought I explained the rules fairly well. What will it be? Another finger? Nah. We did that already. Maybe a toe. . . . I know. Let's take off one of your ears.

He's up. He's looking through the kitchen drawers.

—I swear to you. I do not know what that device is.

—I guess we'll know soon enough. Where are my manners? I forgot to introduce myself. My name is Charles. I believe . . . this will do just fine.

A bread knife. He's coming closer. I can't move! No! No!

—AAAAAAAGGGHHH!!!!

Throbbing pain. I feel the warmth on my cheek, my neck. This sick bastard is taking pleasure in this. No, we are not alike. We made a choice to be different. Our choice.

—There. It's over. You have nice ears. . . . I may be naive, but I think you really have no idea what I'm talking about. I'll be damned. The universe has some sick sense of humor if that's true. For your sake, Sarah, I hope you're lying to me. I really do. Because if you don't know . . . All of this for nothing?

I'll take real pleasure in watching you die, Sarah. I'll make whirligigs with your bones. I'll skin you alive and have your daughter wear you as a coat. You like ancient customs? I'll give you the tub. I'll have you stand in a vat up to your neck in water, then I'll pour milk and honey on your face. The flies will come first, then the maggots. In a day or two, you'll be swimming in your own shit and piss. I'll feed you, of course. I'll feed you over and over so you can shit some more and watch yourself rot. I'll make it last for months.

My head is spinning but I need to be strong. Every minute he spends with me is one he is not hunting Mia. I can keep her safe if I stay strong.

—You can torture me all you want. I will live on.

—How? Do you think you're a god or something? Oh, your daughter! You think *she's* safe? I have some bad news for you, dear, she's not. My brother has her by now. If you don't give me what I want, trust me, she will. When we're done cutting things off, we'll let you see each other. I'll remove your eyelids and have you stare at one another while we take your whole faces off.

He is lying, trying to confuse me. There were two of them but his brother was in the front yard. Mia is smart. She is fast.

—Is that why you have been hunting us? To get to that . . . device?

—Hunting you? You're the one running. We're chasing you because you're a fucking traitor!

—I have betrayed no one. You have murdered hundreds.

—YOU LET YOUR OWN FUCKING KIND DIE! Billions of people! Don't you dare compare yourself to me.

—My kind? What are you talking about?

—You don't know anything, do you? How the hell do you even stay alive? *We*—the two of us—we came together to this place. We came to find a new home before ours ends in a fiery hell. Only you chose to fuck it up and hide the one thing we need to call home.

Is that how it happened? Is that the choice we made? I see no reason for him to lie, but I have no reason to believe him either.

—I think you take pleasure in hunting us. I think you do it for the thrill. Is there some sort of prize for killing one of us?

—You think I'm doing this for a *reward*? Do you know what our people will make of us when they get here? Weird versions of each other, all of us born to a lesser species. They'll think we're an abomination. They'll put us down like stray dogs. That's my reward. I get to die. I get to leave this . . . sty. It's the stench. I have to be born in that smell over and over again, to have one of them as a mother and fff—I get nauseous just thinking about it—and *feed* off her stinking breasts. It wasn't supposed to be like that, you know. We were supposed to mate *together*, not with them.

—You disgust me.

—I didn't mean you and *me* me. You're older than my mother. I meant—you know perfectly well what I meant. Aren't you tired of being someone else? I am. I want to be me, not my father and his father. I want this to end but I need that device first so you're going to give it to me before I cut you into a thousand pieces.

— . . .

—Why are you smiling? Did you hear what I just said? I'm going to slice you up like a ham. What the hell are you smiling at, you crazy witch?

58

Walk—Don't Run

Run from the Tracker. Keep running. Don't look back.

Over the fence. Through the alley. My legs are heavy as dumbbells, my lungs are burning. I'm getting a headache. That's my body running out of fuel, but I need to keep going. Run. Survive at all costs. Remember the rules. That's what Mother would want.

I wonder if she's still alive. She's all alone if she is. He'll kill her for sure, but she would want me to run. No second thoughts, no regrets. I understand. If my daughter were alive, I would want her to live. Run. Never stop.

I wouldn't want my life, and my mother's life, to mean nothing. I wouldn't want my daughter to be the end of us, for all the knowledge to be lost on a whim. I wouldn't be afraid of dying, because I know I would live on through her. We are the Kibsu. I am the mother, the daughter. I am many, and so would my daughter be. I wouldn't want her to be selfish. . . .

I wouldn't want her to think of the lives she'd taken. Throats slit, hearts stabbed. Bodies convulsing on the floor. I would not want her to see Didi's face and wonder if the wrong person died that night. I wouldn't want her to doubt. To slow down. To catch her breath.

. . .

I wouldn't want my daughter to think of what she's lost. Leaving her life behind time and time again. Never saying goodbye. Waking in a strange place, not knowing her name or what language she speaks. I wouldn't want her to relive it. A woman she loved and will never see again. Words never spoken. Kisses never kissed. The utter vastness of an empty bed. No. I wouldn't want her to go through that. An empty womb. Breasts aching, gorged to feed a life that isn't. A promise broken before it was ever made. I wouldn't want my daughter to relive that loss. I wouldn't want her to imagine losing me, because I know what it would do to her. I wouldn't want her to be stubborn, to draw the line and say: "Fuck no. I'm not losing any more."

I wouldn't want her to turn around and head back the way she came—that would be foolish—to take one step, then another. Faster. Her feet beating the ground like a war drum, waking the animal inside her.

It starts with a tingling, hair standing on end. Heightened senses. Everything becomes clearer, crisper.

I wouldn't want her to welcome the beast. To let herself become what she fears the most. I wouldn't do that to her. I'd be afraid she'd lose herself for good. I'd be afraid she'd like it.

I sure as hell wouldn't want her rummaging through the shed looking for a weapon. She wouldn't do that. I know she wouldn't be stupid enough to think a tiki torch was a good idea.

No. I'd tell my daughter to run and to keep running, just like Mother would tell me. Think of all that came before you. Three thousand years of sacrifice on the line. Ninety-nine lives spent making sure you survive. Don't blow it. When I die, you will be the last of us.

Well, fuck all that. I don't have a daughter and Mother's not dead yet.

Last chance to turn around. My heart wants to burst out of my chest.

The back door's still open. Slowly. Don't make a sound. They're in the kitchen. I can see him, one of him. The other must be looking for me.

Mother. What the fuck did he do to her? Her face is all swelled up. She's bleeding all over herself.

Slowly.

I feel the warmth taking hold. I feel the monster waking.

Slowly.

Her eyes are swelled shut but she can see me. He doesn't know what she's looking at as I raise the spike high above his head.

—Why are you smiling? Did you hear what I just said? I'm going to slice you up like a ham. What the hell are you smiling at, you crazy witch?

Let the animal loose, Mia. Let her rage.

59

At Last

—You should not have come back, Mia. I am grateful for what you did but it—

—You're welcome, Mother. Can we do this another time? He was right on our tail a second ago.

I saw him, too. Ford Fairlane, Corinthian white. The Tracker stayed three cars behind the whole way, but I am certain he knows we spotted him.

—Are you sure it is a good idea to stop here? We could keep driving.

—We'll be safe down here. There are soldiers everywhere. Now will you please get inside the elevator?

—How deep are we going?

Part of me is glad we stopped moving. I am still dizzy and I can barely see. I have never been to a missile silo before. Vandenberg is a development launch site, but this is what they will all look like. Three nuclear-capable ICBMs buried underground. On the surface, all we can see are the two-hundred-ton circular doors. Beneath them lies a small maze of tunnels linking the silos to the control room and whatever else is down there.

—It's not that deep, about a hundred and fifty feet.

We have been here for less than a minute and I am claustrophobic already. Good, the control room is just across from the elevator. It is roomier than I thought. I imagined something like a submarine: narrow corridors, low ceilings. There are filing cabinets everywhere, I wonder what they keep in—Oh wait. They are part of the computer.

—This is the machine you were talking about?

—Yes. That's the ATHENA computer. Now you unders—

—What kind of unholy abomination is making that noise?

—They're testing the Titan I. That's why we came here. I knew there'd be soldiers around. What you're hearing is the elevator raising the missile above ground.

—That sound!

—It can lift half a million pounds, but it has its kinks. It won't move sometimes. Still makes that noise, though. They'll raise the missile to the surface to load the liquid oxygen. I'm supposed to make sure the guidance computer and the rocket are talking to each other. They'll do a pretend countdown and abort just before sending the signal to ignite.

—Then what?

—They bring the missile down again, remove the liquid oxygen, and everyone goes home.

I do not like it here. There is only one exit. Nowhere to hide.

—What about us? He will be waiting for us.

—I'll ask for a military escort. We'll figure out where to go. . . . Do you think it's true, what the Tracker was saying?

—Which part?

—That we came together, that our world was dying. Did you believe him?

—I am fairly certain *he* believed it. Whether you and I do does not seem particularly relevant.

—What if it's true? The necklace I'm wearing, did you know it's not from Earth?

—I suspected.

—What if we let our people die by hiding that thing?

—Let us assume for a moment that the device he mentioned does exist. Would you use it if you could? Would you bring billions like him to this world? Besides, I am not hiding anything and neither are—

—What?

—Did you hear that, Mia? It sounded like gunshots.

—Maybe the army will kill him for us.

—How far is the silo from the control room?

—It's . . . at the end of that tunnel on the left.

—Take us there, Mia! We are not waiting for him here.

—He might be dead already.

—He might not be. Go.

—Fine. This way.

There is no one inside the tunnel. There were plenty of soldiers outside, but I have only seen a handful since we went underground.

—Is it always this empty?

—I don't know, I've only been here twice. But these things are designed for a skeleton crew.

—How much farther?

—What did you say?

The noise is getting louder and louder. It sounds like a thousand baby goats are being burned alive.

—I SAID HOW MUCH FARTHER?

I see a door ahead of us. It is much closer than I thought, fifteen hundred feet from where we were at most. If we were above ground, the control room would be miles from the launchpad.

—In here.

This is impressive. Our ceiling is rising along this giant metal structure, no doubt bringing the missile to the surface. It must be near the top now. There. It stopped. I do not know if it is fear or the beating I just took but that noise was driving me mad.

—This is better.

—That platform is holding two hundred thousand pounds of rocket fuel above our heads, Mother. I don't mind the noise as long as it doesn't drop it.

A fair point, though I'm certain it would not take a feat of engineering to quiet this monster down a bit. . . . And now we wait. With any luck, the guards will t—

[Hello? Anyone?]

There is someone here. I did not hear him coming. It could be a soldier, or an engi—

—Mother, it's him.

This one might be a couple of years younger, but he looks the same. Same height. Same cold eyes. Same response. Adrenaline is binding to my heart and arteries. My heartbeat is speeding up; so is my breathing. He is blocking the only doorway out of here, and I do not have a weapon. His is a baton. He must have grabbed it from one of the guards. We will not last five seconds without something to fight with.

[Oh, here you are! I'm so glad to see you both here. So which one of you ladies killed my brother?]

I see an ax next to the fire extinguisher, but it is too slow a weapon. Mia is digging through a toolbox. She grabbed herself a hammer. That is anger talking, not fear. I will take a screwdriver if there is nothing else. Box cutters. Perfect. I prefer short blades.

—Let me take care of this, Mia.

[Take care of this? I just want to know who left a tiki torch inside my brother's skull. I don't think that's too much to ask.]

—That would be me.

—Don't talk to him, Mia. I will keep him occupied. You run.

My hand is killing me but I can still hold a knife. I do not need to kill him. I only need him out of the way. If Mia makes it to the exit, there should be armed soldiers above us.

—Like hell I am, Mother. I'm not leaving you here. We'll take him together.

[You're not holding a grudge because I kicked you off that launch-pad, are you? Fine. I don't feel like talking either. Let's dance.]

—Mia, stand back!

He is swinging his baton. Close the distance. Don't parry. A baton is mechanical leverage. Basic physics. Amplification of the input force is proportional to the distance over which it is applied. Take the hit close to the grip. Slice his forearm.

He is transferring his weight. Walk back and slice again. There is a lot of blood but I am not cutting deep enough. I need to hit muscle and tendon if I am to weaken his arms. Baton again. Walk forward and slice. I cut him deep this time. His right elbow is moving back. He will swing again. He is strong, but predictable. He will not last long if we continue this routine. Baton from above. Walk forward. Slice his fore—Aaaagh. He grabbed me by the hair.

Headbu—

. . .

. . .

. . .

Where am I? I am on the floor, dizzy. I must not have been out long. Mia is running towards him. He raised his baton but she slid on one leg and swung her hammer into his knee.

—I'll kill you for what you did!

His leg buckled. She's behind him now. Crack his head open, Mia! He is walking backwards. He will slam her against the wall.

[*What I did? You just killed my brother, you stupid bitch!*]

They are facing each other again. GET YOUR HANDS UP! Mia took a blow to the temple. She is barely conscious.

[*Is that all you got? How about I rip your ear off so you and your mom match? Then you can be mad.*]

He knocked both of us out in under a minute. Time to face facts.

I need him to come to me before he kills her.

—LEAVE HER ALONE!

[*Hey! You're back!*]

You should have killed me when you had the chance.

[*If you insist.*]

The Tracker is limping towards me. Come at me. Keep coming.

I don't need the knives anymore. . . .

Only now, in the end, do I understand.

It is not our path that brought us here but my straying from it. I let selfishness and doubt distract me. I wanted what other people have and I forgot the treasure we possess. I forgot my purpose.

Hsue-Shen was right. We cannot change what we are. I tried, and the Tracker knocked at our door. I broke the rules, and my daughter paid the price. I pretended to be something I'm not, and Mia lost her child.

Now I get to set things straight. Survive at all costs.

I got the ax off the wall. It is heavy. I can see the Tracker in the corner of my eye, but I am not looking at him. I am staring at the platform hydraulics.

—MOTHER, NO!

Good. Mia knows what I am doing. I wish there were another way but there is not.

— . . .

—NOOOOO! PLEASE, MOTHER, STOP!

One swing of the ax. She will need to run fast. The closest blast door is a quarter mile away. Run, Mia. Always run.

The Tracker stopped dead in his tracks. He does not know what just happened. He sees the cable dancing, spitting oil like an angry snake. He does not understand. He just now realized Mia is gone. He can hear the pump struggling. The platform above us just dropped three feet on one side.

Now, he knows.

[*What have you done?*]

That is a good question. I have lived. I have learned. I have made mistakes. I doubted. I did what I could to honor the ones that came before me. I brought a life into this world. I tried to help. Now I die, but, as my friend said, at least I will die knowing who I am.

272

—I hope I have done enough. Now burn, you fucking piece of shit.

The platform is coming down hard. We will be dead before the fuel tanks rupture and blow this place to hell. There is so much I *have not* done, but I have no regrets, for this is not the end. Ninety-nine of us are gone, but we were born a hundred times.

My name is Sarah Freed, and we are the Kibsu.

CONCLUSION

60

Stand by Me

1961

A handful of fine clouds linger over the ocean, thin and wispy, while the sun dips its toes and sets the sea on fire. I look forward to our time on Mallorca. It will be . . . It will be just that, our time. Me and her and nothing else. No rockets, no computers. I came here to give birth—the Tracker will never find us here. A new life is coming. It's exciting, and scary. We'll make it work. I have it all planned. The three "B"s, I call it. Books, beach, breastfeeding, probably not in that order. I have some time to figure it out. She won't be born for another five months.

I was pregnant a week after Mother died. I was in shock when I came out of that base. I couldn't feel anything. I couldn't think. All I had left were the rules.

Preserve the knowledge.

I ran home, threw our journals in the trunk of the car, and drove east.

Survive at all costs.

I found a shitty bar next to a truck stop and dragged the first man I saw into the bathroom. I don't remember what he looked like. Ugly, I think.

Don't leave a trace.

I torched the car, found a truck on its way to Miami, and hopped on the first boat heading for Europe.

I'm not sure when I cried for the first time. I know it took a while. I still . . . I haven't quite come to terms with Mother's death. It doesn't feel like she's gone. In some ways she's not. She's inside me. She's . . . happy. Happy that I'm alive, that we're alive. It's for her that I—that we're here tonight. I found this secluded cove a few days ago. It's just us, all one hundred of us, looking at the sky.

—Look up, Lola! I know you can't see, but there is a man up there. His name is Yuri. He doesn't know that we're looking at him but I bet you he's looking at us. Not you and me, he's looking at the planet. He's seeing more of it than anyone in history. He can see whole continents. He can see Earth's curvature. Did I tell you we live on a giant ball? We do! And right now, this very minute, there is a tiny tiny spaceship spinning around it with Yuri inside it.

I wonder what he's thinking. Does he know how many lives were spent getting him up there? Can he grasp the sheer amount of work that went into it? I bet you he couldn't care less at the moment. Good for him. He's the first man in space, it would be a crime if he weren't having the time of his life. He left from Baikonur, on *my* rocket. Well, Korolev had something to do with it as well, he and a million others, but there's a bit of me in that rocket. Lots of memories. Not many regrets.

Oh! She's moving.

—You like that, don't you? Someday you'll build ships like this one. You'll send people even farther. Don't worry, not today. There's a lot I need to teach you first.

We'll stay here for a couple of years, then we'll find somewhere I can work. There's lots to do. Mother said it: getting to orbit is only the first step. We need to go farther, much farther. We'll start with the moon, then, another planet. Then . . . Then Lola can figure it out.

Lola . . . I had absolutely no idea what to name her. My one friend here—I made a friend—told me not to worry about it. She said: "Wait until she's born. You'll know when you see her." I laughed. I know exactly what my daughter will look like. I would have named her Sarah, but that'll be weird and creepy when she grows up. Billie, well . . . There's only one Billie. I took out a piece of paper to make a list, but I couldn't come up with a single name I liked. Finally, I wrote down a big "101" and pinned the sheet on the kitchen wall. One morning, I was making eggs and I saw it. I added the "a." 101a. I think it fits. I can see myself as a Lola.

I wonder what she'll think of me. Will she look at her mother the way I looked at mine? Will she see a pillar of strength or the insecure child I still see in the mirror? Now that I'm in her shoes, I often ask myself whether my mother was as sure of herself as I made her out to be, or if we were more alike than I thought all along.

I don't know where we'll go. I don't want to return to the United States, not now. When Lola's older, maybe. If she wants to work on rockets, we'll have to go where the rockets are. Unfortunately, that's also where the computers are. We'll see. Fortunately, I can continue Mother's research anywhere. I will finish what she started. I think I owe her that much.

There's something else I want to do. I want to find out who we are. I want to know if the Tracker was telling the truth. I want to know where we come from, what our world is like. Mother said that we lost the knowledge a long time ago, but I think it's out there somewhere, waiting to be found.

I'm not sure what the future holds for us, but I'm eager to find out. For the first time in my life, I know exactly who I am. I am a mother, a daughter. I am all of those that came before me and all that will follow. I feel . . . very much alive.

—Can you feel it, Lola? We're alive!

We *are* alive. We are the One Hundred.

FURTHER READING
(Not as boring as it sounds, I swear.)

The story's over (for now). I learned a ton writing this book. I knew little of the space race when I began, nothing of rocket science. Writing in the past was the biggest challenge. Basically, nothing exists and women can't do anything. When were women allowed to open a bank account on their own? Was there duct tape in 1945? Was "alpha dog" a thing back then? That said, I love research, and digging into history was a lot of fun. I thought I would share some interesting bits about the people and events that make up this book and throw in some reading suggestions if you want to know more, or if you're looking to pass time while waiting for the next book.

Rather than give you a long list of books, most of which you're never going to read, I picked relatively short documents from good sources that you can read online for free. Of course, just about everything and everyone I mention in the book has a Wikipedia entry.

The OSS
The story begins with Sarah working for the OSS, the Office of Strategic Services. It is, of course, a real thing, and in many ways the ancestor of the CIA. You've seen them or read about them before. In *Cloak and Dagger* (1946) by Fritz Lang, Gary Cooper plays an OSS agent who—drumroll—has to exfiltrate a German scientist. Indiana Jones worked for them, according to *Kingdom of the Crystal Skull*, and Diana Prince, a.k.a. Wonder Woman,

works for Steve Trevor at the OSS. The great thing about the organization is that they were the first espionage agency of their kind,[1] as in there weren't earlier ones that they could model themselves after. They made it up as they went along. The result is sometimes amazing, sometimes really, really weird. They made gizmos and gadgets. Think Sean Connery's James Bond: cameras in the shape of a matchbox, playing cards that hid secret maps, the ever-useful compass hidden inside a uniform button, and explosives disguised as just about everything.

Their hiring practices were interesting, to say the least. They hired baseball catcher Moe Berg after his career with the Red Sox ended, and sent him to Zurich to meet German physicist Werner Heisenberg, to ascertain how close the Germans were to the atomic bomb, and to shoot him if he thought they were close to a breakthrough. Famous chef Julia Child was apparently too tall to enlist in the Women's Army Corps, and so she joined the OSS instead. There, she assisted in developing a shark repellent for the navy. All this is to say that I felt fairly comfortable having them send nineteen-year-old Mia on a mission in Germany.

There were real heroes working for the OSS, men and women braver than any of us—well, me anyway—but in some respects, the agency also resembled what my ten-year-old would come up with if I asked him to start his own spy thing. If you want to read about the OSS, I suggest the publications section on the CIA website.[2] You should also look up Virginia Hall. She's literally a superhero.

Operation Paperclip

Operation Paperclip has to be one of the most famous secret operations in history. Its purpose was to extract German scientists

1. The office of the Coordinator of Information (COI) came before the OSS, but it was much smaller.
2. https://www.cia.gov/library/publications/intelligence-history/oss

and to get them to work for the US. Why Paperclip? The way I heard it, the US put together a big pile-o'-files on German scientists, and researchers would put a paper clip on the ones they thought were of interest. The operation was . . . let's just say controversial. People often talk about Wernher von Braun because he makes for a more sympathetic figure, but hiring people working for Hitler in Nazi Germany significantly increases your chances of ending up with actual Nazis. I won't speculate as to these people's beliefs or motivations, but von Braun wasn't the only one working at NASA who once wore the SS uniform. Kurt Debus, director of the Launch Operations Center at Cape Canaveral, was a member of both Hitler's Brownshirts and the SS. He worked with von Braun at Peenemünde. The gigantic Vertical Assembly Building at Cape Canaveral was designed by Bernhard Tessmann, who helped set up the facilities at Peenemünde. Tessmann was one of the people von Braun asked for help in hiding the V-2 research documents Himmler had ordered destroyed.

The Saturn V rocket, which sent the Apollo astronauts to the moon, was designed by former SS *Sturmbannführer* von Braun, and Arthur Rudolph, who joined the Nazi Party in 1931 and later the Brownshirts. These are the more presentable people the US recruited. Then you have people like Kurt Blome, director of the Nazi biological warfare program. This guy did some really nasty stuff I won't describe here (but you've already guessed where he got his test subjects from). He was later hired by the US to work on . . . chemical warfare.

This book begins with Mia and von Braun during their escape from Germany. Writing it was super fun, because it's all true, more or less. Accounts of the events differ slightly from source to source, even for something that happened not that long ago, but the gist of it is always the same. Von Braun and some of his people decide they want to surrender to the US. The Russians are coming, and they have to leave Peenemünde.

They have a bunch of conflicting orders to pick from, and they choose to go to Bleicherode, but they're worried about their gigantic convoy getting stopped. This is where it gets crazy. Yes, they just happen to have a box of misprinted letterhead on hand, and they use it to make fake papers for this VzBV secret project. Somewhere along the way, von Braun's driver falls asleep at the wheel, and he breaks his arm in a crash. They get to Bleicherode, where they meet Dornberger. They receive orders to burn all their research and take the top five hundred scientists to a camp in Oberammergau. They hide all the research documents inside a mountain instead, because why not. Once in Oberammergau, they convince the SS major in charge that they should disperse in the nearby towns. From there, they use the VzBV letterhead to requisition supplies and go wait it out at a resort in the Alps until von Braun's brother Magnus runs into a certain PFC Schneikert while riding his bicycle. The American soldier points his gun at him, and Magnus says, in broken English: "My name is Magnus von Braun. My brother invented the V-2. We want to surrender!"

I think what I like most about the von Braun story is that he did it all himself, as far as I can tell. Operation Paperclip wasn't always pretty. Truman authorized one thousand German scientists to be held in "temporary, limited military custody." That usually meant scouting and then kidnapping people. Von Braun, on the other hand, *chose* to surrender to the US. He didn't have a Mia helping him. He got his people out of Germany all on his own (with a little help from Dornberger), and he did it in the craziest way.

Before the Saturn rockets used in the Apollo missions, von Braun developed the Redstone, the first large American ballistic missile, which served as the basis for a whole series of rockets. A modified Redstone launched the first US satellite, and the Mercury-Redstone rocket sent the first Americans into space. He did a lot to popularize the concept of space travel. Check out his crazy concept for the "ferry rocket" from the pages of *Collier's* magazine in 1952.[3] Von Braun died of pancreatic cancer in 1977.

Walter Dornberger spent two years in a British prison camp after escaping Germany. The British didn't like him at all. They thought he was a weasel. That didn't stop the US from hiring him in 1947. He worked on a bunch of things, including the ultracool X-20 Dyna-Soar spaceplane. It was never made, but the concept was as awesome as the name. I'll let you google that one.

Korolev and the Soviet Paperclip

In Act III, Mia recruits Sergei Korolev in Germany and brings him back to Russia, along with thousands of German specialists. This was called Operation Osoaviakhim. It pretty much went as I describe it, sans Mia. The Soviets didn't mess around. You want scientists? We'll "recruit" thousands of them at gunpoint, all at the same time, and drag them and their families back to Moscow. The memo Mia reads to her mother is an actual translation of what these people were given.

Korolev is fun to read about. He had it rough, though. Arrested for treason and sabotage, tried and sent to a gulag where he lost all his teeth to scurvy. Saved at the last minute, retried and forced to work in a prison for scientists. When he got out, he ended up as chief designer of long-range missiles at the OKB-1 special design bureau. Korolev, the chief designer, was more or less the face of the Russian missile and space program, but the Soviet Union was a mess under Stalin. There were so many people working on so many different things, it's really hard to keep up. I found a great read on the Soviet space program in the NASA archives.[4] If you have *any* interest in rocket

3. https://www.wired.com/2014/09/wernher-von-brauns-fantastic-vision-ferry-rocket/
4. Asif A. Siddiqi, "Challenge to Apollo: The Soviet Union and the Space Race,

research and all the politics involved, you have to read it. It's fascinating.

Mia introduces herself as Nina, the interpreter, when she meets Korolev in Germany. Korolev was a married man. He had a daughter, Natalya. His marriage eventually fell apart, in part because of an affair with a young English interpreter from the Podlipki office. Her name was Nina Ivanovna Kotenkova. The two tied the knot in 1949.

Korolev's crowning achievement as chief designer had to be the R-7, Mia's perfect rocket. It launched both Sputnik and Yuri Gagarin. You can read the issue of *Life* magazine dedicated to the little satellite that created the space race at Google Books.[5] As Mia predicts, the R-7 was more or less useless as a ballistic missile, and it was only briefly deployed operationally. It was, however, the perfect space launch vehicle, and versions of the R-7 served as the basis for the Soyuz family of launchers, which is still in service, more than sixty years after the R-7 first tested. As of now, it has launched over eighteen hundred times.

Some name dropping. Tons of people were involved in the development of every rocket, including the R-7. The original cluster or packet design came from Mikhail Tikhonravov. He could write, of course, and wrote some very influential papers about rocket technology. His design was improved upon by a fellow named Dmitry Okhotsimsky at the Steklov Institute of Applied Mathematics. He came up with the cluster concept Korolev chose for the R-7. Korolev's right hand, Vasily Mishin, also played a major part in the R-7 project. Unfortunately, Mishin will mostly be remembered for failing to put a man on the moon after he inherited the Soviet N1 program.

1945–1974" (NASA SP-2000–4408, 2000). Part 1: https://history.nasa.gov/SP-4408pt1.pdf. Part 2: https://history.nasa.gov/SP-4408pt2.pdf.
5. https://books.google.ca/books?id=QFYEAAAAMBAJ&pg=PA19&source=gbs_toc_r&redir_esc=y#v=onepage&q&f=false

Kapustin Yar

At the beginning of Act IV, a self-loathing Mia goes to Kapustin Yar to help with test launches for the R-2 and save some dogs. (I know you want to hear about the dogs, but we'll do that later.) Kapustin Yar was created in 1946 for testing jet-propelled weapons starting with captured German V-2s. Nuclear tests were also performed on-site in the late fifties. Understandably, Kapustin Yar was kept secret and didn't appear on any maps. Secret remote location, secret military projects, shitty black-and-white photography. You know where I'm going with this. The site is an all-you-can-eat buffet for conspiracy theorists and is often referred to as the Russian Roswell. Secret underground base. UFO sightings. Alien autopsy, of course. Little green men. There's a "documentary" episode of History's *UFO Files* called "Russian Roswell," which you can find online, or you can read a summary[6] and get the gist of things. There's all sorts of crazy in there (dogfight between an alien ship and fighter planes!), and a lot of it connects to this book, somehow.

There's mention of a giant fireball falling from the sky in 1908 near the town of Tunguska. That part is true. It was the largest impact event on Earth in recorded history. Whatever it was, it flattened two thousand square kilometers of forest. Comet, asteroid, who knows? Of course, if you like conspiracies, you can believe just about anything hit Earth, including little green men in a giant spaceship. As the story goes, a team of scientists was sent to investigate some forty years later by none other than Sergei Korolev. Soon after, the Russian space program made miraculous progress because of some reverse-engineering of the alien spacecraft.

They even talk about Ahmad Ibn Fadlan, the tenth-century Muslim traveler who is said to have "witnessed 'aerial battles' between 'shapes' that moved through the clouds." That is the dude

6. http://www.rolfwaeber.com/mystery/russian-roswell/index.html

the Sixty-Five is traveling with in AD 921 during the fourth en-tr'acte.

The other launchpad I mention in this book is Baikonur, a.k.a. "Gagarinskiy Start" (Gagarin's pad). Both Sputnik 1 and Vostok 1, the first human spaceflight, launched from Baikonur on top of an R-7 rocket. In 1955, during construction, one of the workers fell off the launch platform and impaled himself on a steel rod midway down. Unfortunately for him, he didn't have the Kibsu's superstrength, and he died before they could take him down.

Russian Space Dogs

Happy now? If your priorities are the same as Mia's, you want to find out what happened to the dogs. Everyone's heard about Laika, the first animal to orbit Earth aboard Sputnik 2, but there were lots of dogs before and after. Laika got the short stick. She's the only dog that was sent with no hope of survival. She died soon after liftoff, but she'd have died anyway because, well, you shouldn't put a dog inside a satellite. Sputnik 2 reentered Earth's atmosphere on April 14, 1958, and burned up before it hit the ground. That means that for about six months, there was a dead dog flying over our heads.

The ones Mia tries to save are Dezik and Tsygan. They were the first. Back then, they didn't used pressurized cabins, so the dogs had to wear tiny dog space suits. In July 1951, they were shot up 110 km into the sky on top of a modified R-1 and . . . came back down safely. (Yay!) Dezik made another flight a week later with a dog named Lisa. Unfortunately for Dezik, the parachute didn't deploy that time. In the book, Mia brought Tsygan home, but in real life it was Soviet physicist Anatoli Blagonravov who adopted the dog.

Between 1951 and 1960, at least twenty dogs made suborbital flights on top of a rocket. Here are my three stars:

Smelaya. She ran away (I wonder why) the day before her

launch. They found her, though, and she flew with another dog. Both of them survived.

Bobik. He ran away. They didn't catch him. Go Bobik!

Zib. Zib was a street dog they found running around the barracks. He made a successful flight. ZIB is a Russian acronym for "Substitute for Missing Bobik."

There's a website about Soviet space dogs with more info (and more dogs) and tons of pictures.[7] There's even one of Korolev with one of the dogs. I strongly suggest the story of Damka and Krasavka. It would make a great movie.

The Wikipedia entry[8] has pictures of Belka and Strelka in a museum (I'm not sure if they're stuffed or fake, but they *are* creepy). These two were the real superstars in Russia. They spent a day in orbit with a gray rabbit, forty-two mice, two rats, and some flies (no partridge nor pear tree) and came back alive. That made them better propaganda tools than dead Laika, and soon they were featured in children's books and cartoons and on just about anything from stamps to candy tins and cigarette packs. Then comes the true story of the Cold War romance that prevented World War III. Okay, not quite, but still. Back at the space center, there was a male dog named Pushok. He had never made it to space, but he was not the kind of dog that gave up, or ran away. He had grit, determination. It was those qualities that Strelka recognized, and the two quickly became proud parents of six puppies. Among the litter was little Pushinka (Fluffy), whom Soviet premier Nikita Khrushchev gave to John F. Kennedy's daughter, Caroline. Pushinka could not resist the childish ways of Charlie, one of the Kennedy dogs, and their forbidden love resulted in the birth of Butterfly, Streaker, White Tips, and Blackie, whom Kennedy affectionately called "pupniks."

7. http://www.esdaw.eu/soviet-space-dogs.html
8. https://en.wikipedia.org/wiki/Soviet_space_dogs

Slight change of tone. Much of Act V revolves around Lavrentiy Beria. There were a lot of really bad people in positions of power around the time of the Second World War. Hitler, of course. Stalin was a nasty piece of work. And then there's Lavrentiy Beria. If you make a list of evil people who walked the earth at one point or another, I suggest you leave some room near the top for this guy. He got his start crushing a nationalist uprising in Georgia, got about ten thousand people executed in the process. He met Stalin in 1926 and was a close ally during his rise to power. As chief of the secret police, he supervised the barrier troops, the folks who shot their own soldiers running away from battle. He expanded the gulag labor camps, continued the great purge started by his predecessor. After the war, he helped organize the communist revolutions in several European countries—he liked those as bloody as possible—and he oversaw the development of the atomic bomb for the Soviets. By some accounts, he liked to participate in the butchery himself. He is said to have personally tortured the family of an Abkhaz Communist leader, placing a snake inside his widow's cell and having her watch as he beat her daughter to death.

So this is a man directly responsible for hundreds of thousands of deaths, and what does he do in his spare time? He prowls the streets of Moscow in his limousine and brings young women back to his home, where he rapes them inside his soundproof office. They found a bunch of bones in his backyard, so he apparently didn't stop there. Those who left his home alive were handed a bouquet of flowers, because in his mind nothing says consent like taking flowers from the secret police. People knew about it. Even members of the Politburo warned their daughters to stay away from that asshole.

I read about a woman who was breastfeeding and refused to let Beria touch her. When the secret police mistakenly handed her a bouquet anyway, he apparently said, "Now it's not a bouquet, it's a wreath! May it rot on your grave!" He had the woman arrested the next day. He took a Russian actress to his home and promised her he'd set her father and grandmother free in exchange for sexual favors. He then told her: "Scream or not, it doesn't matter. You are in my power now. So think about that and behave accordingly." She, too, was arrested, and sent to the gulag. Her father and grandmother had died weeks before Beria offered to free them. We know most of this from the mouth of Colonel Rafael Semenovich Sarkisov, one of Beria's most senior bodyguards. During the war, Beria had Sarkisov keep a record of all the women he took back to his house. Sarkisov was supposed to burn it all at some point, but he kept a copy, which he handed to the new head of the MGB when Beria's fall from grace began. I really wanted to let the Kibsu have a go at Beria, but I settled for the bullet in the head he got in real life. For a deeper look into the mind of Stalin and his profoundly messed-up entourage, try Simon Sebag Montefiore's book.[9]

Beria apparently bragged about killing Stalin. There has been a lot of speculation about Stalin's death, and many believe he was poisoned, presumably with warfarin. It was reported that Stalin was drinking diluted Georgian wine on the night he fell into a coma.

Perhaps ironically, it was Beria who requested a new trial for Sergei Korolev after he was sentenced to life in the gulag. Beria had just been named head of the NKVD. He saved Korolev's life to sell himself as a fair and humane leader. It did not last, but Korolev survived because of Beria's actions.

Qian Xuesen, or Hsue-Shen Tsien

The former is a transliteration of his Chinese name, family name first; the latter is the Americanized version he used while

9. Simon Sebag Montefiore, *Stalin: The Court of the Red Tsar* (New York: Alfred A. Knopf, 2007).

in the US. Qian was one of the people behind the Jet Propulsion Laboratory, and a real genius. While in the US, he was temporarily made a colonel so he could go to Germany and debrief Wernher von Braun and others after they surrendered to the Americans. The government later accused him of being a communist during the Red Scare. After spending five years under house arrest, he was finally allowed to return to China, presumably in exchange for some prisoners from the Korean War. The US got rid of an absolutely brilliant man because they were paranoid about communism.

In China, things were dicey at first for Qian. Mao wasn't the most trusting guy. Qian came from the US, and his father-in-law worked for the government the communists had just overthrown. He had to profess loyalty to the party a bunch of times, but things got better for him soon enough. In 1956, he became director of the Fifth Academy of the Ministry of National Defense, where he ran the missile and nuclear development program. He reached his goal in record time, and China tested its first nuclear bomb in 1964. Qian also founded the Chinese space program, so you may hear from him again at some point. Qian never returned to the United States (he was pissed). He died in 2009, at the age of ninety-seven. His work on complex systems was groundbreaking and served as the basis for some of China's social engineering experiments.

The American Space Program

There's been so much written on the subject, lots of movies even, that I chose to focus on smaller, lesser-known events. It's also why the book ends in 1961, before Mercury, Gemini, and Apollo. Some of the events I mention were *huge* when they occurred— the Vanguard rocket explosion, for example. It happened live on national television, at a time when the US was deeply troubled by the Soviet space endeavor. Google "Vanguard explosion" and you can watch it blow up; there are tons of videos online.

When they go back to the US, Mia works at the Jet Propulsion Labs as a human computer. You probably recognized the term from *Hidden Figures*.[10] Little was known about these insanely smart women and the role they played in the space program before Margot Lee Shetterly's book and the movie that followed. Both were huge successes and went a long way in giving these pioneers some of the credit they deserved, even if it came fifty years too late. *Hidden Figures* follows a group of black women working as human computers in a segregated section of NASA's research center at Langley beginning in 1961, right after this book ends. There were, of course, some women working in scientific positions in the early days of rocket science, before the era of spaceflight. Nathalia Holt's book[11] (also nonfiction) follows a handful of women leaving their mark on the other side of the country at JPL during more or less the same timeline as this book.

Mia thinks that, once at JPL, she might work on the Ranger program. Those were unmanned missions, basically trying to hit the moon after taking close-up pictures of the surface and transmitting them to Earth. The first six Ranger missions all failed, leading to a congressional investigation of both NASA and JPL.

At the end, Sarah dies when she causes a Titan missile to fall on her and the Tracker at Vandenberg Air Force Base. That happened, though it was an accident. It must have felt like the world was coming to an end for the people who were there. The blast doors were a mere twelve hundred feet from the explosion, and it was quite the explosion. It destroyed the two-hundred-ton silo

10. Margot Lee Shetterly, *Hidden Figures: The American Dream and the Untold Story of the Black Women Mathematicians Who Helped Win the Space Race* (New York: William Morrow, 2016).
11. Nathalia Holt, *Rise of the Rocket Girls: The Women Who Propelled Us, from Missiles to the Moon to Mars* (New York: Little, Brown, 2016).

doors. Debris flew all the way to the Vandenberg golf course, a few miles away. Miraculously, there were no casualties.[12]

Climate Change

One of the most interesting (and depressing) things one learns reading about climate change is how long we've known about it. There are people today who aren't sure how big a role humans played in the process, but there are also plenty who simply don't believe that the temperature is rising, or that greenhouse gases have anything to do with it. Svante Arrhenius wrote about it in 1896 (you can read his paper online[13] if you're curious), and he wasn't the first. We've known this stuff for over a hundred years.

I really enjoyed reading about ice core research. I just love the simplicity of it. I have no idea who thought about air bubbles trapped in ice first, but I like to think the conversation involved an ice cube tray and sounded a bit like the one between Mia and her mother. The hydrogen and oxygen isotope thing is a bit more complicated, but still very cool. The credit for that belongs to Willi Dansgaard,[14] the Dutch paleontologist Sarah worked with. I drop a few more names throughout the book; feel free to look them up.

Towards the end, Sarah thinks she's found a way to measure the amount of CO_2 in the atmosphere that comes from burning fossil fuel. I didn't let her explain, because I thought it was too technical, but now we're here and I'm filled with regret, so let's science together a bit. We'll start with carbon—that's the C in CO_2. Carbon is awesome. It can make funky things at the temperatures found on Earth, like the sugar found in DNA. That's

12. https://lompocrecord.com/news/local/military/vandenberg/workers-remember -titan-1-explosion/article_009183fa-ff78-11df-9f09-001cc4c03286.html
13. http://www.rsc.org/images/Arrhenius1896_tcm18-173546.pdf
14. http://www.nbi.ku.dk/english/www/willi/dansgaard/

why it's in every living thing we're aware of. It's in the air. It's everywhere. There's also a special kind of radioactive carbon called carbon 14 but we'll call it Steve because that's more fun. Steve is also in the atmosphere. Plants take in some Steve during photosynthesis. That means a banana tree has some Steve in it, and so does a banana. You eat the banana and, you guessed it, there is some Steve in you. (Note that the same is true if something else eats the banana and you eat the something else.) In the end, you and every other living thing has more or less the same amount of Steve in you as there is in the air around you. Then you die. Sorry. When you die, you stop eating bananas. No new Steve comes in, and the Steve that's already in you starts to fall apart because, you see, Steve is not like the other carbons. Steve is unstable. He decays, sloooowly. If you leave Steve alone in a room and come back in 5,730 years, half of Steve will be gone. Because we know how fast Steve decays, we can know how long you've been dead by measuring how much Steve is left in you. That's carbon dating in a nutshell. What's that got to do with fossil fuel, you say? Well, fossil fuel, petroleum for example, is still a bit of a mystery, but we know it comes from decomposed organic matter. Dead things. Very, very dead. We also know that the process takes, like, forever, way longer than it takes for Steve to disappear completely. So when you burn fossil fuel, the CO_2 you throw back into the air contains no Steve at all, and over time, you reduce the Steve concentration in the atmosphere. Tadaa. That effect was discovered by Dr. Suess (that's not funny) in the late fifties. Dr. Hans Suess was an American chemist born in Austria.

Given the current attitudes towards facts and science, trying to imagine the social consequences of rising temperatures and extreme and unpredictable weather is really scary. One only has to look at the past for clues. In the first entr'acte, set in 1608, the Eighty-Seven stumble upon a witch trial on their way back from visiting the first wind-powered sawmill in the Netherlands. The sawmill is real, of course, and that technology would help create the Dutch empire, but the interesting part is the witch trial. Like other parts of this book, it has something to do with the climate. The event takes place at the height of what is known as the Little Ice Age. It's a period of—you guessed it—cooler temperatures. Winters in Europe and America were colder. Rivers froze. The Baltic Sea froze. Winters also lasted longer, by a few weeks, which meant shorter growing seasons, crop failures, famine, etc., etc. Bad things. Science was kind of iffy at the time, so in the absence of a plausible explanation, people looked to the supernatural for answers. Witches. Unmarried women made for easy scapegoats and were singled out for the slightest of reasons, like having a mole. Women were accused of anything from stealing the milk out of starving cows to raising storms with the Devil's magic. In North America, the Salem trials (1692–93) are the most well known, but there were similar trials all over Europe during that period. This wasn't the first time people were killed because of the weather. The Greek myth of Iphigenia, sacrificed by her father to quell the gods' anger and receive favorable winds, is rooted in the customs of the time. In the north, the Vikings performed a *"blót"* to ensure Odin's goodwill about the weather. Scientific ignorance paired with religious extremism leads to all kinds of craziness, including throwing people into rivers to see if they float. There is some interesting new research[15] that suggests that the Little Ice Age might have been caused in part by reforestation after the genocide of native people in the Americas. Following Christopher Columbus's first voyage, Europeans killed about 90 percent of the indigenous population, either directly or by spreading disease. The dead stopped farming, and trees started to grow back, reducing CO_2 concentrations enough to cause a global cooling.

15. https://www.theguardian.com/environment/2019/jan/31/european-colonization-of-americas-helped-cause-climate-change

The Kibsu

Alas. Let's start with the obvious. As far as I know, they don't exist, but I'm the first to admit that there's a whole lot I don't know. If you believe this story, though, they would have come a little over three thousand years ago, most likely somewhere in Mesopotamia. On today's map, that's Iraq and Kuwait, parts of Saudi Arabia, Syria, and Turkey. I know this, of course, because I recognized Kibsu and Rādi Kibsi as words from the Akkadian language, which was spoken in the region at the time. I say they would *most likely* have landed in Mesopotamia, because Akkadian was also the language used for trade in much of the Near East, so, who knows?

According to the online Akkadian dictionary[16] of the Association Assyrophile de France, the word Kibsu can be interpreted in several ways: a footprint, a path, a way of life, a line of reasoning, etc. Rādi Kibsi is the one following the footprints, a tracker.

Mia, Sarah, and her mother leave Germany on September 18, 1932, aboard the SS *Milwaukee* of the Hamburg-Amerika Linie. They cover their tracks as best they can, but if you look at the actual passenger manifest from that day, you will find a Sarah Freed.[17]

In AD 921, a thousand years earlier, the Sixty-Five is part of a delegation sent by the Abbasid caliph to Volga Bulgaria. She travels up the Volga River with a fellow named Ahmad Ibn Fadlan—we talked about him before—who serves as secretary to the ambassador. I tried to set events happening at different times in similar places, and you'll see the Volga in a few places throughout the book. For example, Kapustin Yar, where they built the launchpad for the first Soviet missile, the R-1, is near the river.

16. http://www.assyrianlanguages.org/akkadian/index_en.php
17. https://www.gjenvick.com/PassengerLists/Hamburg-AmericanLine/Westbound/1932-09-18-PassengerList-Milwaukee.html

Ahmad Ibn Fadlan was a real person. He went up the Volga to meet the new king of Volga Bulgaria, and along the way he met himself some Vikings. The cool part is he took some notes. I put a little quote from his journal in the scene, but a lot of it is inspired by what he wrote. The Kibsu ends up marrying Igor of Kiev, son of Oleg of Novgorod. The Varangians, a.k.a. Vikings, ruled over a *massive* part of Europe and Asia at the time. The Kievan Rus' empire, as it was called, was based in Kiev, and we have Igor's dad to thank for that. Olga of Kiev, Igor's wife, was also a real person, and she was not someone you wanted to mess with. We don't know much about her, but the story about burying people alive, killing thousands, and burning a town with pigeons to avenge her husband is a real thing.

We go back another eighteen hundred years to meet the Seven in the third entr'acte. She—her name is Varkida—joins a group of horse-riding warriors before being banished and starting her own all-woman tribe, which you might have recognized as the legendary Amazons. Varkida is the name of an Amazon (*BAPKIΔA*) appearing on a sixth-century red-figure amphora (it means "princess," likely from Proto-Indo-European *wel-*, as in English "weal[th]").[18] Legend aside, there is significant evidence that the Amazons were actually Scythian warriors (sometimes called Saka). The Scythians were badass. They were nomadic tribespeople, incredible horse riders, and absolutely deadly with a bow. And yes, some of them were women. Just google "Scythians"; the connection to the Amazons is cool enough that thousands of people have written about it.

How we go from actual Scythian warriors to Greek myth is even better. Maybe I'm biased because I trained as a linguist, but I think it's objectively cool. OK, so the Greeks travel and they meet a bunch of people they don't know. They find out the names of these people and they go back home and tell everyone.

18. http://www.palaeolexicon.com/Word/Show/26040

A good chunk of what we can read about the Amazons comes from Greek historians. Now, the Greeks back then have some problems, but a small ego isn't one of them. They think their language is *awesome*. So, some Greek fellow gets back to Greece and says he met some women warriors and they were called the Amazons. There are many possible etymologies for the word. The one I picked is reconstructed from Old Persian: *hama-zan*, which would mean "all women." Another option is from Iranian *ha-mazan*. It could mean something as simple as "warrior." There are many that make sense. But one Greek historian, Hellanikos, doesn't speak Old Persian. It's all Greek to him. He sees the Greek *a-*(ἀ-) "without" and *mazos* (μαζός) "breast." BOOM! Without breast. That's how we end up with women who cut their breasts out because, contrary to the millions of women who have used bows throughout history, these ones can't do it without hurting themselves.

The same goes for the Arimaspi (that's what the caravan members called the first tribe Varkida meets). In Early Iranian, the word would probably be a combination of *ariama* ("love") and *aspa* ("horses"), and it would sort of make sense for people to refer to a horse-riding tribe this way. But Herodotus, another Greek historian, thinks it's from the roots for "one" and "eye," and all of a sudden we have a whole tribe of one-eyed people spreading terror up north. In both cases, we have completely absurd myths started not because anyone actually saw anything, but because the guy doing the linguistic analysis was an idiot.

That was my "linguistics is cool" moment. Oh, and the final battle takes place on the banks of the Volga River.

Three generations later, in 825 BC, the Ten settles in the kingdom of Quwê. The Kibsu is still great at breeding horses, of course, and the Ten sells some to the king of Israel. Those of you who studied the Bible would recognize the kingdom from the first book of Kings as the place King Solomon got his horses from: "Solomon's horses were imported from Egypt and from Kue—the royal merchants purchased them from Kue at the current price. They imported a chariot from Egypt for six hundred shekels of silver, and a horse for a hundred and fifty. They also exported them to all the kings of the Hittites and of the Arameans" (1 Kings 10:28–29).

The Kibsu loses all the knowledge in Quwê when the Ten kills herself. The Eleven, and all of those who follow, will spend their lives trying to get it back.

There are a million more historical references in the book, some more subtle than others. I'll let you discover them for yourself.

I really hope you enjoyed this one. I can tell you I had an absolute blast writing it.

Until next time,
Sylvain

PLAYLIST

Chapter	Song
1.	Sentimental Journey, Les Brown and His Orchestra (with Doris Day) (1945)
2.	The Honeydripper, Joe Liggins and His Honeydrippers (1945)
3.	Begin the Beguine, Artie Shaw and His Orchestra (1938)
4.	I Wonder, Cecil Grant (1944)
5.	Crawlin' King Snake, Big Joe Williams (1941)
6.	Lili Marlene, Marlene Dietrich (1938)
7.	God Bless the Child, Billie Holiday (1941)
8.	Hot Time in the Town of Berlin, Bing Crosby and the Andrews Sisters (1944)
9.	Death Valley Blues, Arthur "Big Boy" Crudup (1941)
10.	This Land Is Your Land, Woody Guthrie (1944)
11.	Y'a pas de printemps, Edith Piaf (1944)
12.	Stormy Weather, Lena Horne (1941)
13.	Trouble So Hard, Vera Hall (1937)
14.	Dream, the Pied Pipers (1945)
15.	L'âme au diable, Léo Marjane (1943)
16.	Down, Down, Down, the Mills Brothers (1941)
17.	Going Home, Paul Robeson (1958)
18.	Twilight Time, Les Brown and His Orchestra (1945)
19.	Ac-cent-tchu-ate the Positive, Bing Crosby and the Andrews Sisters (1945)

20. My Mama Don't Allow Me, Arthur "Big Boy" Crudup (1944)
21. Che puro ciel, Kathleen Ferrier (1946)
22. I'm on My Last Go-Round, Lead Belly (1942)
23. Gloomy Sunday, Billie Holiday (1941)
24. "Murder," He Says, Dinah Shore (1943)
25. Songs My Mother Taught Me, Nellie Melba (1916)
26. You Gonna Miss Me When I'm Gone, Tampa Red (1944)
27. La vie en rose, Edith Piaf (1946)
28. It's a Good Day, Peggy Lee (1946)
29. As Time Goes By, Dooley Wilson (1946)
30. Nature Boy, King Cole Trio (1948)
31. Still a Fool, Muddy Waters (1951)
32. East of the Sun (and West of the Moon), Sarah Vaughan (1949)
33. I'm Gonna Dig Myself a Hole, Arthur "Big Boy" Crudup (1951)
34. Unforgettable, Nat "King" Cole (1951)
35. Pink Champagne, Joe Liggins and His Honeydrippers (1950)
36. How High the Moon, Les Paul and Mary Ford (1951)
37. Moanin' at Midnight, Howlin' Wolf (1951)
38. Hey, Good Lookin', Hank Williams (1951)
39. Hymne à l'amour, Edith Piaf (1950)
40. You Belong to Me, Jo Stafford (1952)
41. Night Train, Jimmy Forrest (1952)
42. Thinking and Drinking, Amos Milburn (1952)
43. Blue Moon, Billie Holiday (1952)
44. Hound Dog, Willie Mae "Big Mama" Thornton (1953)
45. All Night Long, Muddy Waters (1952)
46. Songs and Dances of Death: Lullaby, Jennie Tourel and Leonard Bernstein (1950)

47. Jock-A-Mo, Sugar Boy Crawford and His Cane Cutters (1953)
48. Earth Angel, the Penguins (1954)
49. Mr. Sandman, the Chordettes (1954)
50. The Great Pretender, the Platters (1955)
51. Death of an Angel, Donald Woods and the Vel-Aires (1955)
52. Little Bitty Pretty One, Thurston Harris (1957)
53. Great Balls of Fire, Jerry Lee Lewis (1957)
54. Milord, Edith Piaf (1959)
55. Come On, Let's Go, Ritchie Valens (1958)
56. Wonderful World, Sam Cooke (1960)
57. Will You Love Me Tomorrow, the Shirelles (1960)
58. Walk—Don't Run, the Ventures (1960)
59. At Last, Etta James (1960)
60. Stand by Me, Ben E. King (1961)

ACKNOWLEDGMENTS

I want to thank my editor, Lee Harris, for giving my weird slightly-homicidal-alien-clone-space-race story a home. Thank you to the myriad of people at Tor.com who had a hand in making it an actual book. You all rock. On the other side of the pond, I'm grateful to be working with Jillian Taylor and the great team at Michael Joseph again for this series. Thanks to Seth Fishman, my amazing agent, and everyone at the Gernert Company. I'm extremely thankful to the real people whose lives I borrowed from for this story. I also can't help but think of the thousands who helped send humans to space but whose names we'll never know. The mathematicians, the engineers, the welders, the accountants, etc., etc. There are many who strived to build rockets or go to space but never achieved their goals because of funding, or politics, or because they were born in the wrong place, or with the wrong gender or skin color. We remember the von Brauns and the Gagarins and Armstrongs, but I wish we would celebrate the Mercury 13, the selected astronauts who never got to fly, all the scientists and engineers who worked on spacecraft that were never built. They all have one thing in common: they looked to the stars and dared to dream.